Deborah Masson was born and bred in Aberdeen, Scotland. Always restless and fighting against being a responsible adult, she worked in several jobs including secretarial, marketing, reporting for the ~~~~~~~ newspaper and a stint as a p~~~~~~~~~~~~~~

Through it all, she alway~~~~~~~ when motherhood finally ~~~~~ adult (maybe even a respon~~~~~ hand to writing what she lo~~~~ ~~~~~~~ started with short stories and flash fiction whilst her daughter napped and, when she later welcomed her son into the world, she decided to challenge her writing further through online courses with Professional Writing Academy and Faber Academy, where she wrote her award-winning debut novel *Hold Your Tongue*, the first in the DI Eve Hunter series. Since then she has published two more books in the series, *Out for Blood* and *From the Ashes*.

www.penguin.co.uk

9030 00007 9511 1

Also by Deborah Masson

Hold Your Tongue
Out for Blood

FROM THE ASHES

DEBORAH MASSON

PENGUIN BOOKS

TRANSWORLD PUBLISHERS
Penguin Random House, One Embassy Gardens,
8 Viaduct Gardens, London SW11 7BW
www.penguin.co.uk

Transworld is part of the Penguin Random House group of companies
whose addresses can be found at global.penguinrandomhouse.com

Penguin
Random House
UK

First published in Great Britain in 2022 by Penguin Books
an imprint of Transworld Publishers

A CIP catalogue record for this book is available from the British Library.

ISBN
9780552178259

Typeset in 11/14pt ITC Giovanni by Jouve (UK), Milton Keynes.
Printed and bound in Great Britain by Clays Ltd, Elcograf S.p.A.

The auth

For Beverly
The best neighbour a girl could ask for,
especially in a lockdown.

Chapter 1

IT WAS THE SOUND. That's what drew him in. The seconds of silence watching as the flame caught; orange-tinged yellow sparking before growing and picking up speed – the poor bastards inside unaware of the nightmare headed their way.

Then the roar as the beast found its fuel. Crackling, popping rage as it moved, spreading across the floor, licking at the walls; its desire to devour everything in its path. Eager, and wanting more.

The open window of the room where the fire was coming to life glowed orange as he moved. He kept to the edges of the garden, making use of the darkness, knowing he had to get around the building and down the drive, hidden, before the alarms sounded and sleeping neighbours across the road were drawn zombie-like to their windows and doors.

He slunk down the drive, crossed the pavement and turned back towards the house, the tall hedge hiding him from view. He stepped back, branches pressing into his hoodie, leaves rustling against his jeans. His eyes closed, savouring the moment before the chaos, letting the noise wash over him – comfort and excitement as he listened, the fire sounding oddly like torrential rain as it burned, the gush of a river fit to burst its banks. He opened his eyes when the fire alarms sounded, white-grey smoke now billowing from the building as the beast belched.

Time for the fun to begin.

He stared at the building, the only sign of the fire being the smoke visible above the roof. The blaze around the back would be in full flow now. He wanted to feel the heat of it pressing against his face. To stand still as the fire warmed his body and emptied his mind. That was his definition of home.

His eyes watered, fixed on the spot where those inside would spill out on to the driveway – his patience rewarded as the door was thrown open, bodies spilling out into the night; screaming, shouting, crying. Weak.

He smiled and stepped sideways past the drive and out of view of the property. Twigs snapped against his body as it dragged along the hedgerow. He turned his head to look down the street, knowing it was mere minutes before windows and doors would be shoved open, resembling some drug-induced hallucination of an Advent calendar, excitement audible on the breeze as people shouted to neighbours next to them and across the road. Some with arms outstretched holding mobile phones doing what folk did best – bugger all except for making sure it was caught on camera. He stood still for the briefest of moments, not wanting to miss any of the shitstorm in front of him.

That stuff he'd read online was true. He didn't have a bloody clue who'd said it, only *what* they'd said – *Catch on fire and people will come for miles to see you burn*. The idiots in this street wouldn't care if it was wood or flesh burning.

He was so deep in thought at how selfish people could be that he almost missed the best sound of all. The far-off sirens whooped through the air, announcing the arrival of the fire engines.

He should get back but, shit, the buzz of watching the firemen jump from their cabins, fluorescent yellow helmets and beige uniform heavy upon them – the weight of the job ahead more so. Why the hell would he miss that? He wanted to stay. Right where he was. To watch the hoses being freed and hauled from the truck; to listen to the guys as they hollered to one another before the first jets of water hit in the battle against the inferno. But he knew he couldn't.

Knew he wouldn't. Because this wasn't supposed to happen.

Chapter 2

DI EVE HUNTER PULLED at the electrical cord as it caught the edge of the workbench, stumbling a little with the sudden give of the sander. She knelt and rubbed a hand across the dark lacquered wood, the overhead lighting bouncing off it, daylight in the city of Aberdeen still a while away. Eve hoped the dresser would be as beautiful underneath as she'd envisaged. There was only one way to find out.

Noise filled the shed as sandpaper met wood. Welcome noise drowning out everything around her. With a bit of luck, it would do the same to what was going on inside her head. Today of all days.

This was always a difficult day. At least it had been since she'd hit the age of ten. The year her mum had decided Eve was old enough to know the answer to the question about who her dad was and where he'd been all her life. Eve still remembered the giveaway tremble in her mum's hand as she explained about the night a man

4

had pushed her into an alleyway and attacked her, leaving her pregnant with Eve.

Her mother went out of her way to make every birthday special. Later, once Eve knew the truth, it tortured her to think what went through her mum's mind on that day and every other day when she looked into Eve's eyes. How her mother could possibly even try to block out the images of what had happened to her, even though neither she nor Eve's grandparents had ever made her feel anything but loved. Wanted. Never anything less.

No, it was Eve who allowed herself to feel that way.

No matter how irrational it was. Because *his* blood, those dark genes, ran within her and she had no idea who he was. Not a clue what she could be capable of or what problems might lie ahead.

She was aware this had been the driving factor in her joining the force. The want to do better, to *be* better than the person her father had been. She found solace in taking people like him off the streets, putting them behind bars like caged animals. That was the only way she allowed herself to think of him. An animal.

Eve pressed harder against the wood, needing to feel something else, to think about anything else. No need to be worried about how the neighbours would react to her chosen way of escape – Bert one side of her cottage near deaf and Elsie on the other side delighted any time she could hear her, aware she had the protection of a copper next door. Eve glanced over to the workbench, the movement of her mobile phone catching her eye.

She stood and lowered the face mask, her nose

wrinkling against the cloud of sand-coloured dust rising as she switched the sander off. The vibrating mobile phone danced across the bench in front of her, its ringtone now clearly audible.

'Hunter.'

Before a word had been spoken on the other end, she knew it was Colin, the barrel-shaped call handler at HQ. Morbid obesity and a forty-a-day smoking habit gave it away in his breathing every time.

'Sorry to bother you this early,' he wheezed. 'There's been a big fire.'

'Call the fire brigade.' Eve guessed what it meant if she was getting the call. Shoot her if she wanted to steal an extra minute before dealing with the inevitable.

Colin didn't miss a beat. 'Body found. Hastings wants you there.'

Eve looked longingly at the dresser she was working on. The simplicity and escapism of it. Something she'd hoped to immerse herself in for at least another couple of hours before heading into work. 'Whereabouts?' Eve didn't bother with paper or a pen.

'Kids' home up in Kincorth. Name's Wellwood.'

She'd never heard of it and, with what little she knew about the area, could only picture the shopping arcade at the top of Provost Watt Drive – a nearby church and community centre too. Not a kids' home. 'Any details on the body?'

There was a brief silence. 'One of the kids. A boy. You're to ask for Dave McCabe. Incident Commander.'

'Shit.' There was a pang of guilt for her earlier reluctance. 'I take it the fire's under control?'

'Pretty much. It's been going all night. Apparently, staff did everything they could to find the kid. They had to get out. By the time firefighters were able to gain access and do a thorough search . . .'

'How the hell did they manage to lose the kid in the first place?'

'I guess you'll find out when you get there.'

Eve yanked the soiled mask out and up over her head, already moving towards the door of her work shed. 'Get Cooper. Tell him I'll meet him there.'

She didn't wait for an answer before hanging up and stepping out on to the wet grass of her city-centre cottage garden, oblivious to the sudden shower as she tapped at her phone, googling Wellwood and all the while wishing it had been anyone else but a kid.

Chapter 3

DC Scott Ferguson wiped the back of his hand across his sweaty forehead as his feet slowed on the wet pavement and turned into the stone-pillared black iron gates of Duthie Park. Sunrise was creeping through the rain shower and into the park, darkness left behind when he'd come up off the riverside path. He jogged to the foot of the wide, shallow stone steps leading up a grassy slope, his gaze fixed on the usually pink obelisk above and, to the left, the early-morning sun bouncing off the monument, dyeing it orange.

As his eyeline came level with the top of the steps, he took in the Victorian bandstand poised regally in the middle of the large expanse of grass ahead, the weather-vane at its crown tipping and turning lazily in the breeze. The park's glass-walled winter gardens glinted in the distance. Ferguson turned sharp left, following the generous concrete path skirting the edge of the newly cut grass, the only sound in his ears the slap of his trainer soles hitting the ground. The scratched face of his Fitbit said it was 7 a.m. Plenty of time to make it to the mound and up to the top before heading back to his car, home and into work.

He blew breath from his cheeks, mustering energy for the last stint as the flagless pole of the mound came into view through a clump of trees. Maybe he was mad. His boss, DI Eve Hunter, thought so. She'd made it clear she thought getting up at the crack of dawn to exercise was crazy, obsessive even. But, hey, he wasn't doing anything else when his body, without fail, woke him at the same godawful hour every day. The way it had since he was a kid, although the freedom and need to be the best version of himself had only come to him in adulthood. A time in his life he could finally control. Be in charge of his own decisions, his own fate driving him every day: in his work, his hobbies – on this run now.

He pushed a little harder, his thighs responding. He concentrated on the feeling, taking his mind away from wandering into those years before. This is what worked for him: the blood pumping, the escape. His thoughts turned to Eve. He suspected she had coping mechanisms of her own. Just as obsessive as he was, only in a different way. Needing that distraction whilst the rest of Aberdeen slept.

The narrow pale-yellow path of the grassy hill which wound up to its stone top was upon him. He didn't slow, his legs propelling him instead, his breathing ragged now. A rain-sodden dog walker on the way back down grunted Ferguson a good morning as he climbed. He wasn't the only crazy one at this time in the morning.

The smell hit his nostrils as he reached the stone base

of the flagpole. Signalling danger. It was subtle, somewhere off in the distance, but the fire wasn't far enough away for Ferguson to miss the sudden change to the skyline as he hit the summit. He looked across the park towards the suburb of Kincorth. The billowing grey and black clouds above the dwarfed buildings were clearly not the work of nature.

Ferguson bent a moment to catch his breath, his hands cupping his thighs above the knee before straightening. He squinted at the grey houses nestled against the skyline where the smoke was rising, not sure exactly where it was. Above the buildings, he saw the slow plumes, telling him the worst of the blaze was on its way out.

Ferguson swallowed before taking measured breaths, in through the nose, out through the mouth. Grateful the worst years of his life were long gone and that he'd made it this far.

Chapter 4

THE SUBURB OF KINCORTH lay south of Aberdeen, separated from the forty-four-acre greenery of Duthie Park by a granite stone road bridge spanning the picturesque River Dee, the beauty of which was lost on Eve, who was growing impatient with the inevitable early-morning traffic that started before rush hour. She tutted and flicked the switch for the siren, instantly making her unmarked car visible and in demand of attention. Eve dodged in and out of cars, wheels leaving behind wet trails on the road. She was relieved to exit the bridge, nipping over the roundabout on to Provost Watt Drive, and leaving behind the snake of traffic, which either slithered left to the industrial estate of Altens, or right, heading towards the Stonehaven road.

She drove up the road's steep climb, spotting where she needed to be, ahead and to the left. She indicated, only making it over one speed bump before coming up against blue-and-white metallic incident signs and a pinched-faced uniformed officer. Rain dripped off the peak of his hat. Overseeing traffic control was perhaps the least of his worries as Eve spotted three journalists already gathered. Marcie Wade, the local writer she'd dealt with most to date, was one of them.

The officer shooed Marcie away before trying to do the same to Eve, waving aggressively from where he stood in front of the metal-legged warnings which blocked her advancing any further.

Eve's fingers banged a rhythm against the steering wheel as she stared at the officer now striding towards her, obviously put out because she was ignoring him; that his authority was being questioned in front of the press. The man's steely glare slipped, feet faltering, as he peered through the windscreen at her.

His bony cheeks reddened, now clearly seeing whom he was demanding reverse the car. He mumbled an apology, turned and walked back towards the barricade, shifting parts of the cordon to the side, fighting off the now clamouring journalists as he allowed her through.

Eve's car crawled past them. She didn't make eye contact with any of them, but she felt Marcie's stare through the glass as she passed by.

She picked up a little speed, passing a small smattering of shops on the right: a pharmacy, newsagent, fast-food takeaway and barber. Debatable whether they'd open at all today with the street barricaded off. On a normal day, what more would you need within spitting distance of where you lived? The tree-lined pavement to her left fell away to a grassy hill and sloped downwards to granite stone homes. There was no need to check the door numbers in her search for the kids' home; two fire engines, blue lights silently flashing, blocked the narrow residential street ahead, marking the spot.

Eve drove through the residents' cars crammed along both kerbsides, where the detached and semi-detached homes were now level with the road either side. Eve edged into the only available space, noticing her colleague DS Mark Cooper's car two ahead of hers. Cooper stood on the pavement, soaked, stock-still amongst the bustle of activity.

Eve pulled a waterproof jacket from the passenger seat and got out of the car. 'How'd you get here so fast?' she said, coming up alongside Cooper.

Cooper turned and tapped the side of his nose. 'Good morning to you too.'

He didn't wish her a happy birthday – Eve kept that little nugget to herself every year.

'You've got baby sick on your shoulder.'

Cooper looked down, his face reddening as he saw the congealed splurge on his jacket that had held fast even against the rain shower. He rummaged in his pocket before wiping at the spot with a tissue. 'Sorry, bit of a hectic exit this morning.'

The bags were deep beneath his eyes. He and his wife had had two young kids already before the arrival of the new baby, or not so new now. Ryan was six months old and had spent a lot of that time making it clear sleep was not important to him. And yet Cooper had still beaten her here.

She watched him fold the tissue and stuff it back where he'd got it, as if it was normal to have a pocketful of sick. That was Cooper though, hands-on and he loved it.

13

Eve turned back to the building and they stood in silence a moment, staring at the ruined home. The left side was open to the elements, the roof caved in, blackened beams still clinging, grey granite walls now scorched charcoal where the smoke had billowed out.

'Any sign of Dave McCabe?' Eve checked out the sweeping driveway leading to the detached granite dwelling house, identical to other houses on the street, and not what she'd expected a kids' home to look like. Although, to be fair, she'd had no idea what to expect.

Cooper checked his watch. 'The Incident Commander? He's getting an update from the breathing apparatus team before he talks to us.'

Eve zipped the waterproof. 'I hear it's a kid.'

'Eleven years old.' Cooper's Adam's apple bobbed as he said it. 'They were lifting the body out when I arrived. It's in the ambulance at the top of the drive.'

Eve craned her neck, feeling a chill – nothing to do with rain as she saw the end of the black body bag through the half-open ambulance door. The bag appeared too big for its contents, even from there. She couldn't stop studying it. Some kid who hadn't had the best start in life before they'd ended up here. Maybe a child who had found a home of sorts. Hopefully better than their last, with new people to care for them. Except those people had let them down. Seconds turning to minutes trapped in a building as it burned. Missing until it was too late.

Chapter 5

FERGUSON SIGHED AS HE indicated. The driver in front clearly didn't know the accelerator was on the right-hand side. There was no need for him to slow as he turned left and crawled on to the bottom of Crown Street.

Three-storey granite-grey buildings stretched either side of him to blue-grey sky above. Residential flats punctured with signs hanging in doorways and windows shouting out about anything and everything from fast-food delivery and B & Bs to a music store. The store had been there since he was a kid. The drum kit that had once stood in pride of place in the large front window was still as real to him now as it had been all those years ago when he'd stood staring in at it from the pavement, drooling for one beat of its drums. The window was now full of yellowing music manuals propped amongst dust-covered instruments. It was a place that had once meant so much to him, which he now drove past daily without noticing. But it was hard to miss it at today's

15

speed. Ferguson sighed as he followed the car in front. He'd be quicker getting out and walking, wishing he was one of the two vehicles up ahead – a white van leading the pack followed by a souped-up Mini. Neither of which Ferguson would want to drive but at least they were getting somewhere.

A screech of brakes shot straight to Ferguson's ears, followed by a sickening crunch as metal slammed into metal. He braked hard as he heard the squeal of rubber halted by a metallic thud.

Ferguson sat still, gripping the steering wheel, grateful now for the snail-like pace of the driver in front, who had also come to a standstill.

He unclicked his seat belt, opened his door and got out; the Mini up ahead had stopped dead in the middle of the road, black tyre marks left in its wake when the driver had slammed the brakes. Burned rubber hit Ferguson's nostrils. The white van was on the other side of the road, crushed into the side of a car parked kerbside. What had made the car swerve?

He got back into his car and checked his rear-view mirror before reversing and steering to the right: copper instinct kicking in as he blocked both sides of the road and shoved on his hazard lights. He lifted his mobile phone and dialled 999, not taking any chances. Then he was out of the car again, phone clamped to his ear as he made his way to the boot and hauled two warning cones out of the back.

He walked fast back from the car, not stopping as a woman's voice came on the line. Ferguson reeled off his name and officer number. 'I need an ambulance and road traffic to Crown Street. Two-vehicle collision.' He waited a beat for confirmation before hanging up and placing a cone a decent distance away from his car, ensuring, even on the straight, people would slow without hitting his car first.

Then he was running, back and past his car with the remaining cone. The old woman who had been driving in front of him was now out of her car, staring at the scene before her.

'Stay there,' Ferguson shouted as he ran past the woman, who was gripping the top of the open driver's door as if glass and metal would shield her from whatever lay before her.

Ferguson was sprinting now, the cone banging against his thigh which was responding well, given he'd already done his run for the day. He got to the Mini first, crouching to the driver's window, a blonde-haired female wide-eyed and still gripping the wheel.

'You OK?'

She turned her head to the window, eyes focused on Ferguson, which he took to be a good sign. 'I . . . I think I am. I didn't have time to—' She turned back to the windscreen, staring at where the van had come to a standstill.

'Don't worry. Are you injured?'

She shook her head, releasing her grip from the wheel, hands dropping to her lap.

'Stay put. I'm going to check the van driver. There's an ambulance on the way. We'll need a statement from you.'

Ferguson could see the front of the van had crumpled into a black Mercedes. People were pouring out of the many doors, some still in bathrobes, the tallest of them a portly red-faced gent who Ferguson could already tell was the Mercedes owner as he charged towards him, shouting.

'Sir, please. I need to check the driver.'

The man's eyes flickered to the van, his attention before that being fixed only on his own car. Ferguson stuck his head in through the open window; the old guy at the wheel was pressed back against the headrest, eyes closed, moaning. Blood dripped from a nasty cut on his head.

'Sir? Are you OK?'

The man groaned and attempted to nod.

Ferguson pulled back and out of the van, craning his neck over the roof and inhaling sharply as he stared at what had caused the accident.

The old guy in the van now looked positively healthy, compared to what lay in the middle of the road.

Chapter 6

THE THICK SOOT SMEARED across the face of the man who walked down the driveway towards Eve and Cooper failed to hide the exhaustion there. Eve imagined questions were the last thing the guy was in the mood for.

'Dave McCabe?'

The Incident Commander offered his large hand over the cordon dividing them.

Eve shook firmly. 'DI Eve Hunter. This is my colleague, DS Mark Cooper.'

McCabe shook Cooper's hand in turn, his grip dwarfing Cooper's almost as much as it had Eve's. 'I would say nice to meet you . . .'

'What can you tell us?' Eve didn't see any point in mucking about.

'It appears someone poured petrol through the back door letter box, followed by a lit rag soaked in the same.'

'Jesus. Arson. What kind of bastard targets a kids' home?' Eve admired the two wide bay windows either side of the scorched door; a further two skylight windows were tucked into the red-tiled roof. It was obvious how homely the place had been, even in its now-ruined state. She sensed there was a lot more of the building out at the back. Odd that there was a letter box back there.

McCabe pointed to the building. 'The markings in the entranceway and the way it spread, plus how quickly, is what makes us suspect an accelerant was used.'

'Here was me hoping it might be along the lines of an electrical fault.'

'If only.'

McCabe raised the cordon tape flickering in the breeze and motioned for them to duck beneath.

They walked up the driveway, Eve sandwiched between both men, dirty water trickling downhill beneath their feet, a mix of rainwater and the residue of the fire hoses overnight. Her eyes were fixed straight ahead, stuck on the ambulance blocking the drive. The back doors were open, a stretcher visible, the black bag spread on top of it barely covering it. Eve swallowed as McCabe spoke.

'Obviously it's not safe to go inside yet. I'll take you round the back.'

Eve was level with the ambulance. She stopped, notic-ing McCabe intended to keep going and that Cooper was taking his lead. 'I want to see.'

Cooper and McCabe stopped and turned.

McCabe's face softened. 'It's not pretty.'

'I don't expect it to be. I need to see what's in there.' And she did need to see it – to make sure this body was a person to her, not a statistic.

McCabe peered into the ambulance. 'OK.'

Eve pulled gloves from her pocket and took her time putting them on, pretending they were an awkward fit, steeling herself for what she was about to see. She stepped up into the ambulance, her hip brushing against the edge of the stretcher, rocking the bag slightly before she leaned over and pulled at the large zip. The noise as it slid against the teeth bounced off the small space around her. She dipped her head as the smell of soot met her nostrils. The child's face was swollen, scorched red at the eyelids and around the mouth, soot clinging around the nostrils and inside the nose. Black curls of hair were clamped to his forehead, wet like those of a sweaty child sleeping, except this one would never wake again. Murdered. There was no other word for it when the fire had been started deliberately.

'His name was Lucas Fyfe.'

Eve had forgotten McCabe and Cooper were there. 'Did you speak to the staff?'

'They were frantic when we got here. Two guys. Shouting for him. We had to stop one of them from going back in.'

Eve's hand hovered by the boy's cheek. She had an overwhelming urge to offer comfort. She swallowed before zipping the bag back up and disposing of the gloves.

'You OK?' Cooper's voice was soft.

She remained silent as she tilted her face upwards, breathing deeply before she turned and jumped from the ambulance.

Neither man said a word as they walked alongside her

again. Eve broke the silence. 'Do the staff know how the fire started?'

'No, they were moved off site pretty quickly, before we discovered where it had started.'

'Where are the rest of the kids now?'

McCabe wiped a hand against his side, leaving a black smudge behind. 'They've been temporarily moved to a disused youth hostel on Great Western Road. Shut down a couple of years ago. The council kept it for emergencies like this one.'

Eve was distracted by the full extent of the damage now revealing itself as they came around the back of the house. A huge extension out back led on to a large patch of grass, now charcoal-coloured, muddy and dotted with shards of glass and debris where the windows had blown out.

McCabe moved ahead of them. 'Arson, for sure. But it's where we found the boy . . . It makes me think there's a lot more to this.'

'What do you—'

'What the hell's that?' McCabe hollered towards three firefighters heaving what appeared to be a metal drum between them. The men were red-faced as they grasped either end of the drum, and its centre. It thumped on to the grass before the tallest of the three men answered.

'It was down where we found the boy.' He was panting as he spoke. 'Bloody lucky the fire didn't reach it. The thing's covered in hazardous waste warnings. Depending what's in it, the place could've gone up a whole lot worse.'

Eve squinted towards the drum.

McCabe walked over to the drum and knelt to read the labels covering it. He peered at the sealed lid before standing. 'This could be anything. It needs to be X-rayed to see what we're dealing with.'

The three men grumbled, each of them grimacing as they lifted the drum again, carrying it as far away from the property as possible.

McCabe strode back to Eve and Cooper. 'Sorry. Anyway, the boy.'

Cooper was watching the firefighters struggling to move the drum across the scorched grass as Eve spoke. 'They said "down" . . . down where they found the boy.'

McCabe sighed. Eve studied his face, already not liking what he was about to say.

'We found the boy underground.'

'What, the floor had given way?' Eve was seeing the boy's puffy face, feeling the burn of the red marking on his face, hearing his shouts for help from below, and imagining his screams before silence.

'No. The carpet had burned away, exposing a hatch.'

Eve's eyes widened. 'A hatch?'

'There was a ladder down. Kind of like a crawlspace except you can stand freely in this one. More of a basement. It mirrors the rooms above.'

Eve stared at him. 'How the hell did he end up down there?'

McCabe shrugged. 'Your guess is as good as mine.'

There was no way of McCabe knowing but she wanted answers, already impatient to get to the staff who'd better have bloody good ones. 'Couldn't he get out?'

McCabe's focus was on the house. 'The hatch was

closed. No lock beneath but if the carpet had been placed back over then someone of his size would've struggled to push it open.'

Bile bit at the back of Eve's throat. 'He couldn't have put the carpet back if he'd gone down there by himself.'

'Exactly.'

The boy's face was haunting Eve. 'Would he have known there was a fire?' From what she'd seen, he must've but she wanted to hope, at least.

'Oh, he knew. The place was filled with smoke.'

Cooper was looking back towards the ambulance. 'Maybe it knocked him out before too long?'

McCabe's face was slack. 'I wouldn't bet on it. We found him at the bottom of the ladder and by the state of the underside of the hatch and his hands, he'd fought hard to get out.'

24

Chapter 7

THE BODY LAY AT an angle which made it almost impossible to believe it could be human. A young man from what Ferguson could see, blood pooling around his head and spreading out across the road's surface. His left arm and leg were in positions that seemed impossible.

Ferguson stepped closer, doing his best to keep his features neutral in front of the many spectators crowding the pavement, surprised they'd stayed back when there was only him to set and manage boundaries until road traffic arrived. Even the blustering bald guy who'd been ready to rant about his Mercedes had stopped when he spotted the boy on the road.

He crouched by the body, careful not to interfere with it as he stretched for the wrist to take a pulse. His hand stopped mid-air as he spotted the chest rising and falling. *Breathing.*

Ferguson's head bobbed up at the nearby sound of sirens coming from the main strip of Union Street, seconds away from them. Relief as he listened, not moving himself from the boy. Road traffic would not be far away either.

He delved into his pocket with his free hand as his mobile rang. Maybe road traffic had decided to phone him en route. He peered at the screen. *Mearns.*

'Ferguson.'

'Where are you?'

He hadn't been held up too long in getting into the office. But he was punctual. Mearns was aware of that.

'Two-vehicle collision in Crown Street, a pedestrian hit and injured. Young guy.'

'Shit. Were you called out?'

'No, I was a car behind it.'

'You OK?'

'I'm fine. Neither driver appears to be injured badly. The pedestrian is a different story. I'm with him now.'

'Sounds like the ambulance is too.'

'I need to go. I'll be in touch once I know what's happening.' Ferguson hung up as the ambulance stopped short of them. He made eye contact with the driver, signalling him over before his attention snapped back to the boy. His eyes widened as the boy opened his own eyes. Narrowed, dimmed blue eyes.

Ferguson couldn't be sure if the boy was seeing him. He took hold of the dirty, cold hand on the boy's uninjured arm, squeezing gently and staring at the badly inked skull tattoo at the base of the forefinger and thumb. A mobile phone lay beneath the boy's arm, smashed to bits. 'I've got you. Help's here.'

'Don't leave me.' Mumbled but clear.

The boy's hand grasped at his, Ferguson's fingers gripping as hard back as the skull tattoo winked at him and the paramedics sprang from the ambulance. 'I'm not going anywhere.'

And he meant it.

Chapter 8

THE WIDE WOODEN DOUBLE door of the youth hostel creaked open, a smell of mould rushing out through the crack where a middle-aged man with a shock of red-blond hair and bloodshot eyes peered out.

'Stephen Alderton?'

The man dipped his chin.

'DI Eve Hunter.' Eve held up her ID. 'This is my colleague, DS Mark Coo—'

'Have they found Lucas?' The door yanked back on its hinges, the red-cracked whites of Stephen's eyes darting from Eve to Cooper as he stepped backwards, allowing them access. Eve and Cooper entered, closing the door and turning to Stephen, who stared at them.

Eve glanced at Cooper, breaking the intensity of Stephen's glare. 'Is there somewhere we could sit?'

The man's back was already to them, walking away, boot soles echoing in their ears as they followed, mouths breathing in the mouldy waft that wrapped itself around them and mingled with the stale sweat drifting back from Stephen in the draughty hallway. They stopped when he did, watching him push at the round brass doorknob on a heavy, dark, wood-panelled door which led them into a large high-ceilinged room.

The room didn't offer much more than scuffed walls, a large two-paned window too dirty from passing traffic to allow in much light, an old out-of-use fireplace and the large worn table and chairs dominating the centre of the space – six empty chairs around it.

The granite detached building would've been grand in its prime, housed on an affluent street that now boasted B & Bs, florists, wedding-dress shops and cafes.

Stephen went to the closest seat and hovered. Those haunted eyes back on them, no invitation for them to sit.

Cooper pulled out a chair by Eve's side, the bottom of bare wooden chair legs screeching against the floor as Eve joined him and motioned for Stephen to do the same. 'Please, sit.'

Stephen didn't break eye contact as he lowered himself to the chair.

Eve clasped her hands and laid them on the scored table in front of her, the furniture as alien to her as it must be to Stephen. The news she was about to break needed to be done with as much empathy as she could muster, something else alien to her, learned from Cooper. 'I'm sorry to tell you that Lucas is dead.'

Stephen's wide eyes flickered and closed as he dipped his head, too heavy for his neck, the weight bearing down, causing his shoulders to slump too. They let the silence stretch, giving him time to process that one of the kids was gone.

Eve continued. 'He was trapped in the building and sadly died before the emergency services could get to him.'

He dragged a hand through his hair, which shot off in all directions; more of the same red orange sprouted from the open collar of the denim shirt he wore. Eve's nose wrinkled at his body odour as he lowered his arm and, for a moment, she thought she could smell a sharp undertone of alcohol too but couldn't be sure.

Stephen splayed the fingers of his left hand, rubbing at the ring one. Eve clocked there was no band there as she watched his right forefinger and thumb circling flesh. Back and forth. Round and round.

She broke the silence. 'I appreciate things are raw. We need to chat to you about what happened last night. It'll help too if we know more about how Wellwood operated.'

Stephen's forefinger and thumb stopped mid-turn. 'He should've been in his room.'

'You were surprised when he wasn't?'

'Of course we were. We searched everywhere. Jake went back in twice once we got all the rest of the kids out . . . the smoke became too much and they wouldn't let him.'

Stephen raised his head. Lines Eve hadn't noticed moments before now punctured his forehead; his voice was dry and cracking as he spoke. 'Where? Where did they find him?'

'He was found in the basement.'

Stephen froze. His mouth opened and closed; his eyes narrowed to slits with the frown deepening the lines on his face. 'The basement?' Little more than a whisper.

Eve offered nothing more, waiting for Stephen to give her something.

'Are you sure?'

Cooper answered. 'I'm afraid there's no doubt about it. Can I get you a drink of water?' Cooper was up and over to the sink in the corner, rinsing a mug.

Stephen's head was moving from side to side. 'Why would he be down in the. . .' He rubbed at his forehead.

'We were hoping you might be able to help us with that.' It was Eve's turn to stare as Cooper put the mug down.

Stephen lifted it and sipped at its edge, the swallow loud against his dry throat. 'I can't . . . I don't know what to say. Is that where the fire started?'

Cooper sat. 'No. The Incident Commander believes it was started externally as in someone poured petrol through the letter box, followed closely by some kind of lit material.'

'Who the hell would . . .'

'That's what we need to find out. Maybe we could start with whether the kids had access to the space?'

Stephen licked at his lips. 'Of course they didn't. They didn't even know the space existed before three weeks ago.'

'Why three weeks?'

'We had a water issue – Scottish Water had to access the basement for pipework.'

'And the children were there during the work?'

'We kept them in the day room whilst the work was being carried out. They asked a lot of questions.'

'Was Lucas interested?'

31

'Yes. As much as the rest of them.'

'What kind of stuff?'

'If it was a secret. If anyone had ever lived down there. If they could make it into a den. Most of all, if they could go down and see it.'

Cooper's voice was soft. 'I guess it's the stuff of childhood adventures. A space beneath ground and one you can stand and walk around in. My kids would love that.'

'They wouldn't stop talking about it; we took them down with torches after the work was carried out. All safely done and with two members of staff present. We weren't down long. I think the darkness and spiders freaked some of them out in the end, although no one said.'

'Did you and the staff know about the space prior to that?'

'Yes. It wasn't a space we ever accessed, other than for maintenance work.'

'What's down there?'

'Nothing. Exposed pipes overhead and bare brickwork dividing rooms of a sort. With Wellwood being on the hill, the space beneath is substantial. The layout is the same as the floor plan above ground.'

'Quite something then?'

'I guess. Many of the houses and businesses in Kincorth have them.'

Cooper raised his index finger. 'Rings a bell. I heard someone had developed a similar space, the street down from Wellwood. Kincorth Crescent, I'm sure. They made it into a games room of sorts. Another story was a couple who had done it all up with a staircase down to it and their daughter lived there.'

Eve had never heard anything of the sort. 'You were never tempted to develop the space?'

'No, ours was just dirt and rubble. Not having windows and being underground doesn't advertise well for a children's home. Besides, we could only ever dream of that kind of money. We have enough problems keeping ourselves afloat as it is.' Stephen coughed. 'I should let the other staff know. Tell the kids. About Lucas.' Head down again, basement stories forgotten.

Eve unclasped her hands. 'I appreciate the kids' welfare is paramount. They and the staff need to know. But if you could hold off a little longer, tell us how Wellwood operates? Give us some understanding before we start investigating what happened last night.'

Stephen's attention shifted over to the closed door, as if making sure he was free to speak. 'What do you want to know?'

'You said it's difficult keeping yourselves afloat. How do you fund a place like Wellwood?'

'Several ways. We are privately run – community grants, loans from professional bodies who support children's homes, fundraising . . .'

'Give me the basics. The set-up. The staff. The kids.'

He was still staring at the door, maybe willing it to open, to go and see his staff and kids. 'Can this not wait?'

'Please.'

Stephen's gaze came back to Eve and Cooper, resigned. 'Let's start with layout.'

'Wellwood has seven bedrooms with en-suites. There's

33

a living room, recreational area, kitchen/dining room, laundry room and an office.'

'Fairly compact then?'

Stephen nodded. 'Not unlike a large family home.'

'How many staff?'

'I like to keep it intimate and simple. There are four of us. Me as manager, Beth as team leader and Ben and Jake as residential support workers. There are always three of us on day duty and one overnight.'

'You mentioned Jake was working last night?'

Stephen pushed at the mug. 'There happened to be two of us last night. Me and Jake. He was on shift for the kids.'

'And you were?'

Stephen shifted in the chair. 'Working late. I some-times find the quiet at night helps. I have a sofa bed in the office for nights when it's too late to go home.'

'Are you on your own?'

'No. I'm married with two kids. They understand the nature and pressures of the job at times.' Stephen was staring at the table.

Eve stared at the top of his head. 'Does the member of staff on night duty stay awake?'

Stephen shook his head. 'No. We don't have anyone of high risk needing that kind of supervision. We cur-rently have six kids.' Stephen baulked, realizing his error. 'Five kids. One bedroom is used for the overnight staffer. The kids know a member of staff is there if needed.'

'Tell me about the kids.'

Stephen was looking at the door again.

Eve pushed. 'The kids and then we'll let you go speak to them.'

He slumped. 'Like I said, we currently have five. Four are enrolled at Kincorth Academy and one is actively searching for employment.'

'Tell me about them.'

'Darren is the eldest – eighteen – he's been with us four years and is the one searching for a job now.'

'What does he want to do?'

'A trade. Mechanic. He's all about the cars. He was placed with us due to a drug problem in the home. His mum has since died after an overdose. The father has cleaned up a bit through a programme and now gets access fortnightly. Has done for about two and a half years now. The visits were supervised to begin with, but Darren is now of an age to see him by choice, and he does.'

'And the next down from him?'

'Hannah. She's sixteen and has also been with us four years. She was placed with us after neglect at home. She sees her grandma regularly, not her parents. Then there's Sadie. She's fifteen and has been with us six years. She lost her parents in a car accident and sadly no one stepped up to care for her. She has no family contact.'

'Must be tough seeing others meet with family.'

'It is at times. Our aim is to provide a family setting and to be that family. Then we have Charlotte. She's fourteen and has been with us eight years. Underage mother who was not able to care for her properly. There's no relationship there with her or the family.'

Cooper shifted in his seat. Eve knew what his family meant to him and imagined he was finding these kids' plight hard to swallow.

'Matt is twelve and been with us six years. His story is a little removed from the usual reasons. His mother was on her own. She had a form of OCD, you could call it, brought on after pregnancy. To the stage where she feared all germs coming in contact with Matt. All the furniture was wrapped in plastic and she kept him at home instead of nursery and his first two years of school. Social services got involved.'

'Where is she now?'

'Still wrapped up in the same home. She refuses to come and visit Matt and won't let anyone into the home. Mental health services are involved and have been for some time.'

'I can imagine it's a challenge to deal with all the things these kids have experienced.'

'It can be. It's rewarding also. Some kids adapt. They all do in their own way with the right care. The likes of Matt remain affected by those early years.'

'And Lucas?'

Stephen's jaw twitched. 'He was eleven. With us since two. Drugs. His mum died in a fire; Lucas was there at the time. He's been terrified of fire ever since.'

'His dad got him out?'

Stephen's lip curled. 'His dad was the cause of the fire. Left a joint burning in an ashtray and went off to bed, leaving her out of it on the sofa. Both of them had dabbled in a lot more than cannabis that night. By the time the neighbours were fighting to get into the flat, it was too late for the mother.'

'That's heartbreaking.'

'It is when Lucas has a surviving parent but still ends

up here. His dad was a dealer and an addict back then. Still is to my knowledge.'

'He didn't have any contact with the father?'

'No, though the father has tried numerous times. In fact, he was there yesterday. We call the police when he turns up. He's usually off his face and shouting the odds – about how he has rights, that his son needs him. Thankfully Lucas has been at school mostly. Not yesterday.'

'He saw his father?'

'No, he heard him. It took a while for us to comfort him after he'd been removed.'

'He wanted to see his father?'

Stephen chewed on the inside of his cheek. 'He was in love with the idea of his dad. Like a lot of kids in care. Wanting to believe that things can be different.'

'And did he understand they couldn't be?'

'We'd explained in many ways his dad wasn't in a state to be responsible for him.'

'Is that his only family?'

'No, he has a grandmother. His mother's side. She's never shown any interest.'

'Have you spoken to them?'

'No, we didn't know . . . couldn't be sure . . .'

Eve dug into her pocket and took out a notebook. 'I'd appreciate the addresses. We'll go and break the news to the grandmother and have other officers visit the father simultaneously. Make sure we get to them first.'

Stephen stood. 'I can access that info via my phone. I need to go see the kids. Jake is upstairs with the two other members of staff, Ben and Beth.'

Eve stood, stopping Stephen in his tracks. 'I need to ask you one more thing.'

Stephen shoved his hands into his pockets, said nothing.

'What you've told us, about these kids. There's a lot of trauma. Are they happy here?'

Stephen frowned. 'I like to think they are. Why are you asking?'

'We suspect arson.'

Stephen's hands shot out of his pockets. 'And you think one of my kids was responsible?'

'That's not what I'm saying but we can't rule it out. We can't rule anyone from Wellwood out.'

Stephen slammed back down into his chair. 'No one would . . .'

The words hung in the air.

'We are going to have to go through everyone's phones, any computers and so forth.'

'Do you really need to go to those lengths? These kids value their privacy. And there's a lot on the work computers of a sensitive nature. Confidential.'

'And it'll remain so – unless specifically related to this case. We also need to talk to Jake. Could you organize a private space here? Somewhere with no interruption?'

Stephen looked around the room. 'In here?'

'Here is fine. We'd also like to speak with the kids.'

'OK. I'd prefer the kids were spoken to together. They've gone through enough without being pulled apart by the police.' Stephen glanced between them. 'No offence. And maybe up in one of the dorms we've made available to them. Less formal.'

'That's fine. We'll go and tell the family. Give you space to talk to the others. I'll be in touch when we're on the way back. I'd appreciate Jake waiting in here for us when we arrive – and any technology to have been gathered together.'

Eve looked back over her shoulder at Stephen, knowing he must be dreading the chat with the staff and kids; the emotion and exhaustion was raw on his face, the knowledge they all faced a long road ahead.

Chapter 9

Then

THIS IS HIS PLACE. Beneath the bullshit. Away from all the hurt and the lies. A world away from false smiles and high-pitched voices, pretending everything's all right.

Down here he can hide. In the dark. Unseen. Untouched. Away from her. Because above she is everywhere. Like a jaundiced light creeping into every crevice, covering everything in her sickness, exposing things better left hidden.

Rubble flattens beneath his shoe soles, lodging between the grooves there. He'll remove the shoes from his feet at the top of the ladder, in the same way he'll shake off the freedom of darkness as he squints against the harshness of light and prepares to pretend again. He'll hide the shoes away until next time, when he can escape again.

She can never know he comes down here. She doesn't even know it exists. That makes it his. No one else's.

She can never know because she would take it from him. The way she's taken everything else. Making the whole of his life a prison. Trapped.

He's been there before. Imprisoned. Barely space to breathe. Afraid to breathe. Scared to be heard, to be noticed.

Mum demanded he was quiet when the men came. He got good at being silent. Excelled at it. So good she'd forget he was there, her mind somewhere else other than the bottom of the latest bottle she'd drunk, and far away from what each of those men would do to her. Things he'd learned the hard way the men would do to him too if he didn't stay quiet. Hidden.

The day help came, it was like being found in more ways than they knew. People who were kind, who spoke gently to him as they held his head away when they passed his mother's body on the floor.

That day, the day he escaped prison, was the day they brought him here. For the shortest time he'd dared to breathe again. It wasn't long before it dawned on him that he'd only been moved to another cell.

There were no bottles to blame this time, but the place was as dangerous, albeit in a different way.

In time, he grew to realize the bottles had never been to blame. It was his mother's fault and hers alone. She could've stopped what was happening. She could've made things different. Better. Saved him and herself. She didn't.

No, it wasn't bottles he had to fear. Coming here to someone else, to *her*, had taught him that.

It was women he should fear. He knew that now. He'd suffered enough at their hands to know he should never be anything else but terrified of them.

41

Chapter 10

FERGUSON HADN'T MADE IT past Aberdeen Royal Infirmary's A & E's reception area. He'd run in after tailing the ambulance and at the same second a swarm of blue-overalled bodies burst through the scuffed double doors, grabbed the trolley with the young boy whose hand Ferguson had held as he lay broken in the middle of the road, before the same doors swallowed them all whole again.

Ferguson sat by the entrance, able to see everything going on from the row of blue chairs as he shifted from side to side on plastic not built to encourage a long stay.

His discomfort wasn't helped any as he saw DS Ron Miller from road traffic marching through the door, appearing even shorter and more squat than normal next to the wiry officer who looked young enough to be Ron's son.

'What are you doing here, Ferguson?'

Miller had a voice that grated. Loud, clipped and cutting with its own self-importance. Ferguson had crossed paths with him on more than one occasion, none of which had been a pleasure.

Ferguson stood. 'I came in with the boy. The van driver is here. I'm waiting for him to be checked over before I talk with him. Your guys took a statement from the other driver at the scene. I don't expect to be talking with the boy any time soon.'

Ron resembled a bulldog in his current stance. Stumpy legs apart, chest puffed, elbows bent out with his hands in his pockets – marking his territory, ready to piss on Ferguson. 'We got your statement from the boys at the scene. I meant what are you *still* doing here.'

Ferguson glanced at the receptionist behind the glass partition, who hadn't shifted her attention his way once. She now stared out at them, her stern face telling them this was her ground and she'd be the only one marking it.

'It would help for me to be present when you talk to them, what with me knowing what went down.'

Ron dug his hands deeper into his trouser pockets and rocked back on his heels. 'We can take it from here.'

Ferguson didn't want to give up on this easily. He wasn't so concerned about the drivers. But he'd made the boy a promise and he needed to see it through. Making himself involved in the meantime would ensure that. 'I appreciate your position, Ron, but—'

They were interrupted by a stout, bald man in overalls coming through the doors. 'The male driver has been checked over. You can see him now. His name's Arthur.'

It was the first time Ferguson had heard the driver's name.

'His daughter is with him. They're in bay one.'

Ferguson stepped forward, ready and waiting in case Ron tried to block his access. The determination on his face must have been clear as Ron stepped back and turned to the officer by his side. 'Stay here. Doesn't need bloody three of us.'

Chapter 11

'I COULD SWEAR I smelled drink on his breath.' Eve sat in the car passenger seat. Cooper had driven them to the small strip of shops up from the hostel and they were parked outside.

Cooper turned to her. 'Who?'

'Stephen. You didn't smell it?'

Cooper shook his head. 'Maybe it was a quick shot of something after what happened. Would be understandable, wouldn't it?'

Eve's nose wrinkled. 'I doubt he had time to stop by a shop between what happened at Wellwood and getting to the hostel.' She left what that meant hanging in the air. 'The stuff he said about struggling to keep themselves afloat; do you reckon they could've been having financial difficulties?'

'What, and now he's drinking?'

'I was thinking more about the fire.'

Cooper rested the back of his head against the driver's window. 'An insurance job?'

'Stranger things have happened. I'm batting stuff about.'

'Jesus, could you imagine? Finding out the kid was down there?'

Eve's mind was back in the ambulance with Lucas; she'd still be seeing him in her sleep tonight. She shook herself out of it as Cooper went on.

'What do you want?' Cooper tilted his head towards the Co-op outside the car.

'The biggest sarnie you can get me and a large coffee from the machine.' She was under no illusions. They were in for the long haul once they'd visited Lucas's grandmother and returned to talk to the staff. 'I'm going to check in with Hastings, get Mearns and Ferguson to go and break the news to the father.'

She jabbed at the screen on her phone as Cooper got out of the car. DCI Hastings picked up within seconds.

'It's me, sir. Checking in to say we've spoken with management from Wellwood and are going to see Lucas's grandmother. We'll be heading back to speak with the kids and staff afterwards. The boy was only eleven years old.'

'What the hell happened?'

Eve could picture Hastings banging the pen on the desk in front of him as she heard it tapping.

'Arson. A lit rag shoved through the letter box.'

'In a fucking kids' home?'

'No clue yet as to what happened to the boy, Lucas. I assumed he'd got lost in the smoke or something, or maybe they'd miscounted heads in the panic. I hadn't counted on his body being found underground.'

At first there was silence on the other end, before: 'What the hell do you mean, underground?'

'In a basement, sir. I haven't seen it yet. I'm led to believe it's a substantial space. According to the firefighters, it matches the layout of the house and is tall enough to stand in.'

'What the hell was he doing down there?'

'Therein lies the question. The manager of the place is saying he has no idea and the place was out of bounds to the kids.'

'It clearly bloody wasn't . . . How are they all?'

He meant the kids. He was a moody and stern son of a bitch but, like most people, and especially as a father himself, there was a soft spot there when it came to children. 'They'll all be shattered and shaken. Sounds like they've been through a lot in their short lives. The question is whether one of them may be responsible. I'm not ruling out anything at this stage.'

'And the staff are all there today?'

'It's a small set-up. Two of them weren't there last night. We'll take the opportunity to interview them one by one regardless. The manager is setting up a room for us to use.'

'What are you thinking?'

'At the moment? One obviously upset manager but no answers. We'll see what the staff and kids have to say.'

'Do you think one of the staff might've been responsible for him being in there? Some sort of punishment they wouldn't exactly make public knowledge?'

'It's a possibility. It's whether the fire was connected to him being there or not. The hatch was maybe too heavy for Lucas once it was shut. What I'm struggling with is how the fire started. Hard to believe Lucas would've started it deliberately. He had a fear of fire. He lost his mum in one and was there when it happened.'

'The poor wee bugger.'

Eve rested the side of her head against the car-door window. 'He must've been terrified, whatever happened. As I said, I'm not ruling out one of the staff or the kids being responsible. At the moment we have nothing else to tell us otherwise.'

'The mind boggles.'

Eve pulled the phone a little away from her ear as Hastings shifted things about his desk, his voice coming and going as he moved about. 'Anyway, sir, I'll check in with Mearns and Ferguson after this.'

Hastings came back fully on the line. 'Mearns knows about the fire. Not sure you'll get much luck with Ferguson. He ended up at the scene of a road accident on the way in this morning. He's at the hospital with the driver and the kid who was hit.'

'Jesus, it doesn't rain but it pours.' Eve squinted through the window. 'Anyway, Cooper's out of the shop with a bag big enough to feed the thousands. I'll keep you updated.'

Hastings sighed. 'This is a kid, lost and found dead in a kids' home. Underground. And bloody arson responsible for the fire that killed him. The press is going to be all over this. Full focus needed, no shit.'

'I can guarantee that, sir.'

Hastings didn't bother to say goodbye. The loud click of him hanging up told Eve he was already gone.

Chapter 12

MEARNS SHUT OFF THE radio, stabbing at the button a little harder than she'd meant to and making the radio rock back and forth on top of the desk. She was sick of listening to news updates telling her nothing.

What the hell was happening with the fire? So far, it seemed she knew more than the newsreader, who had made no mention yet of the boy who had died. Ferguson's car accident hadn't even made the news.

Mearns stretched back in the chair, frustrated at being here waiting on the others to check in or turn up. Even if it was the way it went sometimes. Her colleagues' days had started before she'd even got here. Eve's and Cooper's had been planned for them via Hastings, and Ferguson's definitely unplanned. It still sucked being stuck here instead of being out there doing *something*.

She jumped forward as the phone rang and snatched it. *Eve.* 'Mearns.'

'I need you to do something.'

Thank God. 'Shoot.'

49

'I need you and Ferguson to go and break the news to the father of the boy who died at Wellwood.'

Not quite the job she was hoping for. She glanced across at the empty seat where Ferguson usually sat. 'What's the story?'

'It's not a good one. Boy's name was Lucas. He was eleven.'

'Jesus.'

'It gets worse. He was found in the basement. Trapped.'

'Did the fire start down there?'

'No, it was a lit rag shoved through the letter box.'

'Someone started it on purpose?'

'No other way to look at it. We're on the way to tell the grandmother. I wanted to be sure they're both told before the press gets hold of it.'

Mearns balanced the phone between her ear and shoulder and grabbed a pen from the desk. 'What's the address?'

'Fifty-one Morven Court.'

Mearns's hand paused in mid-air. She knew the address. Torry. Off Balnagask Road. 'Did he have contact with Lucas?'

'No. Not for lack of trying by the sounds of it but the love of a hit, any kind of hit, stopped that from happening. The mother died in a fire caused by a joint he left burning before they went to bed.'

'Nice.'

'About as nice as the grandmother who never tried to access the boy.'

'The father's mother?'

'No, the mum's.'

For some reason that fact stuck in Mearns's throat more than if it had been on the dad's side.

'I also need you to dig into the history of Wellwood, get us the background. I know nothing about the place. I want the big picture.'

'Sure.' Mearns was already typing into the Google search bar.

'Is Ferguson there now? Hastings told me about the accident.'

'No. I tried him earlier. No luck. He must still be up at the hospital. I'll keep trying and get him to meet me there.' Mearns's eyes were scanning the computer screen.

'Make sure you get him before you go and see this guy. I've no idea what he's like or capable of. It's definitely a two-officer job. We'll be heading back to talk to other members of staff and the kids later.'

'Will do.'

Mearns hung up, clicking to print what little information there was in front of her, and wasting no time before calling Ferguson.

Chapter 13

THE HARSH OVERHEAD STRIP LIGHTS above the A & E bay bounced off the man's liver-spotted scalp, the wispy white comb-over doing little to hide it – or the square white patch plastered to his forehead.

He sat propped up by pillows, a hospital gown baggy on shoulders rounded with age, seeming as if he might be about to fold inside himself – were it not for the plastic cup of coffee he'd been given and held between both hands.

There was a slight tremor in his grip as he stared at Ferguson and Ron, who had invaded his space through the closed curtains around his bed and now stood on either side of him.

Ron had asked his daughter to leave, something Ferguson didn't see as necessary. He wasn't planning on letting Ron be the first to speak. 'Arthur, the head's shaping up better than when I last saw you.' Ferguson ignored Ron's stare across the bed.

The man parted thin dry lips, a top row of perfect, if

slightly yellowed, dentures visible as he answered. 'Feels better too. Four stitches. I was lucky.' He lowered his eyes. 'Wish that was the case for the other guy.' His eyes searched Ferguson's. 'How is he? They haven't told me anything.'

Ferguson felt the mobile in his pocket vibrate with an incoming call. He ignored it.

He looked down at Arthur. 'We haven't heard yet. He's in surgery.'

'Are his family here? I'd be happy to talk with them.'

Ferguson sympathized with the guy, someone simply in the wrong place at the wrong time. 'We've been unable to identify him as yet.'

Arthur's brow creased. 'He's alone?'

'Not alone. I was with him at the scene, and I plan to be here when he's ready for visitors.' He ignored Ron's glare, not even sure if the boy would ever be ready for visitors.

Ron roughly dug a hand into his trouser pocket. 'You need to tell us what happened.'

It wasn't the words but the abrupt tone that made Ferguson baulk. Arthur's double grip tightened on the cup, like a child about to be disciplined.

Ferguson stared at Ron before turning back to Arthur. 'This morning will have been a real shock. I was there. It all happened so fast. Take your time. Tell me what you remember, if you can, as and when you're ready.'

Arthur's fingers relaxed slightly. 'I'd done my pick-up from the bakery. I work for them six mornings a week. Cowan's in King Street.' His voice was as thin as his lips.

Ferguson sat in the plastic chair by the bed as Ron

scowled and remained standing, no seat at his side. Ferguson shifted in the seat as his mobile vibrated again, pulling it out this time and seeing it was Mearns. He pocketed the phone. 'Early starts.'

The man gave a small nod. 'Yes. I drive down in my own car at 5 a.m., help load up the van, and head into the city centre to deliver to businesses. It's not much, a wee job to keep me busy in retirement. I don't drink.' The old man was wide-eyed, keen to get his point across.

Ferguson leaned closer to the bed. 'Don't worry, the breath test is procedure. It was negative.'

The man visibly breathed out. 'I gave up over a decade ago. On too many meds for my diabetes and my ticker.'

Ferguson was surprised the old man's ticker had survived the crash, let alone the sight afterwards.

Ron shifted forward, hands still dug deep in his pockets. 'So, you were driving along Crown Street towards Union Street?' It was clear he was keen to get the facts, not caring about those who were affected.

Arthur turned to Ron and peered up at him. Ferguson was thankful at least that Ron was short and not towering over the bed as he could've been.

'I only have one delivery at the bottom of Crown Street. I get it done first then the rest are Union Street and Rosemount most days. I was coming up to Portland Street and Rosebank Terrace.'

'Driving at the speed limit?' The clipped tone cut between the three of them.

'Thirty on the nose. The van's a walking advertisement for my employer. I wouldn't dare do anything else, traffic or no traffic.' The man paused; pain etched in his features as he swallowed. 'Doesn't matter though, it was still too fast.'

Ron didn't miss a beat. 'You were coming up to Portland Street?'

'Yes. There wasn't another car or a soul going about. He came out of nowhere.'

Ron moved closer, his trouser legs almost touching the bed. 'From which direction?'

'To my left. Rosebank Terrace. You know the dead end?'

Ron cricked his neck. 'I know where you're at.'

'Used to be a good Chinese there, was surpri—' The man stopped.

Ferguson filled the gap, pretending the vibrating wasn't happening in his pocket. 'And he stepped out on to the road?'

'I wish he had; I might have been able to avoid him then. No. He was running. Sprinting even. Right into the path of my bonnet.' The man closed his eyes. 'The sound when he hit . . .'

Ferguson got in before Ron did. 'I can imagine. What did you do?'

'Banged on the brakes, closed my eyes as I swerved right. By then he was bouncing away from the van.'

Ferguson leaned back. It supported the position he had found the van in.

Ron wasn't taking what Arthur said or what Ferguson's statement had said as gospel. 'We'll be able to confirm once forensics are done investigating the scene and CCTV has been checked out.'

The man's head moved from Ron to Ferguson, who said nothing.

'There's not much I could've done.' Arthur's voice cracked.

Ferguson edged forward again. 'We have officers checking CCTV and I'm sure footage will confirm that, as well as the witnesses they've already interviewed.' He didn't say anything about his own statement backing it up as Ron stared at him. 'Please try not to worry.'

The man's bottom lip quivered. 'For me to have hit him like that . . . he must be in a bad way.'

Ferguson chose not to share what he'd seen. He guessed the reality might be worse than Arthur was imagining.

Chapter 14

LUCAS'S GRANDMOTHER, LESLEY, WAS a bony woman with thicker white hair on her chin than on her head. She stood blocking the doorway to her top-floor tenement flat in Mastrick, tugging at her long cable-knit cardigan, her spindly legging-clad limbs sticking out from its hem, as Eve and Cooper finally cleared the stairs and came face to face with her.

'Bit of a climb, isn't it?' Her voice was as rough as sandpaper, and her lips looked just as dry.

Eve licked her own lips as she stared at them. 'Thanks for letting us up.' She breathed a little heavier after the climb, trying not to as she inhaled cat's piss hanging pungent in the air of the hallway.

'What's this about?'

'Could we come in?'

The woman moved aside to let them in, the cloying smell of tobacco taking over now, sticking to them as they stepped into the hallway, jostling for room in the narrow space. The woman closed and locked the door before lifting and rattling the chain across the once silver metal strip, congealed now with dirt. This woman was obviously taking no chances with security before leading them through to the living room. The stench was worse here, a lit cigarette burning orange in the overflowing glass ashtray, the ceiling, once presumably white, now yellow and brown.

'Sit.' It was barked, more like an order than an offer.

Eve couldn't count the number of crumpled newspapers strewn across the faded fabric sofa and opted for an armchair by the window, Cooper taking the other one by the old telly on a stand in the corner. Lesley sat on the sofa, one butt cheek crushing a paper beneath her, the trapped pages rustling as she lurched forward and resumed dragging on the fag.

'We're sorry to have to tell you this but your grandson, Lucas, died in a fire at Wellwood last night.'

Lesley didn't flinch. 'I won't be much help to you. I hardly knew the kid.'

There wasn't a hint of emotion in the woman's voice or face. Her coldness was perhaps down to shock. Or maybe Lesley couldn't care less she'd lost her grandson.

Her lips pursed around the filter, eyes narrowing to slits amid the grey smoke as she exhaled. 'We weren't close, and I won't be made to feel guilty for him being in there.'

Eve's lip curled. An eleven-year-old boy was dead, and all this woman wanted was to make sure she wasn't getting any blame.

'We're not here to make anyone feel guilty. As I said, it was about notifying you. Seeing as we're here, can you tell us anything about Lucas?' Eve needed the boy to be remembered by someone else other than the staff at Wellwood, for this woman to find some small space in her heart, if she even had one, for Lucas.

'I know he never should have been born.'

Cooper visibly tightened in the chair.

'My daughter, his mother, was a junkie. Gave me a life of hell. Never got anything from her but strife. All the thanks I ever got from bringing her into this world was thieving my stuff to feed her filthy habit.'

'How old was she? It must've been hard watching her become addicted.'

'Fourteen. It was a given with the crowd she was running with.'

'People from school?'

'Some of them. Added to the ones around here. Trouble, the lot of them.'

'When did you realize she had a problem?'

'Early doors. She got hooked fast. No thanks to the boyfriend.'

'Boyfriend?'

'Ten years older. Always wondered if it was any kind of relationship or if he liked young blood – both for the drugs to be introduced and in the bedroom.'

Cooper's top lip curled. 'Did you try to stop her seeing him?'

'Of course I bloody did. I'm not stupid. She was headstrong, and he was persuasive – especially because he had the gear she was after.'

Eve could almost feel the heat coming off Cooper. 'He was Lucas's father?'

'I remember the day she came to tell me. Off her face, she was. All this talk about how the guy loved her and they'd get a flat and be a family. I begged her to get rid of it. Said she wasn't in a fit state or of an age to be a mother.'

'She wouldn't be swayed?'

'No, and when I threatened to go after the bastard for meddling with an underage girl, she left.'

Eve wanted the woman to look at her. She was yet to make eye contact. 'Where did she go?'

'God knows. I heard she was sleeping on floors and sofas with the guy. Whoever was willing to take them in. Probably took whatever he was offering for rent.'

'When did you next see her?'

'I didn't. Next I heard was when they found her.'

Eve took a moment to digest that. 'Found her where?'

'Some squat in Sandilands. Went up in flames with a joint he'd left lit. He was in another room with the bairn who was crawling about the place in amongst rubbish and gear with a soiled nappy he'd been wearing for days.'

Cooper shook his head. 'Jesus.'

'Almost three and still not potty-trained.'

Eve wanted to see some kind of emotion from Lesley, for her daughter at least, if not for the baby. 'That's sad.'

'Don't get me wrong. I did feel sorry for the kid but after what she put me through, I wasn't taking on another child. Especially one with the genes of that guy. And drugs in his system from the day he was conceived. Would've been nothing but trouble.'

Had Lesley even tried? 'Did the authorities ever ask you to take him?'

'Och, they tried. I wasn't having any of it.'

Cooper was struggling to keep quiet. 'Weren't you worried about him being left with the father?'

'No. I knew he'd been banged up for stuff found at the flat after the fire.'

Cooper was staring at her. 'Lucas was left with no one?'

'Which is why I agreed to the home.'

Eve spoke as Cooper's fingers flexed. 'Did you ever visit?'

She shook her head. 'No. Thought it was for the best he didn't get attached to me in any way.'

Now it was both of them struggling to keep their mouths shut. Hard to believe anyone could be so heartless.

The woman stared back at them, lighting another fag as she did. 'I did drop a bag into the home they put him in.' She sat straighter, as if the drop-off were something for her to be proud of. 'A picture of his mum before she got herself in a mess. Some clothes folk had given to me for him when they expected me to take him in.'

What could she say to that? Eve opted for the first thing to enter her head. 'I'm sure he was glad of the picture of his mum.'

'No point in me keeping it. Didn't even resemble how I remembered her, and I definitely didn't need the clothes.'

Eve wanted to shake the woman. 'His father was at Wellwood yesterday. Wanting to see Lucas.' Too much of a coincidence that the fire started later that day? Lesley hadn't even asked about the fire.

Lesley didn't miss a beat. 'Pah. He's about as interested as me. To him, Lucas was a free ticket to a flat and benefits.'

Never mind shake her, she wanted to punch her. 'What about the funeral?'

Lesley leaned forward to stub the fag out in the ashtray, grey and white ash spilling over the glass edges and on to the littered coffee table. 'As in will I be paying?' She laughed, a cruel sound. 'What with? Buttons?'

'I meant will you attend?'

'I haven't seen him in over nine years. I went to her funeral. Didn't pay for that either. Council picked up the tab.'

Eve was already standing, ready to drag Cooper with her if need be, not sure either of them would be able to contain themselves if they stayed any longer.

She made sure Cooper was up out of the seat before she spoke. 'We'll be going now. Lucas will have the staff and kids from Wellwood at his funeral and neither I nor Cooper here would dream of not being there. He was a good kid who deserved more. Much more. And he has people who loved him and will miss him.'

Eve made her way to the living-room door, not waiting to be shown out. She glanced back to see Cooper was with her, not surprised to see the woman still seated and pulling out another fag before lifting the TV remote.

Chapter 15

'YEAH?'

'Finally, I've been trying you for bloody ages.'

Ferguson held the phone away from Mearns's rant. 'I was in talking to the driver with Ron Miller stepping on my toes.'

The silence on the other end stretched long enough for Ferguson to take the phone away from his ear to check he still had a connection. Mearns spoke. 'How's the boy?'

'I'm waiting on an update from the doc.'

'You'll have to leave your number as I need you at Morven Court.'

'Why?'

'Eve and Cooper have been out at a fire this morning. An eleven-year-old boy died. We've got to go and tell the father.'

Ferguson shifted the phone from his ear as a woman strode into the waiting room and called his name. 'I need to go.'

'Ferguson, I'm waiting for you in the car at the guy's house.' Mearns's voice was tinny. He pressed the phone back against his ear.

'Fine, text me the address.' Ferguson hung up.

'That's me.' He stood, catching the doc's attention.

She was a middle-aged, tall, slender woman with a nose too sharp for her soft face.

'You came in with the boy earlier?' She poked gold-framed glasses up the bridge of her nose.

'Yes. How is he?'

'He's in the intensive care unit. Before any of that, how do you know him?'

'I don't. I happened to be there. On my way to work. I wasn't there in an official capacity.'

'Official capacity?'

'I'm with the police. I've already spoken to the driver who hit him.'

'I see. Did you see anything at the scene that might help us ID him – a bag or a wallet?'

Ferguson shook his head. 'Nothing. He had no ID on him.'

The doctor frowned.

'There was a phone in the road, smashed. Forensics will have it; hopefully they'll be able to get something from it. And a tattoo; did you see the tattoo on his hand?'

'Yes. Maybe you'll get some joy from that. I hope so because he's not good. He's sustained multiple fractures to his right arm and leg. He also took a hit to his head; arrived here unconscious and unresponsive. Scans have shown swelling on the brain. We don't believe it to be too serious, but we've taken the precaution of placing him in a medically induced coma until the swelling sub-sides and we know what we're dealing with.' She shuffled Ferguson off to the side of the seating, which had got busier with people suffering minor injuries and concerned relatives in the time he'd been waiting.

Ferguson swallowed. 'How long will he be under?'

'I don't see it being more than a couple of days. It'll be a case of close monitoring until we see improvement.'

Ferguson could see his outline in the polished floor as he listened. 'He spoke to me when I found him. A good sign, right? Do you know if he said anything in the ambulance or once he got here?'

The doctor shook her head. 'I'm surprised he managed to say anything to you. He was in a lot of pain in the ambulance before becoming non-responsive. Morphine was given for that pain and the shock. He was out of it by the time he got here.'

'Hopefully someone might be missing him and will phone into the station or here.' Ferguson pictured the dirty hands and nails on the boy, the greasy hair and the worn trainers. 'This induced coma; can he hear what's going on around him? Is he aware of what's happening?'

'Again, it's a hard one to call. In a medically induced coma, the brain will continue to work at a minimal level. Basic functions like respiration, circulation and digestion continue. Many people gain comfort from talking to someone in that state and believe it helps them whilst under. Some patients who have come around from a coma say they remember sounds and conversations whilst they were unconscious. Others don't.'

'Will he feel pain when he's under?' Ferguson needed to ask, wanting to know someone at least cared what was happening to the boy.

'We hope not. By monitoring his vitals, we should be able to ensure he's comfortable. There can also be reflexive movements of the limbs and responses to touch or pain.'

'What will happen once you see improvement?'

'When levels return to normal, we'll withdraw the medication gradually until he regains consciousness.'

Ferguson didn't want to think any further than that at the moment. 'OK. Listen, I'm not family. You know the story there. When he comes around, I will want to talk with him in an official capacity. In the meantime, can I come and see him?'

The doctor's mouth tightened to a thin line.

'I want to be there. I found him. I'd hate to think he has no one. To chat to him or let him know someone is there. I won't say I'm a police officer whilst he's unconscious; I won't even say anything about the crash.'

'Like I say, it may help him whilst he's under. General chit-chat. Nothing to pressurize or distress him.'

'You have my word. I need to go into work, but I will be back tonight. Can I leave my card with you? I'd appreciate any updates you can give me.'

'Fine. Be aware, even when he does come around, it's not uncommon for short-term memory to be shot.'

Ferguson sighed. Nothing was going to be simple with this boy. 'OK. In the meantime, I'll do my best to find out who he is.'

The doctor took his card and glanced at it before

placing it in the top pocket of her white coat, the thin cardboard jostling for space amongst the pens and other things hooked there. 'I'll let you know.'

'Thanks.' Ferguson headed to the door, hoping it wouldn't take too long to get across town. Mearns had been waiting long enough already.

Chapter 16

'THEY TELL ME A little boy died in the fire.'

Eve scowled as she and Cooper exited the main door of the council tenement, not surprised to see Marcie Wade standing at the bottom of the litter-strewn path. Tailing them like a sniffer dog on the trail of a good tit-bit. Eve hoped Marcie hadn't been following her since Wellwood, otherwise she'd know where the staff and kids were now. Eve stopped short of where Marcie stood blocking access to the pavement.

'Sadly, yes I can confirm a minor died in the fire at Wellwood.'

'How old?'

'Eleven.' Eve's focus shifted over Marcie's shoulder to the playground opposite, two teenagers bunking off school with cans of Monster, not a care in the world who saw them as they sat on a couple of swings outside the Mastrick Community Centre and library.

'Name?' Marcie's pen was poised in one hand, the other gripping a notepad on which Eve could read some scribbled descriptions of ruined property. Eve remembered a time not long ago when Marcie had been a breath of fresh air compared to her predecessor, Claire Jenkins. The feeling was to be short-lived. The woman was finding her feet in her first reporter job. Still, Eve was surprised how quickly she'd found the hunger for a story at any cost.

Eve met her steely glare, saw that hunger in her eyes now. 'You know the score, Marcie. Can't give you anything until we've spoken to family members.'

'He had family?'

Eve watched as Marcie pushed back a tendril of hair which had come loose from her hair clip. Did the reporter ever consider having her own family or, like her, was it all about the job?

'Yes.'

'Why was he in a home?' The breeze blew at the bottom of the floral shift dress Marcie wore over black leggings. Rocking the look of a mum on the school run. Soft. Approachable.

'We both know it's not that black and white.'

Eve walked towards Marcie, Cooper trailing her. She was forced to stop when Marcie didn't budge, lips twitching with her next question. 'What happened? How did the fire start? Why did the little boy not get out when everyone else did?'

Eve puffed out her chest and took a small step, which was all she could manage in the space between them. It wouldn't be long before Marcie would find out it was arson. She wasn't going to hand that fact to her.

Marcie stepped to the side of the narrow path and

turned, following Eve and Cooper as they made towards the Mastrick shops, back to the car parked outside the bakery. 'Did he get stuck somewhere in the fire? Did they not realize the little boy was still in there?'

A little old woman with a battered shopping trolley stared as they passed the bookies. Eve was glad to see the car up ahead.

Eve didn't miss that Marcie kept using the term 'little boy'. That little boy would make for a big story. 'We are currently investigating both how the fire started and what happened to the boy. We can't give you anything else for now. There'll be a press release in due course.' Eve tugged at the handle of the driver's door.

'A member of his family lives there?' Marcie motioned her head back towards the building.

'Don't even think about it, Marcie. Have some decency.' Eve wasn't saying it to protect Lucas's grandmother; she had the strong suspicion that, if payment was involved, Lesley would have no problem spilling everything she knew about her grandson's death. She was now glad the woman hadn't asked about the fire. It was a headache they didn't need right now.

Marcie turned, her back to them, staring at the tenement in the distance. It wouldn't take many tries of the communal buzzer before she'd figure out which door she needed to be knocking on.

Eve got in the car and slammed the door. Her mobile phone was at her ear before Cooper had joined her.

'Mearns?'

'Yeah?'

'Have you spoken to Lucas's dad, to James Fyfe?'

70

'Not yet, I'm waiting for Ferguson outside Fyfe's flat. He's on his way. I had a quick delve into Wellwood. It was privately run from the mid-sixties to the nineties by a Ms Sally Fields.'

'Is that not the name of the actress – the one who starred in that movie *Sybil*?'

'Exactly what I thought. I watched it as a kid and it still gives me the shivers now.'

'Same. Listen, tell Ferguson to move his backside. Marcie's sniffing.'

Chapter 17

Then

SHE DOESN'T WALK INTO the room, she strides. All attitude and fizz, energy popping and spilling out of every pore.

I'm staring, seeing my mother when one bottle used to be enough. Every other kid in the room is staring too. Silent as we watch this force spin into our space.

Her faded bubblegum-pink leggings dance beneath a torn puffball skirt. She gives a little twirl, lace lifting inches above the curve of her bum.

She's happy. Something this place has forgotten how to be.

My Adam's apple bounces at the same time as she does, down on to the sofa beside me.

This girl screams danger. Everything I learned from my mother – this being the first time I've truly had to remember the lesson.

My body is stiff, not wanting to come across as soft if I move my foot that now touches the side of her leg off the sofa. Heat melting our limbs together.

I have to remind myself that I don't care what this girl

or any girl thinks. She flicks her blonde straight hair over her milky-white shoulder, bare where the oversized T-shirt she's wearing has slid off. No bra strap there.

She smiles, face electric, enjoying all eyes on her. She focuses hers only on mine. Two metal discs drawn to a magnet.

I'm in control.

'I'm Danny.' She grins now and drops her hand. It's resting on my foot. Limbs upon limbs.

For the briefest of moments, I'm sure I can smell drink on her breath. I tell myself I'm remembering my mother. Smelling her whenever I saw her behave like this – whenever I see anyone behave like this.

My cheeks burn as hot as my toes beneath her touch. I let them. I could stop it if I wanted. 'Hi.'

She stares. I don't look away. Chatter starts again in the room. The others recognizing there is no room for anything else in-between us. The way there was never room for me in a room with Mum. With her bottles and her men.

'Who said you could come through here?' The chatter halts as Ms Fields' voice slices through the room, her icy black stare fixed on Danny.

Danny kicks back lazily. 'You were on the phone. I thought I'd take a look around.'

The room holds its breath. Waiting. Faces turning away. Pretending they haven't noticed this girl. That they know better.

Ms Fields blocks the door, her silhouette looming bigger, more of a threat against the light behind her. Everyone already knowing the threat she poses, regardless of size.

She glares at Danny, lips tight, fingers curled. Surprises us all by turning on her heel and leaving the room.

Someone will pay though, and they won't be made to wait long.

Because this girl screams danger, and Ms Fields knows it as much as I do.

Chapter 18

THE BITTER BLACK SCENT of smoke found its way into Darren's nostrils from where it lay trapped in the fibres of his clothing, its grime blocking the pores of his dark skin. The shrill of fire alarms and the holler of voices still echoed in his ears, an unwelcome soundtrack to Stephen's voice as he'd told them Lucas was gone. Darren was wrestling with what had happened. Scenarios spinning in his mind.

No one had uttered a word since Stephen left. Only the odd muffled sniffle and a shuffle of skin against the cheap polyester sleeping bags they'd been given. Darren shifted in the narrow upper bunk that squeezed at his large frame and peered over the metal frame at where Matt sat hunched on a plastic chair pushed hard against the steel grey lockers lining one wall. As removed from the room as he could be.

'You OK?'

Matt lifted his head and coughed as he pushed silver-framed glasses up his nose. He barked again, probably already in the throes of some other unknown new allergy.

'I can't sleep on those pillows.' He looked nervously at the bed beneath Darren's, his eyes wide as his voice whined, as if the pillow lying there might attack him. 'And God knows what all this smoke on me is doing to my breathing.'

Hannah stepped back from one of the two windows in the room and turned to him, wiping at red eyes as she did. 'Have a shower.'

Matt tutted. 'And catch pneumonia or whatever the hell's lurking on those towels?' He stared at the towels piled high on the other plastic chair. Towels that Beth had found and they'd been told to use for a shower before they tried to get some rest.

Hannah scowled. 'Seriously? That's all you're worried about? Are you forgetting about Lucas?'

Darren could see Matt's point about the shower. *Take a shower*, Jake had said to them before Stephen came upstairs. No chance. Not when they'd found the water running cold from the taps, dribbling icy drops from the mouldy shower heads of the two bathrooms on offer. The towels and bedding pulled from a deep cupboard lay unused at the foot of each of their beds, smelling worse than their clothing.

Matt pushed further back into the chair. 'I didn't mean . . . Lucas was my friend.' He sniffed as he pushed his glasses again.

'When it suited.' Hannah was never one to mince her words. 'Well, you've lost your so-called friend and I've news for you, that's not all as far as you and your stupid rules go, because I doubt there's an allergy-free anything to be saved at Wellwood either.'

Darren peered over the railing. 'Hannah . . .'

She stared at him, the only sound the low buzz of a bluebottle bashing against the window where she resumed her position.

Charlotte kicked the scuffed trainer peeping out of the bottom of her pyjama bottoms at the foot of the metal frame where Darren lay, the tinny thud echoing around the room, vibrating in Darren's tail bone.

'The place stinks.' Her thick black eyebrows furrowed on her pale forehead.

'It's not bad. At least we have a bed each.' Sadie jumped down from one of the other three bunks.

Darren gritted his teeth at her sing-song voice as she swept her long, straight blonde hair over her shoulder. Hair which usually hung perfectly against her narrow back, framing the face of a doll. Big blue eyes with eyelashes like spider legs above a perfect nose and a full, plump-pink mouth.

The opposite of Charlotte with her unruly black hair bouncing above her shoulders, refusing to be tamed by any brush. Her eyes, at times, almost black beneath her eyebrows.

Charlotte glowered at Sadie. 'It's the pits. Hasn't even got a telly.'

'They do. Down in the day room. This is where we'll sleep.' Sadie twirled around the end of the bunk and gathered up the corner of the sleeping bag draped over the edge and placed it back on the bed. 'We might be here a while. We should make the most of it.'

Hannah turned from the window again. 'Sure, let's make the most out of a death.'

Darren watched the girls stare each other out. Sadie broke eye contact and batted her long eyelashes towards him. 'What do you think he was doing down there?'

Darren pulled himself up and dangled his legs over the top bunk, dark hairs sprouting from his shins as his pyjama bottoms hitched. 'He hadn't stopped talking about the place. You know he'd been down there again. Jesus, most of you had been down with him.'

Matt was rubbing at something invisible on his thigh. 'I didn't.'

Hannah didn't turn; the distaste in her voice was clear without the others having to see her face. 'You wouldn't even go down when we went as a group with Stephen and Beth, let alone any time after.'

Darren's body stiffened. 'OK. OK. Listen, none of you can say anything about that – about being down there again. Not to Stephen or anyone and definitely not to the police.'

'Why not?' Sadie's eyes were wide.

This time Hannah did turn. 'Sadie, do you think being thick as shit is payback for being beautiful?'

Sadie's fists clenched. 'Sod you, Hannah.'

Hannah smirked. 'Don't you mean "Fuck you" or is that too nasty for those pretty lips of yours?'

Darren jumped from the bunk, and both of them shut up. 'I told you when I found out you had all been there again that I'd cover your arses but not to do it again. But you did and, like a dick, I said nothing again. There's no need to tell them. It'll only cause shit – for me and Matt too, when neither of us were involved.'

Charlotte had stopped kicking at the bed frame. 'We

only went down for a laugh. Hung out for a little while. What's the problem?'

Darren shook his head. 'The problem? Lucas died down there. Something or maybe even someone started that fire. Do any of you want to be in the frame?'

Matt was biting at his lip. 'Do you think Lucas started the fire?'

Charlotte scrunched her features. 'And what? Couldn't get out?'

Matt nodded. Everyone was staring at him now.

Hannah frowned. 'We don't even know where or how the fire started. Say it was down there, why would he and what with?'

Matt was warming to his theme. 'Maybe he found something down there. He maybe didn't mean to start it.'

Hannah was buying into it. 'There was no way it would've been intentional. Not with his past.'

Darren frowned. 'Lucas didn't start that fire.'

Charlotte was kicking again. 'Then who did?'

Darren shrugged. 'I don't know. Stephen says the police are coming back to talk to us. Don't say anything about the basement.'

One by one they nodded as scenarios spun in Darren's mind like a roulette wheel – that little silver ball landing in the same place every time.

Chapter 19

'WHAT THE HELL TOOK you so long?' Mearns was waiting on the cracked pavement in the shadow of the Morven Court high-rise as Ferguson pulled up and got out of his car.

'I was talking to the doc.'

Ferguson brushed past Mearns and headed to the main door of the building. A door doing much better since the council estate had had a bit of a facelift. She strode to keep up. 'Ferguson, why are you so concerned about this kid?'

Ferguson stopped, not bothering to turn towards her. 'Listen, it's not good. Broken limbs are the least of it. He has a head injury that's meant putting him into an induced coma.'

'Shit!' Mearns came level with him. 'You got a name?'

Ferguson started walking again. 'He wasn't carrying any ID. Only distinguishing feature I know of is a skull tattoo on his hand.'

They came to the door and Mearns pushed the number

on the intercom of the flat they were headed for. The speaker crackled. 'Yeah?' The voice was deep with a rasp.

'James Fyfe?'

'Who's asking?'

'My name is DS Jo Mearns.'

'You're a long way from home, aren't ya?'

Mearns didn't flinch, well used to the jibes about her strong Bolton accent which hadn't changed any since relocating to Aberdeen. 'You could say that.'

'What d'ya want?'

'It would be easier if you let me in.'

There was a brief silence before the door buzzed. Mearns pushed at it, Ferguson following her in. She glanced at the wall board, figuring out they were looking for the tenth floor. 'Come on.' She walked towards the lift. 'I'll update you on the way up.'

Ferguson stared straight ahead at the closed doors as the lift lurched upwards. Mearns stood a little back from him, the narrow space not lending itself to them being side by side comfortably. 'The fire was at a kids' home. Wellwood. Up in Kincorth.'

Ferguson said nothing. Mearns didn't miss his fist tightening on the keys he was holding. They all knew anything involving kids was never good. 'The boy's name was Lucas. Lucas Fyfe. Believe it or not, they found him in a basement beneath the place. They reckon it was arson.'

Ferguson's cheek twitched.

'Eve wants us to look into the place. All I know is that it's privately run, currently by a guy called Stephen Alderton.'

Ferguson stepped towards the door as the lift slowed. 'Prior to that it was owned by a Sally Fields.'

Ferguson didn't wait for the door to fully open before he was stepping out into the corridor. It smelled as if it had been a good while since a window had been opened.

Mearns stepped out after him, watching her colleague's back as he strode ahead, the grip on his keys still not loosening. 'Ferguson?'

He spoke without turning. 'I heard you. Which door?'

Lucas's dad looked and sounded like the stereotypical junkie. Knock-off designer gear, greasy hair, nicotine-stained fingers and a voice that spoke of too many joints and hits of methadone amongst God knew what else. By the state of the glaze in his eyes, Mearns figured he wasn't long back from his daily dose at the local chemist.

She moved clear of the Staffy sniffing at her feet, the silver chain lead still around its neck and trailing across the dirty carpet. 'It might be better if you sit.'

He squatted, backside hitting the edge of an armchair that had once been a different colour. His concentration was on the Rizla papers he was rolling between dirty fingers and scar-marked knuckles. 'What is it you want?'

'I'm sorry to tell you that your son Lucas is dead.'

His fingers froze, his stare on the rollie. 'You're having a laugh.'

Mearns watched his hands. 'There was a fire last night at Wellwood. I'm sorry.'

Ferguson stood stock-still by her side.

The unfinished roll-up fell to the floor as James jumped up, the Staffy scurrying to the nearest corner and cowering. 'What the fuck do you mean he's dead?'

James's hands were shaking, barely contained rage showing in them and the clamped teeth as he glared at them.

'Please.' Mearns motioned to the seat. 'Sit. I know this will be a shock.'

James backed up to the seat, his trainers crushing the roll-up on the floor as he slammed his backside to the cushion. 'The amount of times I've tried to see my kid. That bastard Stephen wouldn't let me see him. Wouldn't let me talk to my own son. And what? Now he's fucking gone. Nah, mate, that can't be right.' He pulled at the peak of his baseball cap.

'This is raw. We can arrange for a family liaison officer to see you.'

'Like some twat's going to help. What the hell happened?'

'He was found underground.'

James rubbed at his thigh. 'Underground? What the fuck do you mean, underground?'

'He was in a basement. We don't know why or how he got down there. There's evidence the fire was arson.'

James shot from the seat. 'My fucking son was underground, in a home where he was supposed to be cared for, and someone started a fire? They murdered my son?'

Mearns stepped forward. 'James, please sit.' Regardless of the man's troubles he was right in what he was saying. His anger was more than justified.

Mearns glanced at Ferguson as she guided James back

to the seat. 'I hope you don't mind me asking, but when's the last time you saw Lucas?'

'I ain't seen him in years. Not properly. The social won't let me and neither would that Stephen. Any time I've tried it's been through a fucking window before they dragged me or him away.'

'You've never seen him face to face since he lost his mum?'

'Hey, I lost my blonde. Her and him. I was getting clean until then.' He glowered at them. 'I was. And if they'd given me any hope that I'd get my boy then I would've got clean again.' He pawed for the Rizla packet again.

There was nothing about the man in front of her or the hovel around her to say he'd even tried. 'What had you hoped for?'

'To speak to him. To let him know he could come and kip at mine.'

Mearns studied the place: the litter on the floor, the overflowing ashtrays, the inch-thick dust on the windowsill. No place for a kid, especially when the adult didn't appear to be able to take care of himself, never mind anyone else.

James tapped the fag-papers packet against his palm. 'Those bastards aren't going to get away with this. I'll sue their arses.'

Mearns could still hear the rage. It was emotion that was missing. Mearns didn't want to judge but she sensed the rage wasn't about his son. She'd met people like James Fyfe before. No, this was about the loss of a quick buck. What having to provide for a kid whilst being unemployed would've opened up to him in the way of benefits. The first thing on his mind at the news of his son's death being what he could financially gain from holding Wellwood responsible for that death.

Any sympathy she'd had was dispersing. Still, she was shocked when Ferguson spoke.

'If you'd been any kind of half-decent parent, Lucas would never have ended up in a place like Wellwood.'

Mearns barely had time to glare at Ferguson before James was on his feet again, dirty fist clenched and raised. Ferguson stepped forward, but backed off as Mearns came between them. 'Enough.' She was reeling from Ferguson's unprofessionalism, trying to gain back some ground. 'As I said, we'll arrange for a family liaison officer to come around. Help you come to terms with what's happened.' He didn't give a shit about what had happened – not in the way a parent should – but it wasn't their place to say that. Not Ferguson's, for sure.

She turned, jostling Ferguson to the door, her own teeth clamped together now. Hoping to hell James Fyfe wasn't about to put in a complaint as they closed the door behind them.

'What the hell was that?' The lift door had barely closed before Mearns was ripping into Ferguson.

He stared at the neon numbers flashing as they passed floors on the way down. 'Can't be arsed with twats like that.'

'Jesus, Ferguson. Few of us can be but you know the score. You've been dealing with twats for years. Daily.' Mearns was staring at his cheek side-on, willing him to look at her. He didn't budge. The creak of the lift as it lowered was the only sound between them.

Whatever he'd seen this morning, whatever had happened to that kid, had hit him hard.

The lift doors opened, Ferguson marching forward, keen to get away from her. Something told her there was more to this boy from the accident he'd witnessed today. More than Ferguson was willing to say. But if this was how he was going to be, then she didn't fancy being around him, let alone working with him.

The problem was she had no choice, but she'd have to keep him close. Because if Eve caught wind of it, all hell would break loose.

Chapter 20

'HOW ARE THE CHILDREN?' Eve moved in her seat, wishing the furniture was more comfortable and the place warmer as she smiled at Jake, who sat opposite them.

He made the chair look like a piece of dolls' furniture, his shoulders and narrow head towering above its washable cushioned back. His face was long, high-coloured and slim, a shock of prematurely grey hair spiking from his scalp making him bizarrely resemble a rubber-topped pencil.

Jake scratched at his ear. 'As you'd expect. Upset. Quiet. Tired, as they've been up most of the night.'

'They know about Lucas?'

Jake's jaw twitched at the mention of the boy. 'They do now. We were all expecting the worst, you know, when we couldn't find Lucas.' His sharp intake of breath sucked at the air between them. 'We'd all hoped . . .' Jake rubbed at his eyes with a forefinger and thumb.

Cooper silently checked in with Eve before settling his attention back on Jake. Cooper, who was good at saying the right thing. 'I'm sorry for what's happened. It must be difficult talking about it this soon. We need to make sense of what's happened. Could we maybe start with you running us through what happened last night? What do you remember from the hours before the fire started?'

Jake leaned back against the chair before he crossed his legs at the ankle. 'From like teatime?'

'Me and DS Cooper here know very little about how a place like Wellwood works. Anything would be great.'

'Nothing different from any other day. It was Matt's turn to cook. We work it on a rota. Different kid each night with the team member who's on nights, which was me. Nothing fancy. Macaroni cheese. Always a winner with the kids.'

'What do the other kids do whilst that's going on?'

Jake rubbed the tip of his nose. 'Homework, computer games, telly. Some of them like to go out for a while. They all know grub's up at five thirty sharp and they're seldom late for that.' Jake half smiled, a flash of straight white teeth. 'Everyone was there. Tea happened as normal, dishes were done, and they were back to their own time. Nothing eventful. The odd squabble in the telly room as usual about who's watching what and afterwards they headed to their rooms.'

Cooper was scribbling in a notebook. 'Is there a set time for that?'

'Not set in stone. Obviously earlier on a weeknight than a weekend but we don't have a lights-out. Not now the kids are all older. We work on trust and we want the kids to be independent.' Jake ran a hand through his grey hair, leaving it sticking up on end from the residue of old gel.

'Do you check on them once they're in their rooms?'

'No, they're left to it. They are aware the night member of staff is there if they need them.'

'And do they ever need you?'

'Very rarely. Once in a blue moon if they're ill or maybe have a nightmare or something.'

Eve imagined from what little Stephen had told her about the kids that nightmares might happen at places like Wellwood more often than others.

Jake tilted forward in the chair. 'There was a time Lucas sleepwalked.' He paused, running a hand through his hair again. 'He was a lot younger then though.'

Eve's interest was piqued. 'Often? What kind of thing would he get up to?'

'I saw him two or three times. Kinda freaky. His eyes would be half open and he'd talk. A few words. One time he went to the toilet, another time he went to the fridge and made a cold meat sandwich.'

'Really?' Cooper sounded as surprised as Eve felt.

'I'd stay back and keep an eye on him. They say you should never wake them, don't they?'

'Must've been a bit of a worry to be the one on night shift, knowing he might wander.'

Jake nodded. 'It was the night that Ben found him headed for the back door. Thankfully there were no keys in the lock. After that we fitted sensors on his bedroom door to set off an alarm in the office. A year went by with no incidents. They were removed.'

'When?'

'About six months ago.'

Eve glanced at Cooper and back at Jake. 'So it could be a possibility he sleepwalked last night.' It was a stretch for him to have lifted a carpet, a hatch and climbed down a ladder but . . . making a sandwich wasn't something she'd been expecting.

Jake rubbed at his chin. 'I guess he could've.'

'You didn't hear anything out of the ordinary?'

Jake shook his head. 'I was reading in the telly room. I must admit I fell asleep on the sofa.' He shifted focus between Eve and Cooper. 'Not that it's frowned upon. All the kids were in bed and most of the time the night person goes to the spare room. They're free to get shut-eye if they want as there are no high-risk kids and they all know where to get us.'

'And Stephen last night?'

'What do you mean?'

'He said he was working late. Did you spend any time with him?'

'No, I leave him to it if he's working late.'

'Is it common for him to be working late?'

'It can be.'

'And he stayed last night?'

'Eh . . . I'm not sure if he was planning on staying. It was only gone midnight when the alarms went off.'

'Take us from there.'

'As I said, I fell asleep. Nearly fell off the sofa when the fire alarms went off. Didn't know what was happening at first, then the adrenaline kicked in as I knew there was no planned drill practice.

'I ran into the hallways, saw the smoke and realized it

was for real. Stephen was coming out of his office as I got to him. We ran for the kids' rooms. We've had multiple practice runs and the kids are familiar with the drill and where to head for the fire escape but panic sets in and you want to make sure they're up and out.'

'Who checked which rooms?'

'I went for Darren and Lucas.' Jake's lips twitched; he wiped at them. 'I found Darren in his room, no problem. It was getting him out of there that was the issue. You have to understand, some of these kids have next to no possessions from their "before". Darren is the eldest and he's precious about his stuff. I get that he wants to save whatever he can. I was trying to tell him the priority was getting him out – that if we didn't save him then nothing else was worth sav—' Jake paused. 'Anyway, it took a few minutes for him to see it. Matt came to the door panicking and I told him to run for the fire escape – it's a side door to the property, out on to the drive – and we'd be out as soon as.'

'Stephen wasn't with Matt?'

'No, he was rounding up the others.'

'Did Darren end up taking anything?'

Jake didn't need to think before answering. 'A photo of his mum.'

Eve sensed Cooper tensing beside her before he spoke. 'And you both went to Lucas's room after?'

'No. I told Darren to head to the fire escape as I knew Stephen already had Hannah, Charlotte and Sadie out as they'd gone past us whilst Darren was mucking about in his room. I ran to Lucas's room and he wasn't there.' Jake swallowed. 'The smoke was getting bad by then. I ran to the fire escape hoping he was already out. There was no sign of him. I shouted to Stephen and the kids, told them I was going back in.' Jake rubbed at his eyes and bent forward, his elbow resting on his thigh as he sighed. His voice cracked when he spoke. 'I was shouting, hollering, but those damned alarms. I couldn't hear myself think, never mind anything else.'

'What did you do then?'

'I figured the only option was to go further into the house, that maybe he'd gone somewhere else for whatever reason.'

'Was it possible for you to get much further into the house?'

'No, by that time it was getting bad. I got to the telly room. The smoke got too much. I was still shouting and shouting for him. Hoarse with shouting, and it was getting hard to breathe.' Jake closed his eyes. 'Nothing.'

Eve saw Lucas beneath the hatch. Thought about the fact that the fire had started at the back door where the access to the basement was. Not a hope Jake would've made it anywhere near there, no way of hearing Lucas's screams – if he had even been conscious and able to scream.

Jake seemed to have shrunk. 'If I'd gone towards the back door when the alarms went off, I might have heard Lucas shouting. I might have been able to get to him.'

Eve saw the pain etched on the man's face. 'Jake, there's no way you could've got to him. That hatch was directly behind the back door where the petrol was spilled and the fire was started. We don't know what happened to Lucas yet.' The post-mortem would tell them the truth.

Tears welled in Jake's eyes. 'What if it didn't? What if he suffered every second he was still alive? I came into this job because I had a rough upbringing. I wanted to make a difference. I should've protected him. That was my job. I was his key worker.'

'Yes, you were his key worker and you guys must've known the kids better than anyone.' Eve was choosing her words carefully. 'Do you think any of these kids would've been capable of starting the fire?'

Jake's mouth hung open. 'No, not for one minute. From what Stephen told me, that rag was posted through the door. Doesn't that mean it was someone from the outside? You don't actually think . . .' He stopped, unable to finish.

Eve said nothing.

Chapter 21

MEARNS STARED AT FERGUSON across the desk as she put down the phone. 'Eve and Cooper are going to speak to the kids, and then they'll be heading back.'

Ferguson didn't break his concentration fixed on the computer screen.

'What are you doing?'

'Doing a run-through of missing persons. Seeing if I can get a match for the boy's description. Hoping that tattoo will throw up something.'

'Ferguson, let Ron Miller and his team do their thing.'

This time he did shift his head. 'And what? Let them fuck it up?'

Mearns met his glare. 'I know you've got past beef with Ron but he's good at his job.'

'I am too. I was there.'

Mearns didn't say anything about how he'd handled James Fyfe earlier, knowing it wasn't Ferguson's usual style, aware that whatever he'd been through that morning had hit him hard. It was *why* she couldn't figure out. Not when they dealt with what they did every day.

'Ferguson, what is it with this kid?'

Ferguson chewed at the inside of his cheek, avoiding making eye contact with her again. 'I was there. With him lying on that road. He asked me not to leave him. No one else has come forward yet. Nobody has missed him. He might not have anyone and I'm not going to let that happen.'

'I get it, but Eve wants us all on board with this case at Wellwood.'

Ferguson stared at her. 'Another kid. What makes him any more important than the boy lying up in that hospital bed?'

'Ferguson . . .' Mearns sensed she had to tread carefully. 'This one is dead. His case is ours. The other boy, the one in that bed, isn't. He's Ron's.'

Ferguson snatched the cup of coffee by his computer and sipped, making an exaggerated show of swallowing as he banged it down again. 'That kid is dead because someone wasn't listening at the fire-drill practice.'

Mearns baulked at the coldness in his voice.

Ferguson stabbed at a key on his keyboard. 'This kid is my case, whether or not it says so on a goddamn computer screen.' He stood.

'Ferguson, are you OK?'

'I need to nip out.'

'Where? What do I tell the boss when she gets back?'

'I won't be long. I'm thinking maybe the kid was homeless. Maybe someone on the street might recognize a description of him – the tattoo. No harm in trying.' Ferguson lifted his jacket from the back of the chair.

Mearns wasn't sure what she could do, short of physically stopping him from leaving. 'They'll be doing all that, as well as the usual – CCTV, door-to-door, scene investigation. You know they will.' She was still trying for eye contact with Ferguson. 'I mean, what are you going to do? Go about and ask anyone sitting in a doorway?'

'That's exactly what I'm going to do. I'm not sitting here doing nothing whilst we wait for the boss to get back and hand out the jobs. Don't worry, I'll be back for that.'

Mearns stood. 'Ferguson, let them do their jobs.'

He turned. 'I'm not asking you to cover my arse. You want to tell Ron I'm interfering, go ahead. You want to grass me up to Eve, then do it. I need to do this.'

Mearns stepped towards him, but stopped when she saw his face. Not a look she'd ever seen before. She watched him walk towards the door without another word or glance in her direction, his coffee left to go cold.

Chapter 22

EVE STEPPED ASIDE, CLEAR of the dorm door, to let Cooper follow her in. The space felt cramped and airless, with three sets of bunk beds, a hard-backed chair by each one and a wall covered by floor-to-ceiling grey steel lockers.

Everyone in the room had frozen, four statues standing by the bunks, one sculpted by the lockers.

'Hi. I'm DI Eve Hunter and this is my colleague, DS Mark Cooper. Can we pull up a chair?'

The kids studied one another. No one spoke as Eve moved two chairs into the free floor space in front of the lockers. The boy who sat by the lockers stood and scurried over to stand by one of the bunks, as the others disappeared into them.

Cooper sat, resting forearms on thighs, his hands clasped and his features soft. Eve was happy to let him take the lead. Being a dad, he'd be more comfortable talking with the kids than she would.

'You must all be pretty shaken up.' He stopped to take

each of them in, in turn, their wide eyes staring out from upper metal railings or beds beneath.

Eve figured these kids were far from shy but what they'd been through overnight, plus perhaps a wariness of the police given their backgrounds, meant their silence and need to hide were no surprise.

Cooper continued. 'It's an OK set-up here. You've all got a bed at least.' He smiled the smallest of smiles.

The sickly pale, skinny kid who'd chosen to stand by the bunk stared at both of the empty beds. 'There would have been a bed in here for Lucas if he'd made it.'

Cooper swallowed. 'I'm sorry to hear about Lucas.'

The boy dipped his head.

'Could I go around the room and find out your names? I like to know who I'm talking with and it would be good to get to know you all a little better.' He stared at the boy. 'Since we're already chatting, what's yours?'

The boy put his hands in his pockets. 'I don't like it here. It stinks.' He rubbed at his small nose, which struggled to keep the glasses he wore in place.

Cooper continued to watch him. 'It's been a while since the place was used. The smell will go as you guys make it your own. It's not Wellwood but I'm glad they've managed to keep you all together. Anyway, what's your name?'

Before the boy said anything, Eve knew it was Matt. The story of his mother's obsession with cleanliness and the repercussions of that were obvious to see in her son as he sniffed and stared with disgust at the lower bunk.

'Matt.'

'Nice to meet you, Matt.'

Cooper tilted his chin upwards, seeing more of a man rather than a boy on the top bunk. Darren. The one who wanted to be a mechanic. The stubble on his chin and upper lip was visible even at this distance – black and thick against Darren's smooth brown skin. He was a handsome guy, long, dark eyelashes framing hazelnut eyes that would make a girl, or boy, go weak at the knees. 'And you?'

'Darren.'

'And you must be the oldest?'

Darren nodded.

Cooper turned his head to the next bunk, ducking slightly to make out the face peering out from the lower bed. Bushy brown eyebrows dipped beneath long thick curly hair.

'What's your name?'

'Charlotte.' It was spat rather than said.

'Nice name.' Cooper raised his head to the top bunk. 'And yours?'

'Hannah.' Barely audible, the whites of her eyes bright against her dark skin.

Cooper squirmed in his chair at the sound of his own daughter's name, the plight of these kids hitting home a little harder. He shifted his attention to the final bunk where only one girl sat. She was perched on the bottom mattress, her head slightly bent forward, clear of the wooden slats above. Her bare legs hung beneath a nightie over the edge of the bed. She swept her long blonde hair over one shoulder.

'And yours?'

'Sadie. It's nice to meet you.' She smiled.

'You too.'

Cooper sat back. 'It must have been hard hearing about Lucas. Even harder now knowing where he was found. It's our job to figure out what happened. To get to the bottom of why he was down there and why this fire started.'

The room remained silent.

Cooper glanced at Eve. 'Let's start with the obvious question.'

Bed springs creaked as the kids moved. Maybe uneasy with the chat, perhaps trying to get comfortable in a strange place.

Cooper carried on. 'Stephen told us you guys were first aware of the basement space about three weeks ago. He said all of you were excited about it. I know I would've been when I was a kid. He also told us the place was out of bounds, other than the one time they took you down to see it.'

No one made a sound.

Cooper sat back. 'Is that the case? Did it remain out of bounds?'

Silence.

Cooper tried again. 'Let me be clear here. If it didn't remain the case, if someone did go down there again, no one is in trouble. What's important is that we find out what happened to Lucas.'

The only sound came from Matt as he lifted his hand and grasped the metal pole of the bed, then released his hand quickly before rubbing it against his pyjama bottoms with disdain clouding his features.

Cooper glanced around the room. 'I'll take that as a no to anyone being aware of someone being down there since.'

Eve sensed they were going to get nowhere fast. 'Did anyone know he was out of his room last night?'

The silence stretched.

Eve looked at each of them in turn. 'I don't necessarily mean as in where he *was*. Maybe one of you left your room for some reason . . .?'

Darren sat up in the top bunk, his close-shaved head falling just centimetres short of the ceiling, and stared around the room.

Eve tried again. 'Did one of you have a room next to Lucas?'

Matt kicked gently at the bed frame, obviously seeing it as a better option than touching it with his hands. 'My room was next to his.'

Eve was grateful for some response, at least. 'That must've been great with you being friends.'

Matt's foot stopped. 'All I heard last night was the usual noises like the kettle boiling in the kitchen or the telly on in the day room.'

Eve changed tack. 'Did you ever hear Lucas next door?'

Matt resumed kicking at the pole – more effort this time, glancing up at Darren before he spoke. 'I'd sometimes hear him next door. He was pretty quiet though. He loved reading. Even though we don't have a lights-out, he told me he would read under the covers by torchlight. I never heard anything last night.'

Eve shifted. 'Thanks, Matt.' She evaluated the room and Cooper. He probably hadn't missed Matt staring up at Darren.

She brought her trousered leg up, resting one ankle on her other thigh. 'Was Lucas ever known to leave his room at night?'

More shifting in the bunks before Sadie appeared, her head clear of the railing above, long hair falling from her shoulder and draping either side of her face. 'He'd sleep-walked once or twice.'

Eve's eyes were drawn again to Darren, who was frowning, his features softening as he locked eyes with her. She looked at Sadie again.

'Jake told us about that. He said it hadn't happened for some time. Had any of you seen him sleepwalking before?'

Nothing.

Cooper stretched, figuring out where to go next. 'The facts are Lucas did leave his room last night and he was found down in that basement. Tell me what he was like. How he was after finding out about the basement. I mean, was he adventurous? Could Lucas have been tempted to take a peek?'

Matt shifted the glasses up his nose, sniffing as he did so. 'Lucas was much braver than me. Maybe he might've looked.'

Darren's and Hannah's heads snapped round at the same time. It was Darren who spoke. 'He wouldn't have.'

Cooper's smooth voice did little to ease the tension in the room. 'Can you be sure? Had he spoken to any of you about wanting to go down there again?'

The room was deathly silent.

'Maybe none of you imagined he'd ever go down

102

there alone. Maybe one of you dared him as a joke, never believing he would do it?'

The buzz of a bluebottle was the only sound.

Eve tried: 'You wouldn't have known what was to happen. How could you have?'

The kids' eyes were now darting between each other.

Charlotte broke the silence. 'How did the fire start?'

Eve waited a beat. 'The fire service believes someone poured petrol through the letter box at the back door. Lit it.'

Hannah's eyes were wide. 'Someone did it on purpose?'

Eve let Hannah's words sink in with those in the room. 'What I'm about to ask will be hard to hear and perhaps even harder to answer. Do any of you know of anyone who might've had something against Wellwood? Maybe against someone *in* Wellwood?'

The children's heads turned, wide eyes scared and searching for something amongst them all that they'd maybe never imagined. It was Darren who spoke.

'You're not just asking if one of us might've known why Lucas was down there, you're asking if one of us started that fire.'

Eve wasn't about to insult them by denying it. 'We have to.'

Matt squeaked from the corner. 'Is that why we had to hand in our phones and iPads?'

'Yes. It's procedure in any case like this. We need to look into everything. There's no reason to worry if you have nothing to hide.' Eve could see the kids weren't convinced. 'What we don't know is whether Lucas being

103

down that hatch inside the back door was connected to the fire starting. Whether someone knew he had gone down there. If someone had taken him down there. Maybe it was coincidence only; there's every chance the fire and Lucas being in the basement had nothing to do with each other.'

Hannah was fiddling with the edge of the sleeping bag beneath her. 'If someone started the fire on purpose and knew Lucas was down there, then . . .'

The girl didn't have to finish.

Eve turned to Matt. 'You said Lucas loved reading, that he would read by torchlight. Is it possible he went down there to read?'

Darren was shaking his head, speaking before Matt could answer. 'He wouldn't have done that.'

Eve stared at him. 'Perhaps not, but he was down there whatever the reason.'

Darren's head was still shaking. 'I don't understand why. What happened to him, the way his mother died. He hated fire. He was scared of it.'

Eve was aware of Cooper's silence, remembering what McCabe had said. About the wood beneath the hatch. How Lucas had scratched and clawed to get out. Knowing any kid would've been scared, feeling sick at how much more terrified Lucas must've been.

Was someone in this room right now terrified and scared of that being seen?

Chapter 23

Then

'I LIKE YOU.' DANNY grins as she passes me half of the ham sandwich she's made, both of us sneaking through to the kitchen after seeing Ms Fields leave the driveway. It wouldn't be for long; it never was. We'd make the most of what time we had.

I take it, not hungry, wary of Danny's smile and kindness. It reminds me of my mother. Smiling, teasing, shaking her arse at the latest guy as she swigged from a glass bottle.

Two weeks Danny's been here, and she's been nothing but friendly. She hasn't escaped Ms Fields' wrath, but nothing has dampened her energy, her enthusiasm for life. I watch her giggle at nothing. No bottle in hand and no offer of payment, of anything, from me. But she's after something.

'What do you say?'

That smell again. Of alcohol. Memories refusing to let me see a woman any other way than how my mother made me feel. But that was the past.

I take a bite of the sandwich, watching her and seeing my mother there. Parading her wares. Working her magic whilst I stayed quiet and watched from wherever I hid.

She tuts, her face playful. 'Are you going to answer?' Her back's pressed up against the fridge, one knee bent and the sole of her boot against the fridge door.

I chew, never taking my eyes from hers. I shrug. 'You're all right, I guess.'

She huffs, breaks a chunk of bread away and chucks it at me. I let it hit and bounce off me, both of us watching it land on the floor between us. I look up, electricity crackling in the space between us, deciding there and then to play the game. Safe to do so when I'm the one in control, letting her believe the opposite. 'Let's say I like you.'

Her face grows serious. I watch as she puts down what's left of her sandwich on the worktop, never taking her eyes from me as she slowly makes her way over. Like my mother. Working it for money. My pulse is throbbing in my neck. I could stop it if I chose to. I don't want to take my gaze from her. Again, I could.

I feel the heat of her as she comes close, snaking her arm around the back of me, the other hand running fingers through my hair. I almost explode as her lips part. I allow myself to feel the pressure build as her tongue dances across her teeth. She holds me by the back of my neck now, her eyes boring into mine. I don't dare to breathe. Like I'm hiding again. Watching.

I want to kiss her. Badly. To see what it is that made

those men come to my mum. The difference here being I'm the one in control.

Danny grins again, enjoying herself, believing she's in charge. 'You like me? What are we going to do about that?'

Chapter 24

FERGUSON LOOKED AT HIS watch. He'd been gone an hour, and, in that time, he'd walked from Queen Street HQ into Union Street, stopping to talk to anyone sitting on the street, and their dog – literally. Every one of them had acted antsy or given him a bit of aggro, expecting to be moved on for begging, not relaxing much when he'd told them he was searching for someone. So far, no one had admitted to knowing anything, but he wasn't going to stop trying yet.

He focused ahead, saw the bedraggled guy he'd seen many times sitting in the same old place – between HMV and Boots on the corner of Bridge Street. Prime location for passing shoppers and workers out for a bite to eat, the bridge's edge across the road now barricaded after too many instances of people jumping from it on to the train tracks beneath.

Ferguson stopped, his shoes inches from the stained sleeping bag snaking out from beneath the guy in the doorway. The upturned baseball cap at the man's feet held a smattering of coppers.

'Aw, come on, mate, give me a break.' He spoke with the same rasping voice as James Fyfe; his hands were just as filthy. Ferguson counted about four teeth in the man's head as shoppers bustled past, their hands full of bags, no time to stop to drop change.

'I'm hoping you'll give me a break.'

The guy tilted his head far back to accommodate Ferguson's height. 'Eh?'

'I'm looking for someone. Young guy. Brown hair. Wearing a washed-out Stone Roses T-shirt, jeans ripped at the knees.' Ferguson was sure those jeans hadn't been ripped in the accident.

'Doesn't ring a bell, mate.' He broke eye contact, leaned forward to pet the dog's head, and repositioned his baseball cap as he sat back.

Ferguson fished inside his pocket and pulled out his wallet, taking a crisp ten-pound note from inside its folds. He held it above the guy's head. 'What if I said he has a skull tattoo. A bad one, at the base of his forefinger and thumb.'

The guy rubbed at the stubble on his chin. 'Hmmm . . . that maybe changes things.'

Ferguson stroked the note between his fingers. 'Now, you and I know that I'll come back if what you're about to tell me turns out to be bollocks.'

'I promise ya, it ain't bollocks.' He was almost salivating at the note, his back straightening, trying to get closer to it.

'And?'

'Sounds like a guy I sometimes see up at Cyrenians.'

'In Summer Street?'

'Yeah.'

'Remember, if you're spinning me a line . . .'

'I'm not. Go ask them.'

Ferguson dropped the tenner into the baseball cap; not a second passed before the guy lunged forward and pocketed it. It would scupper the rest of his day if folk saw it. 'I will. Now. And if you're lying, you'd better not be here on my way back.'

Chapter 25

'WHERE'S FERGUSON?'

Mearns looked at the door as Eve spoke, willing him to walk through it. 'Erm, he had to nip out. Something about them wanting to check over details in his statement from this morning.'

Eve picked up the pen from the ledge beneath the whiteboard and turned. 'What's happening there anyway?'

Mearns picked at the edge of the desk. 'The boy isn't great. They've had to put him in an induced coma.'

'Family been notified and with him?'

'There was no ID on him.'

Eve rolled the pen between both hands. 'Nothing?'

'Nothing. Ferguson says he has a tattoo. There's hope something'll come from that.'

'I'm sure they're on it. The Wellwood case has to take priority. We're not only dealing with the loss of a child, we're also investigating arson, which makes Lucas's death murder.'

Mearns stopped picking. 'I get that. Ferguson feels a little more involved than usual, what with being on the scene and following the boy up to the hospital.'

Eve removed the cap from the pen. 'It was good he was there. It'll help road traffic have a clear picture. But we'll have to leave them to get on with it as I need you all on deck once he's sorted out whatever it is he's off sorting out.' Eve turned to the board and scribbled *Wellwood* at the top. 'Let's start with what we've got. Mearns, I'll leave you to update Ferguson.' She wrote *Lucas Fyfe* underneath Wellwood and his age, underscoring it twice before turning to Mearns and Cooper.

Mearns focused, putting Ferguson to the back of her mind for now.

'Lucas was found in the basement beneath Wellwood. McCabe from the fire service has told us they believe the fire was started by an accelerant being poured through the letter box, likely followed by some sort of lit material.' Eve scribbled more on the board. 'The hatch to the basement was situated behind that same door. At the moment we have no idea who posted the material through the door or why Lucas was down there. Whether the two are connected is another thing. Cooper, do you want to take Mearns through where we're at with the staff and kids?'

'Sure. We've met with the manager, Stephen Alderton. He told us the kids only recently learned about the space, as recently as three weeks ago when maintenance works were being carried out. Obviously, the kids were animated about this basement. It's huge, the height and width of the home above. Stephen and a member of staff took them down to explore. According to him, the kids were aware it was otherwise off limits and, as far as he knew, no one had been down again.'

Mearns frowned. 'Clearly that isn't the case.'

Eve was pacing. 'Clearly. This is a long shot, but Stephen said that maintenance work, and the resulting accessing of the basement, was due to a water problem. I want you to track down the Scottish Water engineers who were there. Arrange for me and Cooper to go and talk to them. Maybe they saw something down there. Something that'll tell us whether those kids really only found out about the place once they'd been to carry out the work.'

Mearns finished scribbling. 'What are the other kids saying?'

Eve sat. 'Nothing. Yet. The eldest kid, Darren, is the leader of the pack. I'm not convinced they don't know something but he's keeping them quiet.'

Mearns pushed back on her chair, the two front legs lifting from the floor as she rocked on it. 'Maybe they've all been down there. Maybe it was a dare gone wrong. Getting Lucas to go down alone, not knowing what was going to happen.'

Eve stood. 'Maybe. We've taken all technology off both the kids and the staff. Forensics are going to run through it. We'll see what that throws up. I'm going to try and get access to the basement tomorrow, see if McCabe lets me go down. It'll help to see the place.'

Mearns landed the front legs with a thump. 'Supposedly no one knew Lucas was out of his room?'

Cooper answered. 'Nope. They operate on a trust and

independence approach. No lights-out and no night check now the kids are all older. It was assumed after tea and telly that they'd all gone to their rooms and stayed in them. Jake, the member of staff on overnight, said there was no movement that he was aware of, although he did admit to falling asleep on the sofa.'

'You're kidding?' Mearns was staring at Cooper.

'No. It's not frowned upon as none of the kids are deemed high risk. The overnight person is there purely for supervision and free to go to the spare room for sleep, with the kids knowing they are there.'

'Some supervision,' Mearns mumbled.

Eve was popping the cap on and off the pen. 'Stephen, the manager, was there too. He's often in the office late, sometimes staying overnight. He told us he has a sofa there to sleep on.'

Mearns wrinkled her nose. 'That's a bit full on.'

'The guy has the weight of the world on his shoulders. The place is privately run. He made a comment about keeping themselves afloat. I said to Cooper I thought I smelled drink on his breath.'

'Seriously?' Mearns turned to Cooper.

'It might be innocent enough. You know, maybe a stiff swig of something, given what had happened.'

Eve sat back on the desk again. 'I'm not convinced. We should delve a little deeper into Wellwood. Run financials and see what the story of the place is, both before Stephen came and during his time there. Mearns, I'd appreciate you and Ferguson tackling that in the meantime.'

Mearns nodded.

'How did you get on with the father?'

'He was a real peach.'

Cooper ran a hand through his hair. 'After meeting the grandmother, I can imagine.'

Mearns opened her notebook where she'd jotted stuff down once back at the office. 'The place was a pit. Token Staffy, the lot. He appeared to be under the influence of something. Eyes were glazed.'

Eve placed the pen on the table. 'How did he take it?'

'Not the way we were expecting. Angry more than anything. Didn't appear upset. He was spouting about suing them.'

Cooper tutted. 'Wouldn't want to miss the opportunity of a fast buck.'

Mearns turned to him. 'That's the impression I got. Even when he spoke about trying to get access to his son, it seemed more for what financial gain he could get, instead of wanting to be there for him.'

Eve was walking back and forth in front of the desk. 'Stephen said he'd turned up at the home more than once, always escorted away by police. He was there yesterday. Did he tell you that?'

Mearns shook her head. 'You reckon he had something to do with it?'

Eve stopped pacing. 'We can't rule anything out – even the disruption he caused to Lucas having a knock-on effect on why Lucas went down there. I want you to establish where James Fyfe was last night.'

Mearns scribbled in her notebook.

Cooper watched her as he spoke. 'At least the father made a half-hearted attempt to see Lucas. The grandmother didn't even to try to hide her total lack of interest or involvement.'

Mearns stopped writing. 'Jesus, the poor kid.'

The room fell silent.

'Guys, we need to eat.' Eve stood and fished her car keys from inside her pocket. 'Go home. Both of you. Mearns, when you hear from Ferguson update him and get on the other stuff tomorrow. Cooper, I'll give you a ring first thing. Hopefully we'll be heading to Wellwood.'

Mearns and Cooper stood as Eve turned to the whiteboard.

'I want that board filled with answers. Lucas deserves that at least.'

Chapter 26

FERGUSON WAITED IN THE entranceway of Aberdeen Cyrenians, listening to the hubbub of cutlery and plates clanging together and the hum of chatter behind closed doors.

It was a building on Summer Street he'd gone past many times, but had never noticed. Hidden in plain sight on the opposite side of the road from a small stretch of restaurants and pubs – the well-known sports and karaoke bar, McNasty's, dominating the space – and there was also a casino and an eighties nightclub a stone's throw away.

Cyrenians was invisible to the revellers frequenting the street at nights; it was only those with no reason to party who knew where its doors were.

The man who walked towards him held out a hand in front of him, a broad welcoming smile on his face. 'Hi, I'm Toby.'

Ferguson took the man's hand and shook firmly. 'Thanks for seeing me.'

'No problem. Maureen says you're looking for someone.'

'I'm DC Scott Ferguson. There was a road accident this morning in Crown Street. A pedestrian was hit, a young male. He was badly hurt and is up at Aberdeen Royal Infirmary. He wasn't carrying ID. I can't be sure but I'm going with a hunch that he may have been struggling, homeless even. Could I give you a description?'

'Sure. We get a lot of people coming through those doors.' Toby peered over Ferguson's shoulder. 'Some are a one-off, others dip in and out, then there are those you can set your watch by.'

'This guy, I'd say late teens, twenty maybe. Brown hair, blue eyes. He was wearing a washed-out Stone Roses T-shirt and a pair of jeans ripped at the knees.'

'Not much to go on.'

'He did have a tattoo. A visible one. On his hand. Something people would've seen.'

Toby looked unconvinced.

Ferguson flexed his forefinger and thumb, pointing at the web of skin between them. 'Here. A small skull. A bad one. Homemade, I reckon.'

Toby stared at Ferguson's hand, recognition flickering in his features. 'Archie.'

'Archie? You sure?'

'You're right. It's a shocking tattoo. One I wouldn't forget.'

Adrenaline coursed through Ferguson. 'When's the last time you saw him and what's his story?'

Toby rubbed at his chin. 'Eh, two days ago. He's a regular at lunch. Has been for about the last two months.

Keeps himself to himself, doesn't sit with any of the others.'

'Have you spoken to him?'

'No. Small talk when I'm serving up or being present in the hall.'

'Can you remember anything he's ever said? Maybe a mention of where he's from? Family? Friends?'

'No, nothing like that.' Toby dipped his head down, but lifted it again just as fast. 'Actually, he appeared on edge the last time I saw him. Came in here quickly, earlier than usual, bright red. Sweaty. I asked what was chasing him and laughed. He didn't say anything, but his eyes never left the doors.'

'Sounds like he was running from something.'

'Maybe. Nothing new for a lot of folks who come here.'

Ferguson turned and looked at the doors he'd come through. 'Do you have CCTV?'

'Why?'

'Would you still have footage from two days ago?'

'Yeah.'

Ferguson paused as his phone rang in his pocket. He put his hand in, ignoring it, bringing a card back out instead. 'Any chance you could check it out for me? Find when Archie arrived and whether there was anyone else hanging about?'

'I guess.' Toby took the card, reading it as Ferguson continued:

'I'd appreciate it. Even footage of him if there's nothing else.'

'I'll take a look once I'm finished up.'

'Thank you.'

Toby was staring at Ferguson's leg where the phone was still ringing.

Ferguson patted his pocket. 'I'd better take this. Thanks again.'

Ferguson stepped out into the fresh air as he checked his phone for the missed call. *Mearns*.

He checked his watch. *Shit*. He knew before he'd even dialled Mearns that he'd missed Eve's update.

Chapter 27

THE CONTINUOUS BEEP DOMINATED the claustrophobic heat of the room where the boy lay in the bed, transparent tubes sprouting from his broken body. His right arm was strapped tightly to his chest, his leg hoisted on a pulley and in a cast. Ferguson knew there were metal pins beneath.

Seven a.m. Ferguson stretched his body and yawned. His gaze was drawn again to the red folder clipped to the end of the hospital bed, shouting out for the unknown body lying there. The colour red was only ever used as a marker for unidentified patients.

Unidentified except for a first name. Archie. Even that one piece of information was banking on nothing more than a tattoo he'd described, but he was willing to take it.

The boy's smooth face was pale against the starched white sheets. Pure. Innocent. Young. Too young for someone not to have missed him yet.

What were Ron Miller and his team doing? He should tell Ron what he'd found out about the boy. But that would mean explaining why he was trying to do their job, and why he was sitting here, determined to see the boy before he went into work. Wanting the boy to know, even subconsciously, that he wasn't alone.

Ron he could put off. Mearns was another matter. She'd been pissed off with him on the phone last night, but calmed down enough to tell him what had been covered at the meeting and what they were expected to do today. He'd have to be there sharp and ready to concentrate on the case he should be working on.

What was the alternative? Tell Mearns the truth? Admit his presence here for Archie was about much more than him being there when the boy was hit? How the hell was he supposed to do that when he couldn't explain it to himself?

Except he could. If he wanted to. But it would mean opening up things within him that he'd closed down years ago.

He shot forward as Archie's eyelid moved. He'd reacted to every twitch, every tremor from him in the same way, hoping the boy would come round.

Ferguson slumped back against the chair. The doctor had told him to expect the movements. They were reflexive. Nothing more. The medical team would decide when it was time for him to be brought round.

He stared at the monitor, watching the rise and fall of the line indicating life. Death had always been such a large part of his history. Long before he worked in the police. His parents for starters. Left alone at such a young age. The fear that without them no one would care. Believing it in the years that followed. The fear shaping him and forcing him to make decisions – ones he had no idea back then he'd forever regret.

And he did regret them. Every day. Fear turning to terror in the dead of night at the thought of people finding out. What would happen if the past caught up with him? And now it had.

Ferguson cupped his hand over the boy's thin fingers. They were cold to the touch. He hoped the boy could feel the contact, that he knew someone was there. For him.

Ferguson stared at the boy's features and saw himself. Himself 'before' and, for some reason he couldn't begin to fathom, he felt inside (without knowing anything about this boy) that Archie deserved his 'after' as much as Ferguson did.

Eight a.m. He should head off. Face up to what was going on at work. Outside this room and the boy.

He wasn't ready. Fear was creeping in again, tightening around his throat.

His biggest fear being whether, if the truth came out, Eve and the team would believe he'd ever deserved his 'after'.

Chapter 28

Eve dangled her legs down the hatch and stared into the darkness beneath, white-suit-covered calves pressing against the ladder rungs.

'I'm finding it hard to believe any kid would want to come down here.' She looked up at McCabe and Cooper, who stood at the other side of the hatch from where she sat.

McCabe had made quick work of getting her access when she'd rung late last night. He motioned to the hatch. 'I'm happy to go before you.'

Cooper smiled. 'I know someone she would gladly put down there.'

McCabe smiled at Eve. 'Who's that then?'

'A reporter I'd happily strangle.'

'Ah, the story on the front page this morning. "Boy Left for Dead in Basement". Felt sorry for the grandmother.'

'Don't get me started.'

McCabe tilted his head towards the hatch. 'You sure you don't want me to go down with you?'

Eve's right foot found a rung, her body turning awkwardly in the narrow width of the floor opening. 'No, honestly, I want to see it for myself. Make sure Cooper here follows me down though and doesn't chicken out.' She took the torch McCabe was offering and didn't say the reason she wanted McCabe up here was in case the hatch fell shut. She'd seen that scenario enough in her dreams last night.

Eve lowered herself into the darkness, one rung at a time, stopping to wipe at the back of her neck and cheeks as strands of spider web brushed against her skin. She breathed in, dropping the torch by her side with one hand, illuminating the uneven ground beneath. Seeing Lucas lying there. Imagining his small body on the very ladder where she stood, smoke all around him as he screamed and scratched to get out.

The smell of soot still hung in the air and sweat clung to the base of her back as she continued down, only breathing out once she'd placed both feet on the floor. She turned. It took a moment for her eyesight to adjust to the thin shaft of light ahead of her, white hitting against grey as she took in the brick-walled corridor, the floor little more than rubble sticking to the soles of her shoes. Hairs of silver glinted in the torchlight. She shouted over her shoulder: 'The spiders have been busy down here.'

Eve relaxed a little as she heard Cooper shuffling into the hatch and on to the ladder. She turned back, directing the torch towards his legs as they descended, shining it to the corners of the ceiling, seeing pipes and wires tangled together above her and beneath the home which she tried to picture overhead. Stephen's description of the place had been bang on.

Cooper stepped from the ladder. 'Jesus, this place is something else.'

'Eerie as hell. You wouldn't catch me down here for fun.' Eve turned and shuffled forward, ghosts all around her. Not that she believed in that stuff, but a boy had died here. Her heart quickened as a gaping black hole broke the brickwork to her right. She was on edge and she had no idea why. She turned her head and stepped into the space, light bouncing back off the granite-grey stone pillars dominating the deep room.

'You OK?'

She jumped as Cooper spoke, glad the place was mostly in darkness and he couldn't see her reaction. 'Yeah.' Whispered. For whose benefit she wasn't sure.

Silence pressed against her ears as she shone the torch around the room, Cooper now by her side. In her mind, she heard small animals and insects scurrying for cover. She moved her arm holding the torch from left to right, light finding an old tarpaulin, a couple of ancient paint tins, a dusty leather boot. No sign of the other one.

Eve stepped back out of the room and turned her head to see further along the corridor again. Stephen had said it was a mirror image of the house layout above. She could see gaps in the walls leading into other rooms. She had no desire to explore them. 'Don't know about you, Cooper, but I've seen enough.'

'What do you mean?'

'It makes what Lucas must've gone through much

worse. Do you think he would've come down here alone?' She shone the torch towards Cooper, his face reflecting her own fears.

'There's no way of telling. The alternative is that someone else was here too.'

Together they walked back towards the ladder. Eve was glad when Cooper motioned for her to go first.

McCabe stepped back as they came back up into the light. 'Got a better idea now you've seen it?'

Eve brushed herself down. 'Too clear an idea.'

'I've got something for you.' McCabe opened his hand, a small square plastic pocket protecting the contents that lay in his palm. White strands.

Eve, alongside Cooper, peered at the pocket. 'What's that?'

McCabe turned it over in his hand. 'Remember I told you the material that had been lit and used to fuel the fire was away with forensics?'

'Yes.'

'We found these snagged on the inside of the letter box. Fibres. Relatively undamaged given they were caught between both letter boxes and with it being a fire door.'

'Can I?' Eve picked up the small envelope of plastic. 'Do you know what they are from?'

McCabe nodded. 'A tea towel. We found the rest of it in the skip by the side of the property. The scissor cut is obvious where they took enough to soak it and fit it through the letter box.'

'And threw it in the skip right beside the place? Clever.' Sarcasm dripped from Eve's voice.

'It's gone to forensics also. Obviously, there's no chance of fingerprints. They might be able to lift something though.'

'Good.' She nudged Cooper. 'In the meantime, we should pay the hostel another visit.'

Chapter 29

'WOW, YOU'RE ON TIME.'

'I am indeed, and if you quit with the sarky remarks while you're ahead, I'll give you this coffee I brought in for you.'

Mearns managed a smile as Ferguson placed the drink in front of her. 'Eve's been on the phone. She and Cooper started out at Wellwood this morning with access to the basement. She says it's not something she'd want to repeat. The fire Incident Commander, McCabe, spoke to them about something to do with the ignition of the fire; they're headed to the hostel to talk to Stephen.'

'And we've got all the fun jobs.' Ferguson laid down his own cup and shrugged out of his jacket.

'Financials are going to be a pain in the backside. Private company. Hopefully we'll have a little clout on getting current and past credit accounts, overdrafts and the like. I've phoned Scottish Water. They're going to find out who was assigned the job at Wellwood and get back to me. I'm happy to take both of those if you want to dig into Wellwood?'

Ferguson bit at his lip before removing the plastic lid on his coffee. 'What kind of stuff is she after?'

'When it was established. Who ran it. How it was run. Any info since Stephen took over. Anything.'

Ferguson blew on his coffee. 'Not sure who has the more exciting job out of the two of us.'

'I'm glad you're here today to share the load.'

'I can still take that coffee back, you know.'

Mearns picked up the cup and sipped. Slowly. On purpose. 'You are here for the day, aren't you?'

'Yeah.'

'Good. Eve's getting antsy about how urgent this case is.' Mearns wanted to add more but decided to trust what Ferguson was saying, and to show interest in what she knew was on his mind. 'You heard how the boy is doing?'

'Archie. I think his name is Archie.' Ferguson filled Mearns in on how he'd found that out.

'Have you told Ron?'

'Nope.'

'Don't you think you should?'

'Let me see what the guy comes back with about the CCTV. The guy might have got it wrong about the tattoo.'

Mearns stared at Ferguson. Even though he was here in the office, she wondered whether his head was really in the game. There was no sure way of knowing as Ferguson fired up his monitor and started banging away at the keyboard.

Chapter 30

EVE ANSWERED HER RINGING mobile as Cooper pulled the car into the youth hostel car park.

'It's MacLean.' She pushed a button and laid the phone on her lap – the pathologist would be heard throughout the car. 'Shoot. You're on speaker, MacLean, I've got Cooper here.'

'I've finished looking at the boy.'

It was clear in MacLean's voice how much the small body on the table had affected him, regardless of all the years he'd worked in the mortuary.

'I could find no injury to his body, self-inflicted or otherwise.'

Eve shifted the phone as she moved in the seat. 'I'd been hoping for something – anything that might've told us if he'd perhaps fallen down into that basement or had been thrown down.'

MacLean's voice sounded tinny as it echoed around the inside of the car. 'I'm afraid not.'

Eve looked at Cooper as she asked the next question. 'Cause of death?'

'Smoke inhalation. Plain and simple. He died as a direct result of the fire.'

'Thanks, MacLean.' Eve hung up. 'Let's go and find Stephen.'

Eve and Cooper stood on the doorstep of the hostel, deafened by the passing morning-commute traffic behind them. Eve knocked again, stepping back as the door was finally opened by a tall, dark-haired man who appeared to be as confused as she felt.

'Hi. We were looking for Stephen?'

'He's not here. Can I help?'

Eve took out her ID. 'DI Eve Hunter. We were here yesterday.'

The man peered at the rectangular piece of plastic Eve held up. 'Ah. Come in.' He stepped back, clear of the door.

Eve and Cooper stood in the hallway as the door clanged shut behind them.

'Sorry, I'm Ben. One of the residential workers.'

Cooper shook the hand he was offered. 'DS Mark Cooper. Stephen did mention you. Will he be gone long?'

'He's downtown sorting some stuff out. Hard to tell when none of us have got phones back yet.'

Eve heard the accusation in Ben's tone. 'We should have them back later today. I appreciate how inconvenient it is.' She looked towards the stairwell. 'How're the kids?'

132

'OK, considering. They're all back at school today. We thought it best to keep routine.'

'Which school do they go to?'

'Lochside Academy in Altens. They used to go to Kincorth before it closed.'

At that, an older woman appeared at the top of the stairs. 'Oh, hello. I did't realize we had visitors.' She was carrying a pile of sheets, peeking out from the side of them as she came down the steps.

'Here, let me help you with those.' Ben jogged forward and took the pile from her, placing them on the dresser beside them. 'This is DI Eve Hunter and DS Mark Cooper. They were here yesterday and came back to talk to Stephen.' He turned towards Eve. 'This is Beth.'

Beth pulled at her greying side plait and patted it before taking a tissue from her cuff and dabbing at her nose.

It was only then that Eve noticed how red her eyes were. 'Sorry if we've caught you at a bad time.'

Beth did her best to smile. 'No, I'm sorry. It's still fresh. It'll be a bad time for us all for some time to come.'

Eve noted her lightly tanned face, not missing the wrinkles showing a love of the outdoors and laughter, whilst her bright, clashing clothes hinted at a passion for life in colour. Eve was always amazed by how much could be told by so little.

She imagined Beth spending endless time baking and making arts and crafts, between long walks along the Aberdeen beachfront. Carefree, her hairstyle and whole demeanour suggesting age was but a number and life was to be lived. The only thing that jarred were the tears running down her cheeks again and the snot from her nose she was dabbing at; the brutality and reality of life affected anyone and everyone, no matter how they chose to live.

'It would be good to chat to both of you since we're here. Is there somewhere we could go?'

Ben looked along the hallway. 'I was in the middle of tidying away the chaos of packed lunches this morning – why don't you come through to the kitchen? There's a table and seats there. Can stretch to a cup of tea too, if you like.'

The kitchen was only slightly smaller than the room they had met with Stephen in yesterday. Half-opened packs of ham and cheese spilled all over the worktop, a trail of breadcrumbs connecting the many butter-smeared knives lying between them.

Ben filled and put the kettle on, pulling out four clean mugs from amongst the debris before setting about clearing the place up whilst the kettle boiled.

Beth sat opposite Eve and Cooper, blowing her nose. 'Sorry, I don't know what you must think.' She lifted the end of the chiffon scarf that had fallen from around her neck, flicking it back over her shoulder; the material clashed brightly with the multicoloured knitted cardigan she wore.

Cooper, his forearms on the table, leaned closer to Beth, comforting, as he did so well where Eve usually failed. 'Don't be daft. To lose a child is unimaginable, but in these circumstances? No wonder you're struggling.'

Beth lowered her hands to the table, still clasping the tissue. 'Thank you. They say you shouldn't have favourites . . . Lucas came to us young. He was only two. They become like one of your own.' Beth was now wringing the tissue between her fingers.

Cooper watched the tissue. 'I can imagine. I have three of my own and I don't know if I'd ever come back from it if something happened to one of them.'

'Exactly.' Beth sniffed. 'It's not only the loss of Lucas. It's the knock-on effect on all of us, especially the kids.'

Eve pulled her chair closer to the table. 'The kids are close then.'

She nodded. 'In their own way. They've all had struggles that have shaped them, but they are a family – the closest thing to it most of them have got.'

Ben put the full mugs down and Eve pulled one of them towards her, stretching for the milk jug that followed. 'Do you take milk, Beth?'

'Yes, please.'

'Sugar?'

'No, thanks.'

Eve lifted the mug and placed it in front of Beth before seeing to herself, leaving Cooper to do the same as Ben sat with his own drink.

Beth lifted the tea, cradling it in her hands, the tissue crumpled against the handle. 'Thank you. I used to read to Lucas when he was younger. Harry Potter. The first one. Over and over again. I worry most for Matt; they were good friends.'

Eve pictured the pale boy she'd met, the one whose mother's fears had clearly rubbed off on him. What effect would Lucas's death have on him? The poor kid. Too much experienced in such a short life.

'What were you wanting to see Stephen about? Can we help?' Ben blew at his mug and put it down without drinking.

'It's a development we got from the fire service.' Beth cleared her throat. 'I offered to go with him. He wouldn't have it. The usual. Wanting to do everything on his own. Sort anything needing sorted. It's not possible and why he ended up sleeping at Wellwood at nights. I don't think Audrey could take it any more.'

'Audrey?' Eve glanced at Cooper.

'His wife.'

Ben coughed and stood. 'Anyone for a biscuit?'

Eve shook her head. 'Are things not good with his wife?'

Beth put down her mug. 'Sorry, I shouldn't have said. It's nothing to do with anyone but him and Audrey.'

Ben put an unopened packet of digestives in the middle of the table. 'I think that's one of his biggest stresses and not one he would've told us about readily, had it not been for one of us always being rostered to be on overnight.'

'What happened?' Cooper pulled at the biscuits, ripping them open and taking two.

Beth seemed to check with Ben before she spoke. 'Stephen has always been all about the place. He was when Audrey met him. I think she believed that once they had kids, he'd step back a little. I guess that didn't happen. Then there's the financial struggles of trying to keep a place like Wellwood running.'

Cooper spoke through a mouthful of crumbs, as easy as chatting over a coffee with friends. It was intentional. 'Why didn't he step back?'

'I don't think he could. Wellwood had always been in his life.'

Eve looked up at Beth. 'He was a kid at Wellwood himself?'

Beth shook her head. 'No, no. Well, yes, kind of. His father played a big part in running it back then.'

Ben went for the biscuits. 'Anyway, what was it you wanted to talk to Stephen about?'

Eve could see Ben was a lot more uncomfortable talking about his boss's personal life than Beth was. 'I take it Stephen told you about how the fire started?'

Ben shoved the packet away without taking a biscuit. 'I still can't believe someone could do that. I mean, why? A letter box at a kids' home, for Christ's sake. There are some sick folk out there.'

'Stephen said there are no enemies as such. Maybe this is a random attack and Lucas being down in that basement was a case of being in the wrong place at the wrong time. I'm not sure.'

Ben stared at her. 'What do you mean?'

'Let's say I'm not a big believer in coincidence. Anyway, the fire service found something. Inside the letter box. Fibres from the material that was posted through the door, after the petrol.'

'And?'

'And they found the rest of the material in the skip at the side of the home.'

Ben shook his head. 'Brass neck or what.'

'Or stupid.' Eve dug into her jacket pocket. 'Forensics have managed to determine it was a tea towel. Something with black and white in it.' She placed the plastic envelope on the table, her gaze darting towards Beth as the woman's hand flew to her mouth.

'What?' Cooper said it before her.

Beth's eyes were wide; Ben was staring as hard at what lay in front of them.

Beth took her hand from her mouth. 'All of the tea towels at Wellwood were black and white.'

Eve's hand froze on the table, Cooper stock-still beside her. It seemed the sick perpetrator might have come from inside Wellwood after all.

Chapter 31

EVE AND COOPER SAT with Beth at the table, an empty chair left behind when Ben had gone with the minibus to get the kids out of school. Beth had called Jake at home. He was on his way and the hope was Stephen wouldn't be far behind him. Questions needed to be asked and everyone had to be there ready to answer them.

Beth visibly jumped when Eve's mobile rang. She stood, removing herself from the room when she saw it was MacLean calling. She closed the door and walked further down the hallway.

'Yeah?'

'Hello to you too.'

'I'm kind of tied up at the moment. What've you got?'

'I need you to come down.'

'I can't.'

'Believe me, you need to.'

Eve sighed. 'What? Are you missing me or something?'

'Definitely not. I am phoning with something as unlikely.'

'Tell me.'

'Like I said, this is something best seen.'

Eve looked back at the kitchen door. 'MacLean, you're worrying me. Not like you to want me around any more than necessary.'

'As usual, I don't have a choice in the matter.'

Eve hung up, pocketing her phone as she walked back into the kitchen. 'Cooper, MacLean wants us.'

He frowned at her. 'But . . .'

'Beth, we shouldn't be more than an hour. Ben knows not to say anything to the kids until they're back here. Could you do the same with Stephen and Jake? I'd rather we spoke to everyone at once.'

Eve wanted to see reactions to the news of the tea towel herself. Guilt was hard to hide.

MacLean was standing in the middle of the room, a white-coated arm lifted to the overhead light, his face tilted upwards, studying an X-ray in his hand, his squint more pronounced in his concentration. He lowered his arm on hearing them enter.

Eve stopped dead as her gaze hit what lay in the corner of the room. Cooper did the same mere seconds later.

The labels were still plastered all over the steel, the same ones Dave McCabe had crouched to read. There was no mistaking the oil drum she'd seen being lifted out of Wellwood the morning after the fire.

'What's that doing here?' Her head shifted from the drum to Cooper to MacLean.

MacLean held the X-ray by his side. 'I asked the same

when it arrived, by police escort no less. This answers the question.' MacLean raised his arm towards the light again.

Eve and Cooper joined his side and peered upwards in the same pose as MacLean when they'd found him.

Eve spoke first. 'What is it?'

'An X-ray.'

'Smart, MacLean.'

'From the chemical waste company where the drum was sent for investigation.'

Eve remembered McCabe's instruction to the fire-fighters not to open the drum as it would have to be sent away. Not for one second had she seen it ending up here.

'What are we looking at?' Her words were murmured as her eyes studied the X-ray. The image was brown in colour, three horizontal ridges darker and clear across it, which Eve took to be the sections of the drum. It was what dominated the X-ray that she was struggling to decipher.

It appeared to be a large X at the forefront, the shape brighter than whatever was behind and above it. Eve peered, eyes widening and horror creeping up and over her head at the realization of what they might be study-ing. 'Jesus, MacLean. Are those legs?'

'I'm afraid they are.'

Cooper said nothing, perhaps stunned into silence. The legs crossed over, crammed in tight, the mass behind them and above now revealing itself and presenting more like a body as Eve studied the X-ray. Ribs visible, then thin lines by the side of the legs. The bones of the arm. 'A whole body intact?'

'Yes. But that's not all.'

'*Jesus.*' It was as much as Cooper could muster.

Eve glowered at MacLean. How the hell could there be anything more than a body?

'Look past the legs.'

She leaned closer to the image. What she could see through the X of the crossed legs was beginning to knit together in her brain. Surely, she couldn't be seeing right. Because to her it looked like a skull. Tiny, but a skull, nevertheless. Which meant . . .

'No . . .' She blanched.

Cooper was still staring.

MacLean turned to Eve, the X-ray shifting in his hand, making it seem as if the bones were moving in some macabre dance. 'I'll confirm once forensics have removed the contents from the drum. I'm pretty sure what we're looking at is a woman. And one who was pregnant when she was put in that drum.'

Chapter 32

Then

I WATCH HER ACROSS the room. In profile. The way her nose tilts upwards at the end, slightly, as if it's smiling along with her mouth. She pushes hair back from her face, concentrating on the book she holds in her hand. I want her to myself. He watches her too and sometimes she smiles at him and it tugs at my heart, tightens my throat, but I know she's different – no longer seeing my mother there but something good. Something I'm beginning to believe might exist. *Someone.* A woman who doesn't want to hurt me.

I go over, slowly. Quietly. Past the other kids in the day room pretending to be busy, staying silent. Ms Fields is never far away.

I lean by the sofa she sits on, make out I'm pulling a magazine from the rack there before I whisper next to her ear: 'I've something I want to show you.'

'Have you?' She doesn't take her gaze from the pages of the book, but the smile is there, twitching on the edge of her lips.

'No one else knows, though. You have to keep it to yourself.'

'Oooh, a secret. When do I get to see it?' Now she dares to glance sideways, eyes wide.

'Tonight, when everyone's gone to bed.'

'We're sneaking out?' The book is in her lap now, the words forgotten.

'More a case of sneaking down.'

She frowns. 'You've lost me.'

'You're going to love it.' I straighten and walk back to my seat, knowing she's mine and she's watching, knowing I'm in control. Happy.

Chapter 33

'Come in,' DCI Jim Hastings hollered from behind the closed door. Before Eve had even pushed open the door, she was under no illusions as to what she'd see at this time of day.

Sure enough, the healthy packed lunch made by his wife Sheila that morning lay on the windowsill and, as guaranteed as night turning to day, a greasy, half-eaten bacon butty sat on a napkin on his desk. Sheila would only know about one of them.

Eve didn't sit, stepping forward to rest her hands on the back of the chair facing Hastings's desk instead. 'Shit's hit the fan with Wellwood, sir.'

Hastings's head shot up, a smear of brown sauce at the edge of his mouth. 'I thought it already had. We lost a life.'

'How about another one?'

Hastings straightened. 'You're shitting me?'

'Wish I was.'

He dropped the stack of paper he was holding. 'Another kid since the fire?'

'No, sir. Before it. A woman, years before.'

The lines in Hastings's greasy forehead deepened. 'You've lost me.'

'It didn't seem important at the time, so I never mentioned it. Firefighters found an old oil drum beneath Wellwood, whilst Cooper and I were at the scene. It was found in the same basement as Lucas was. The drum was plastered in hazardous warning stickers so Dave McCabe, the Incident Commander, told the firefighters it would have to be sent off for X-ray before being opened. MacLean's shown me the X-ray.'

Hastings sank his skinny frame into his chair. 'You're telling me there was a body in the drum?'

'Yes, sir. A woman. And MacLean believes she was pregnant.'

Hastings bent forward and pushed the butty away. 'What the . . . Do we know who she was?'

'Not yet, sir. We've not long found out. I've come from MacLean.'

'Jesus. Does he have any idea of how long they'd been in that thing?'

'No, he's waiting for forensics to remove the remains. He'll examine them.'

Hastings shook his head. 'I . . . The press is going to have a field day with this. Arson. A possible murder as a result and now an unexplained death.'

It sounded worse hearing it out loud, if it was indeed possible for it to be any worse. 'The best we can do is be upfront because there's no way we're going to be able to keep something like this under wraps.'

Hastings was squeezing at his forehead.

'I've got to head back to the youth hostel after this with Cooper to talk to the staff.'

'About this?'

'Yes, but also because it appears the material used to start the fire came from inside Wellwood.'

Hastings stared at her, his skin looking almost green in the overhead lights – the hue that had earned him the nickname the Grinch. Not that he knew about it. 'You couldn't write this shit. How did that little nugget come about?'

'Forensics identified the material that was lit and pushed through the letter box. Turns out the rest of it was in a skip outside the property. A tea towel. Same as others used in the home.'

'We're looking at arson by someone from inside the bloody place?'

'It appears that way.'

'For fuck's sake. They're going to be slithering all over this one.'

'I'll get Mearns and Ferguson to set up a press briefing for later this afternoon.'

'This shit stinks, Hunter. We're two bodies in now and both of them found underground. In a kids' home for fuc—'

'We're on it, sir, I can promise you that.'

Chapter 34

MEARNS LOOKED UP AS Cooper entered the office. His face was pale, slack, as though he'd seen a ghost. 'What's up with you?'

Cooper banged into the seat at the spare desk next to Mearns's and Ferguson's, as if his legs had given way.

'Cooper?'

Ferguson had stopped typing and was staring at him as hard as Mearns was.

'We've come up from MacLean. There was an oil drum in the basement where Lucas was found. It was sent off for X-ray due to hazardous warnings all over it.'

'And?' The hairs were raised on Mearns's neck as she listened to how slowly Cooper was talking – and saw the haunted look in his eyes.

'And there's a body in it. MacLean believes it to be a woman. A woman who was carrying a child.'

Mearns was struggling to process what was being said. 'In a drum? In the same basement?'

Cooper was silent.

Ferguson's mouth opened and closed, his face chalk white.

'Eve's in with Hastings now. We were heading back to the hostel anyway about developments with something found at the scene of the fire. A bloody tea towel used to light the fire. A tea towel that came from the kitchen of Wellwood.'

Now it was Mearns's turn to open and close her mouth, unable to find any words.

Cooper wiped at his lips. 'Eve needs you and Ferguson to organize a press briefing for this afternoon. She's clearing it with Hastings.'

'Oh my God, they're going to go crazy.'

They both turned as Ferguson's phone rang, sitting in silence as he answered.

'Brilliant. Thanks. I'll head up now and take a look.' Ferguson stood. 'I need to nip out for an hour.'

Mearns's hackles were up, knowing what Ferguson was heading out for. 'Ferguson, I need you to—'

'I'll be no more than an hour.'

Cooper studied the two of them. 'What's going on?'

Ferguson was staring at Mearns, his eyes asking her something Cooper couldn't hear.

She glared back at him as she answered Cooper. 'It's someone who can tell him more about the history of Wellwood.'

She swallowed the lie as Ferguson left.

Chapter 35

FERGUSON WATCHED AS IMAGES from Summer Street outside moved at speed as Toby from the shelter fast-forwarded through footage on the screen.

'Here.' Toby pointed at the screen.

Ferguson wheeled his chair closer, relief and excitement flooding through him as he recognized the boy standing there. Archie was his name. He stood by a tall male, kitted out in all black, his face as battered as a boxer's. Archie was animated, hands flying as he spoke. The guy seemed to be having none of it. 'It looks like they're arguing.'

'I'd say.'

Ferguson watched as the guy lunged for Archie, missing him by inches as Archie ducked and ran past him. The guy gave chase, but stopped short of the Cyrenians building, shouting something as Archie fled up the steps. 'Can you zoom in on the guy?'

Toby clicked at the mouse, the guy's face coming closer, blurring the more he zoomed.

'Back a bit. There. Can you print that for me?'

Toby confirmed he could as the printer kicked into life.

Ferguson watched as the image spewed out of the printer. He had no idea who the guy was. Hopefully calling in a favour might tell him.

Chapter 36

STEPHEN SMOOTHED THE DENIM shirt against his stomach, seemingly trying for some order in a place and situation alien to him. Eve had pulled him away from the kids and the rest of the staff, what they'd found out taking precedence over anything else. She watched him pull his chair closer to the table, the same table they had first met him at, the man looking worse than he had then.

'There's been a development.'

Stephen picked at the button at his belly. 'Beth said. I thought you wanted to talk to all of us.'

'This is something else. Something we found out.' Eve was glad at least he was sitting.

'It can't be worse than losing Lucas.'

Eve glanced at Cooper. 'There was another thing found in the basement with Lucas. A barrel. One of those old oil drums.'

'That drum's been there ever since I took over, along with old broken tools and paint pots. Stuff I've never bothered to move. As I said, the only time the place is accessed is for maintenance works.' He was shaking his head. 'I don't understand . . . What's that got to do with . . .' His brow furrowed.

'The drum was removed for investigation. X-rayed. The remains of a woman were found inside.'

Colour drained from Stephen's face. 'What do you mean . . .?' His hands dropped to his lap, shaking as they landed. 'A woman?' His voice quivered. 'What woman? How did she get stuck in a . . .?'

Eve looked at Cooper and back at Stephen. 'She didn't seal that lid from the inside.'

'She was *put* in there?'

'It would appear so.'

'Jesus.' He leaned forward, elbow banging on to the table, hand supporting his head as it dropped.

'I'm afraid that's not all.'

Stephen's head shot up, eyes wide.

'It appears she may have been pregnant.'

'Oh my God.'

Eve gave him a moment to take in what she was telling him. 'Stephen?' She dipped her head, trying for eye contact from him. 'The pathologist has yet to examine the remains. I need you to tell me what you know about that barrel.'

Stephen raised his face, his skin translucent. 'It's always been there. I assumed it was empty. I never gave it any thought.'

Cooper spoke. 'Beth was saying your father used to run this place?'

'Yes, I . . . My father and I didn't have a relationship.

153

He left my mother when I was six. For the woman who ran this place.'

'How did you come to run it?'

'He didn't plan it. It was privatized, as it is now. Sally Fields initially owned it. When she and my father got together, they co-owned it. When she died, she left it to my father. Then when he died, it fell to me as next of kin.'

'Do you have records of any of the kids homed at Wellwood back then?'

Stephen shook his head. 'No.' Colour had not returned to his face. 'The place was lying empty when I got it. As I said, I had no relationship with my father, no knowledge of the place. I had no idea it was where he worked before I inherited it.'

'What made you want to reopen it?'

'I was a youth worker. Helping underprivileged kids. My childhood hadn't been a great one. I thought I had something to bring to them. This place was the next step in doing that. It's not been an easy ride.'

'Do you know what might've happened to those records?'

'I have no idea. My father shut down and cleared the place when he became ill. Terminal cancer. I'd hope social services would still have files of what happened to the kids after that, but back then it wasn't a legal requirement to hold records past when the child was twenty-one. Many case files were destroyed. But someone can't just disappear. Not like that.'

Eve wasn't sure. 'People disappear every day.'

'People must've noticed.'

'After, I'm sure they did. But we both know someone can disappear down there without anyone knowing.'

Stephen twitched as if he'd been slapped.

'We're going to have to release this information.'

Stephen was rocking in the chair. 'Please. No, is there not some way . . .?'

'We'll make it clear that it was before your time here.'

'But Lucas . . .'

'I'm sorry: we can't make any of this go away. I'm afraid, as far as Lucas is concerned, it's about to get much worse.'

'What?'

Eve relayed what she'd told Beth and Ben about the towel.

Stephen's face had a green sheen to it. 'There's no way it can be one of ours who started that fire.'

'We think the towel may have come from the kitchen at Wellwood.'

Stephen didn't have an answer to that one but Eve was hoping someone else might.

The kids, standing in their black school uniforms, appeared shell-shocked both at the news of the fire and at the fact they'd been sleeping above a dead woman and her unborn child. Eve had left Cooper to break that news. He would do it with sensitivity and appropriately, bearing the younger kids in mind.

They were all gathered in the dining room – staff, kids, Eve and Cooper.

Eve took in the room. 'I need you all to think and to tell me the truth. We think that towel came from the kitchen at Wellwood. Not some random passer-by or someone bearing a grudge. Someone has to know what happened.'

Charlotte was picking at her fingernail. 'Wellwood was our home. None of us would have done something like that.'

'Explain the towel.'

Darren stepped forward, towering above the kids behind him, and the staff. 'What about Lucas's dad? He was there that day.'

'I was led to believe he wasn't inside the property.'

'He wasn't,' Ben confirmed.

Jake stood up from the table. 'Guys, this is serious. I'm not saying one of you started the fire but if anyone knows about that towel, you have to speak up.'

Eve saw Matt chewing at his bottom lip, his gaze fixed on the floor, as it had been since they'd come into the room. 'Matt?'

His bottom lip quivered.

'Don't be scared to say if you have something to tell us. If it's something you know about someone else. We are here to protect you.'

Matt rubbed a hand against his trouser leg. 'It was me who took the towel.'

Everyone's head whipped towards him.

'I didn't start the fire; you have to believe me.' He was crying.

Cooper went to him and led him to a seat. 'Tell us what happened.'

'I was helping make the tea. Macaroni. Jake had gone to see to something, and I put the towel on the cooker. I didn't know the ring was on until I smelled the burning. The towel was all brown. I thought I'd get into trouble. I hid it, sneaked out after tea and put it in the skip.'

Jake was shaking his head at Matt. 'I wouldn't have given you grief. It was an accident.'

Matt was sobbing. 'I wish I had told you. Whoever started the fire wouldn't have found that towel.'

Cooper was rubbing the boy's arm. 'They would've found something else.'

Eve watched snot drop from Matt's nose, wanting to cry herself. The monster was back outside. But it didn't dampen her determination to find them.

157

Chapter 37

CHARLOTTE SAT PICKING HER toenails in the bottom bunk. 'Lucas was a little shit. He was. Folk say you shouldn't speak ill of the dead but I reckon just because you've croaked it, that doesn't change who you were.'

Darren scowled. 'Jesus, Char, he didn't deserve to die. He was a pain in the arse at times but not that bad. Not annoying enough to snuff it in a fire.'

Char threw a piece of nail on to the floor. 'Maybe someone thought so.'

Hannah was positioned by the window, where she could be found most of the time. 'This is where we should be able to say easily who that might've been. A process of elimination: he liked him; he didn't. She loved him; she didn't. The thing is, we can't. Not when he'd pissed off all of us at some point.'

Matt's face was still wet with tears. 'Is that what the police are doing? Trying to pin it on one of us?'

Sadie rolled her eyes. 'Of course they are. They nearly pinned it on you with that bloody towel.'

Darren slipped from his bed. 'It's not bloody funny. We've spent all this time keeping our mouths shut about what's been going on here. Wanting to stay together, for Wellwood not to be taken away from us. And now this. Is it connected to that, to what we've been worrying about all this time?'

Charlotte stopped picking at her feet. 'Do you reckon he could've done it?'

Sadie spoke. 'If not him, then who?'

Darren pulled at the stubble on his chin. 'It would be an easy way out.'

Sadie shifted on her bed. 'Did everyone delete our texts about Wellwood before the police took our phones?' She looked around the room as everyone nodded.

Hannah turned from the window. 'What's to say one of us didn't do it?'

Everyone glanced around the room, meeting gazes and then dragging gazes away.

Sadie broke the uncomfortable silence. 'Don't be daft.'

Matt piped up from the corner. 'What if Lucas did start that fire?'

Darren curled his lip. 'Matt, for Christ's sake.'

'You saw how he was when he found out his dad had been there. What if he did want to be with him? Maybe he started the fire thinking if he went underground it wouldn't come near him – that we'd all get out.'

Charlotte attempted to throw a bitten nail in Matt's direction. 'You're full of shit, Matt.'

'You're not coming up with anything better. He could've. What about the things he did do? He was always winding me up. Reading up stuff on the internet

159

about germs and freaking me out. Remember that time he spilt something on my hypoallergenic pillow right before bed? Or the time he hid the only cup I'd drink out of?'

Hannah took the baton. 'Or the time he waited for everyone to fall asleep before creeping over to my bed with a pair of scissors. Those bloody blue plastic-handled scissors he took when no one else was watching.

'He cut a chunk from my fringe at the side of my head. I screamed all the way down the hall that morning while everyone laughed. It took me months to grow it back after Beth cut the other side to match it.

Darren leaned against one of the lockers. 'Remember that time with the photo of my mum? Missing. For two days. Then out of nowhere, it appeared on my bed one night. The same night, everyone was crowded around the telly watching and I saw Lucas leave the room under the excuse of needing a pee.'

Sadie's sing-song voice travelled across the room. 'He was forever messing up my stuff.'

Hannah tutted. 'That's because you've got OCD. You're in danger of spinning out of the room, the tizzy you get yourself in if someone moves your stuff. The thing that let Lucas get away with it was his face. He was cute. No denying it.'

Charlotte chimed in: 'Almost as cute as Sadie's beautiful – and as fucking annoying. Both sickening in their own ways.'

'Bog off, Charlotte.' Sadie flounced on to the chair and they all fell into an uneasy silence.

Chapter 38

THE PRESS ROOM WAS muggy, the smell of wet coats and sweat mingling together in the air. Eve's gaze was drawn to the brightest coat in the room. Mustard in colour. Not to be missed. So it was no surprise to see Marcie Wade standing there wrapped up in it.

Eve sat between Cooper and Hastings, trying her best not to breathe in the body odour wafting from the DCI.

Hastings stood, prompting a hush to fall over the room. 'As has already been reported, on Monday the seventh of March, officers responded to a fire at the Wellwood Children's Home in the Kincorth area of the city. Sadly, one of the children there, since confirmed as eleven-year-old Lucas Fyfe, lost his life. During the investigation of the scene, firefighters removed a sealed fifty-five-gallon oil drum from the basement beneath the property which they believed contained hazardous substances. They cleared the barrel from the site and it was sent off for analysis before being opened to determine the contents.'

No one moved. Every reporter in the room hanging off each and every word Hastings said. Eve could see the hunger on their faces. They'd be on their feet moments from now, shouting and scrabbling over one another for the story.

Eve glanced sideways at Hastings; his pause length-ened as she found herself as desperate as the reporters to hear what he was going to say next, even though she knew what was coming.

'The report showed evidence of human remains.'

Eve watched the room erupt, rising like a flood, a sea of faces crashing towards them.

'SIT.' Hastings's bellow broke through the chaos, some of the reporters adhering to his instruction and finding their seats, others staying upright, but quietening down.

'I want to stress that these remains have been down there for some time. Exactly how long is still to be deter-mined. It is safe for me to say we know it to be before the time of the current staff and children at Wellwood. I ask you to remain aware and respectful of that fact.'

Eve surveyed the room. It was like telling dogs not to go sniffing each other's backsides. Not a chance.

'I have time for a few questions.'

A greasy-haired guy at the front, who appeared to have had a rough night, shouted loudest: 'Is it another child in that drum?'

Hastings looked the reporter dead in the eye. 'We don't know at this time.'

It had been decided to detail human remains only. The fallout from it being a woman and child could come later.

162

A mousey, slouched woman who didn't fool Eve raised her hand.

Hastings pointed to her. 'Yes?'

'How could the current staff not have known about the drum?'

'The staff *were* aware of the drum, as it had been there since they took over the building. It was down with many other old tools and the contents were never questioned.'

That fact would not be reported accurately.

A wiry older guy spoke up from the back. 'Why was the drum found during the fire examination? Had the floor burned through?'

Eve stiffened.

Marcie Wade stepped forward and cleared her throat, interrupting before the other reporter's question had been answered. 'Is there any truth to the rumour that Lucas's body was found in the same area as the drum – also underground?'

The rush of noise was deafening. Eve caught the glint in Marcie's eye and bit the inside of her cheek to contain her outburst.

Hastings sighed, the noise clear on the speaker. 'I can confirm that is the case.'

Marcie looked around the room, eyebrows high, playing her audience as they danced alongside her. 'We have a dead child, found beneath ground where another body had lain undiscovered for years. And both of those tragedies have been highlighted by a fire that was not an accident.'

Eve stiffened, not sure where Marcie had got her information.

Hastings didn't flinch. 'Yes, and it is a tragic set of circumstances, but don't make this into a witch-hunt. As I said, respect that part of those circumstances is nothing to do with the current staff of Wellwood.'

Marcie sneered. 'Maybe, but the death . . . *murder* of a child on their watch is – and don't forget that the person who started the fire has not been found or identified as not having anything to do with them.'

Hastings's shoulders sagged as the pack leaped forward again.

Eve stepped back from the chaos as her pocket vibrated. She edged the mobile out of her pocket, glancing at it in an attempt not to draw attention to the move. *Forensics. Done with the technology from Wellwood.*

The baying of the crowd grew louder and Eve closed her eyes. It was only going to get worse from here on in.

Chapter 39

EVE AND COOPER EDGED into the front room, led by Ben. Chaos was the only word for it. Jake stood by the table – all the kids seated and chatting as they scooped at the food on their plates as if they hadn't been fed in days.

Eve couldn't believe they were back here again, only hours since they'd pulled the kids out of school. The place was becoming like a second home to her, the amount of time she was spending in it.

'Guys. GUYS.' The din settled on Ben's second attempt.

Eve and Cooper lifted the plastic pockets containing the children's phones and iPads, and the room erupted into madness again.

Eve placed the evidence bags on the sideboard. 'Thanks for your patience. Don't worry, we have no idea what personal stuff was on the phones, that was forensics' job, and they were only interested in anything that might help us. The rest remains confidential.' The relief on the kids' faces was evident. Eve got it; she couldn't imagine how she would've felt at the same age if someone had delved into her secrets. But she was going to have to do exactly that to one of the kids sitting in front of her.

She watched as Ben approached Matt, barely noticing as the kids elbowed one another in an attempt to get to their devices. Jake was herding them off, handing them out one at a time.

Matt's gaze flickered to Eve as he stood up from the table and followed Ben over to them and out into the corridor, another room already waiting for them.

Matt sat alongside Ben, pulling at the sleeves of his jumper.

Eve shuffled the chair closer to the table. 'Don't be worried. We want a little chat about some texts on your phone.'

Matt glanced at Ben, who smiled at him, but the fear in the boy's face did not lessen any.

'I remember you saying you were good friends with Lucas. That's pretty clear from the message history between the two of you. What you had was pretty special.' Eve could hear Matt's nails scratching against the material of his cuffs. She focused on the phone on the table, still lying in the evidence bag. 'There are messages on there that make for some hard reading. Texts from Lucas at times when his dad had tried to see him. He was torn, wanting to see him, but knowing it wasn't the right thing for him.'

Matt neither confirmed nor denied it.

Cooper fingered the plastic bag. 'Did he talk to you about needing space ever? He might've gone down to the basement that night because of how he felt after his dad attempted to see him.'

Matt's voice was a whisper. 'He was upset. When he got like that, he didn't like to be alone.'

'Did he try to spend time with you?'

'Yes, until it was time for bed.' Matt looked straight at Cooper. 'Maybe if I'd stayed with him this wouldn't have happened.'

Cooper shook his head. 'You can't think like that. What happened wasn't your fault. None of us know why he was down there, or how he got there. We thought he might've said something – or maybe you know it was somewhere he liked to go. With what's happened, I understand why you might not want to tell us.'

Matt stared at the table, silent.

Eve saw the struggle at the loss of his friend, the pain clear in his features. 'There were a couple of other texts on there. Between you and Lucas. About fear of what would go down if something happened at Wellwood.'

Ben frowned, turning to stare at Matt.

Eve dipped her head, trying to make eye contact with Matt. 'What made you scared of that? Did you think something might happen?'

Matt's hands disappeared below the table, the material at his shoulders stretching as he continued pulling at his sleeves. 'Wellwood was all we had. We sometimes got scared about not having one another.' His eyes were brimming.

'It must be hard having lost Lucas. I can't imagine. Why did you think something might happen to Wellwood?'

Matt turned to Ben, as if seeking permission to talk,

visibly relaxing when he saw the softness in Ben's face. 'Sometimes Stephen seemed sad. Tired. Snappy. He wasn't always like that. Lucas and I thought maybe he'd had enough. That he didn't want to look after us any more.'

Ben was shaking his head. 'Matt, Stephen loves you guys. We all do. Why didn't you talk to us about this?'

Matt shrugged. 'Maybe we were scared if we said it to others then it would make it real.'

'Do you think Lucas could've had anything to do with the fire? Maybe in his fear he thought it would mean you would all be rehomed somewhere together, or maybe it would show Stephen cared?'

A tear dropped to Matt's cheek. 'I guess we might be rehomed now if we can't go back to Wellwood, but Lucas won't be there.' He was sobbing now. 'He would've told me. I mean, if he'd been thinking anything like that. And it's like Darren said, he was terrified of fire. He wouldn't have had the guts.' Matt raised his head. 'I don't know why he was down there, and I wish I did.'

Chapter 40

Wednesday, 9 March

EVE TOSSED THE *ABERDEEN Enquirer* newspaper into the passenger footwell of the car, lifting her feet and pressing down on it for good measure. 'Pile of shit.' She stared out of the window at the passing shopfronts in Union Street.

Cooper turned to her as he indicated left at Holburn Junction. 'You might think so. I kinda like the car.' He glanced at the crumpled mass at Eve's feet.

'Funny.' Eve tutted. 'I mean, Jesus . . . "Bodies in the Basement". Could they have made the headline any bigger? And as for that family of Lucas's. Not that you can call them that.'

Cooper didn't disagree. 'Wonder how much Lucas's grandmother got?'

'Whatever it was, they should've chucked in an award for best actress at the same time. "Heartbroken. Unable to sleep. Tortured thinking about what his last moments were like. The guilt felt at having him living somewhere where evil lurked."' Eve's fists were clenched on her thighs. 'What a crock of shit. The only evil is her and her bullshit.'

Cooper pulled off Holburn, turning right and driving past the Ashvale Chipper towards the hostel. 'Unfortunately shit like that sells papers and anybody remotely connected to that kid was going to be a scoop. Even Lucas's dad got in on the act, albeit only with a short quote.'

'Lucas's grandmother didn't care about that kid. Neither did he. Yet they're going to be rolled out all the way through this investigation and beyond.' Eve saw the hostel up ahead to the left. 'It doesn't look good but from what I've seen of the staff, the kids, I'm finding it hard to believe that Lucas's death was the result of poor care. That he was down there as some kind of ongoing abuse. The historic case with the barrel is clouding things. Put them together and they make the place seem evil, before any of these staff or kids were there. But I think we're looking at more.'

'Like what?'

'Lucas is our main focus. Him and the fire on the night he died. And they should be. However, I'm sure finding out what happened to that woman in the barrel is going to give us the breakthrough we need to find the person responsible for Lucas's death.'

Cooper turned to her. 'You believe they're linked? After saying it was before their time, and with Hastings asking the press to respect that?'

Eve didn't look at him. 'I'm finding it hard to believe they're not linked – that's a lot of bad luck and suspicious circumstances for one place. No wonder the press and no one else are buying it. I'm not saying Stephen or

170

anyone else at Wellwood knew about what was in that barrel, but maybe someone else did.'

Cooper took his eyes from the road again. 'In that someone set the fire to finish what they'd started all those years ago?'

'Far-fetched. But think about it: that basement was opened up three weeks ago, for the first time in years for all we know. Those kids were interested. They all went down there. If someone had spent years believing they had got away with murder and concealment, wouldn't you be panicking?'

Cooper didn't disagree.

'Lucas got trapped down there somehow. Either by himself or at the hands of someone else. What if that someone knew about those bodies underground and Lucas got in the way? Maybe the fire was meant to cover it all up.'

Cooper tapped at the wheel, waiting for the lights to change. 'Then we are after someone historic. Someone who was at Wellwood back when Fields owned it. Staff or a child. Bit of a push, don't you think?'

Eve sighed. 'Maybe it's all unconnected and a cruel twist of fate how it's landed. A lot of the time kids like these have come from nothing. When they were shown the basement, maybe Lucas felt it was a place that could be his own. Especially after the upset of seeing his father that day. He maybe wanted to get away somewhere, to think. It could be that simple. Still, it doesn't explain the fire.'

Cooper pulled into the hostel car park and stopped. 'I don't know what to think.'

Eve released her seat belt and opened the car door. 'You're not the only one. I want to go down to that basement again. Today. Straight after we check in with Stephen. I need to see where those bodies were.'

Stephen was half the man he had been yesterday. He sat slouched at the table, his polo shirt crumpled as if someone had attempted to fold it into one of those old paper fans. The local morning paper lay spread out in front of him.

'I'd hoped to get to you before you saw that.'

Stephen raised his head. Eve was shocked at the depth of the dark circles beneath his eyes. When he spoke, his voice was tinged with pain. 'They think we weren't looking after the kids properly.'

Eve didn't say she'd thought the same thing when she'd first been told about Lucas. 'You weren't here yesterday, when we gave back the phones and laptops. We spoke to Matt. About messages on his phone.'

'Yes. Yes, Ben told me.'

'Were you aware the boys were feeling like that?'

Stephen shook his head. 'No.' His voice cracked. 'All I've ever tried to do is to be there for the kids. And now everything is falling apart. Out of my control.'

Eve had no idea what to say. 'The press will always go for blame; it helps stoke the scandal and that, I'm afraid, sells the papers.'

'You've seen how we work. You know it's not true.'

Eve had said more or less the same to Cooper. But facts were facts: the kids had felt a shift in the dynamics at the home and, whatever had happened, Lucas had

172

found himself trapped underground before perishing in a fire. On their watch. And no one had a clue what had happened.

Stephen pushed the paper away from him. 'And the stuff about that barrel . . . I didn't see any clear line saying it's unconnected and before our time here.'

'It wouldn't sound as scandalous if it had. You have to ignore what's being written.'

Stephen shoved the paper further across the desk. 'Like I'm going to be able to do that. The way they're going on about how the fire started, as if one of our own was responsible.'

'We can't rule that out.'

Stephen shook his head. 'There's no way.'

'The truth will out, as they say.'

Stephen looked unconvinced and Eve knew it would have to stay that way until they found out what the truth was.

173

Chapter 41

Then

IT'S DARK. HE DOESN'T need any light to know where it is. He signals to her to stay quiet by his side as he crouches by the back door, a door barely used, and begins to pull at the carpet there. Up and towards him. She edges back, the white carrier bag in her hand banging against her thigh. Making a noise. A clink that makes him freeze, and not because the noise may let someone know they're there.

She hisses. 'What are you do—?'

'Shhhh.' He moves and kneels on the folded-back corner of the carpet before leaning forward to the black rubber mat that's now uncovered and stuck to the wooden floorboards. He picks at the edge of the mat, suction popping as it lifts from the floor exposing a roughly cut square panel in the floor, almost the length and width of the mat. He enjoys the wonder on her face, illuminated by the security light coming through the frosted-glass panel of the door. He forces a finger into the edge of the square panel and lifts, resting the wood against the wall before patting at his pocket for the torch. He whispers for her to kneel and, together, they peer into the darkness before he turns the torch on, already knowing what they'll see.

He watches her as she stares at the ladder, nothing else visible except the floor where it stops. She lifts her head to him.

'Surprise.' A whisper and a secret between them. Making her his.

And she smiles.

Chapter 42

Eve had been brave enough to come down herself this time – if only because McCabe was unavailable. But she needed to know Cooper was at the top of that hatch. In the light. Above ground.

There was a black void on the left, towards the end of the narrow corridor. Where she was headed. She crept along, her lungs struggling against the air that was being sucked backwards past her and up the ladder into the light above. Dust whispered at her nose. A couple more steps and she'd be where she needed to be. Where *they* had been. In the dark. Gone.

Light bounced off the pillars as she stepped forward into the space, fragments of broken glass glinting amidst the rubble on the floor. She glanced right, the torch showing the chimney stack that continued above ground up to the broken roof of the home; brickwork rose to the ceiling here whence she pictured it travelling upwards through to where there had once been carpet and wallpaper. Eve dipped her head and saw it.

A circular indent in the floor where the drum had stood, the rubble around it disturbed when it was dragged out.

Eve almost didn't want to interfere with the rubble any more than it already had been. Out of respect. But many people had been here already – measuring, assessing, photographing. Their goal was no longer only about respect. It was about justice too.

Eve edged closer to the round groove in the floor, seeing the X-ray image in her mind. Seeing Lucas's face in that body bag. The ghosts were swarming now, trying to tell her their stories. Wanting her to help them to be heard.

Eve imagined a young woman tenderly cradling her growing bump, perhaps laughing in wonder at the secret space beneath her home. Or had she been scared, crying as she'd been shoved forward into this space?

Had Lucas seen the drum? If he had, at least he couldn't have known what was inside it.

She swallowed. This cold, dank place had been the last thing Lucas and this poor unknown woman had seen.

Had they struggled and screamed? Lucas unheard in the din of fire alarms; the woman silenced as the lid was hammered down and sealed?

Underground. In the dark. Forgotten.

Eve fought to imagine who could do something like this, her mind's eye seeing a faceless male, someone who had taken advantage of that young woman. A monster who had wanted her gone. Someone who had perhaps known about the baby and wanted them gone too.

Eve blinked back unexpected tears. 'I promise you,'

she said to the ghosts in the room, 'I promise you I'll find out who did this.'

Eve sat at the front of the room, unsure whether her legs would support her after what she'd seen down in that basement. Or, rather, what being down in the basement, knowing what she knew now, had conjured up in her imagination. 'Feels like a lifetime since we were all here together.' Eve looked at Mearns, Ferguson and Cooper in front of her. 'Let's start with an update so we're all on the same page. As you know, Dave McCabe, the Incident Commander, gave us a potential lead as to the material that was used to light the accelerant. Turns out it was a tea towel from Wellwood's kitchen. Half of it found in the skip outside.'

Mearns's eyes widened. 'You're shitting me?'

'No. Called the staff and the kids in, out of school, fearing this was going to be internal after all, hoping someone would crack. Then Matt, one of the kids, goes and starts blubbing and tells us he burned it by accident in the kitchen and binned it for fear of getting into trouble.'

Cooper was shaking his head.

Eve straightened in the chair. 'We did get a chance to chat with the other two members of staff we hadn't met – Beth and Ben. You'll remember I told you Stephen spoke about staying overnight if he had lots of work on?'

Ferguson and Mearns waited.

'That may be a crock. According to Beth, he's been sleeping there because of some problems at home. As in friction with his wife. I'm not saying that's got anything to do with anything but maybe it explains the drink I'm sure I smelled on his breath the first time we met. Maybe there's more to the whole thing. Mearns, have you got the financials yet?'

Mearns shook her head. 'I chased them earlier. Hopefully should get my hands on them later today.'

'Fine. Let me know as soon as you have them.'

'What about James Fyfe, Lucas's dad? Did you get an alibi?'

'I've phoned several times. No joy.'

'Can you not turn up at his?' Eve didn't miss the look between Mearns and Ferguson.

Mearns shifted in her chair. 'It's been fitting in a time when we were both available to go.'

Eve turned to Ferguson. 'What's made you busy?'

Ferguson opened the notebook in front of him. 'It's been a bit of a nightmare getting history on the place. The best I've got is that it was privately run by a Ms Sally Fields and a Mr William Alderton from the mid-sixties to the mid-nineties. In terms of getting access to historical records of the children who were at Wellwood during that time, I'm coming up against brick walls.'

Eve saw Mearns's head whip around to Ferguson as he delivered what he'd found. Eve spoke. 'I take it you've made the connection?'

Ferguson seemed panicked for a second. 'The connection?'

'Alderton. The same surname as Stephen.'

Ferguson coughed. 'Stephen is related to William Alderton?'

'It was his father. We got the details you gave us from

a chat with him. Mearns, did you not make the connection either?'

Mearns was frowning at Ferguson. 'I wasn't aware he had the information. We hadn't updated one another before you arrived.'

Eve glared at them. 'Come on, guys, we need to be more with it than that. Have you seen the papers today?'

Mearns looked to the floor, her jaw tight.

Something was going on. 'What about Scottish Water?'

At that, Mearns perked up a little. 'They got back this morning. The woman has identified the engineer who was tasked with the Wellwood job.' She flicked open her notebook. 'It was a Mr Keith Brydon. I've asked if he'll be available today; she's going to get back to me. I'm happy to see him if you can't.'

'Fine. In the meantime, I need you both to go see James Fyfe. Mearns, I need you to keep on top of those financials, and Ferguson, get me more than we already know about Well—' Eve stopped as Ferguson's mobile rang.

She watched him turn away towards the wall mumbling, before he spun round again and was out of his seat. 'That was the hospital. They're reducing the boy's meds, trying to bring him out of the coma. I need to be there when he comes around.'

Cooper swung around. 'Ferguson, the nursing staff will be there for that. I'm sure those working the case will be there when allowed, too.'

Ferguson was already lifting his jacket from the chair. 'I promised him I wouldn't leave him.'

Cooper's head whipped towards Eve and back to

Ferguson. 'Ferguson, the press is all over this and we have no clue what the hell has happened – with Lucas, the fire, or with the bodies found in the barrel. I'd say that takes priority for now.'

Ferguson was walking towards the door.

Cooper was standing now. 'Ferguson, what the hell? We're talking about a kids' home here.'

Ferguson stopped. 'This is a kid too. Doesn't make him any less important.'

Eve rose and stepped forward. 'It doesn't but he isn't your case.'

Ferguson stood strong. 'I'm not asking to work on it. I'm asking to go and see a boy who has no one. A boy who was hit, wounded and ended up in hospital when I was there.'

Eve could see the determination on his face. 'You can't be pissing about like this.' She paused. 'Go see him. But make it the only time you do it on our time, and make it quick.'

Ferguson didn't need to be told twice.

Eve turned to Cooper and Mearns; Cooper had a face like he'd sucked a sour sweetie. 'I get it, but he'd be no use to anyone right now. You go and see Fyfe with Mearns. I'll update Hastings. Mearns, let me know about Scottish Water as soon as you hear.'

Eve straightened, steeling herself for what Hastings would have to say.

Chapter 43

JAMES FYFE HAD THE same glazed expression as the last time Mearns had seen him. At least the roll-up was already made this time.

He lit it, drawing hard on the filter as he peered up at Mearns and Cooper.

Mearns took the lead. 'We've had a development with the fire at Wellwood.'

'Have you found the bastard who started it?'

'No. But we do need to confirm where you were the night of the fire.'

The Staffy who had been sitting at James Fyfe's feet trotted over to Cooper and jumped on his leg. Cooper bent to pet him as James shouted, 'Rocky. Down, you little shit.'

Mearns watched Cooper pat the dog's head regardless. The dog was probably begging to come with them.

'You're asking me where I was?' He pointed at himself, ash falling from the fag on to his Bench T-shirt.

'Yes. Although you didn't disclose it last time I was

here, we were told you turned up at Wellwood that day.'

'And what? I started a fire that killed my son?'

Mearns didn't offer any disagreement. Given his suspected desire to make money out of the kid, maybe it was his way of making sure Lucas had no place else to go.

'We need to know where you were that night between the hours of ten p.m. and midnight.'

James wiped at his nose. 'Fucking unbelievable. Well, if you must know, I was off my face. Pissed off after being taken away from my son. I went on a bender. Got in a fight with some guy in Union Street, up by Rose Street. I'd say about that time. Battered him, got a kebab, came home. Crashed. That enough for you?'

Cooper pursed his lips. 'It'll do us. You're sure though?'

'Guy's probably still limping.'

Cooper looked at the ceiling. 'Beside Rose Street, you said?'

'Yeah.'

'OK, we'll check it out.'

'What, CCTV?'

Cooper sighed. 'It comes in handy sometimes.'

James took another draw. 'Get me a copy. I kicked the guy's arse.'

Mearns had never been so glad to be back in the car.

Cooper groaned. 'I see what you mean about him being a real peach. That poor kid.'

'You think he's telling the truth?'

'We'll get them to study the cameras; they'll answer that question.' Cooper started the engine and pulled away from the kerb. 'What's the story with Ferguson?'

Mearns stared straight ahead. 'There's no story.'

'Bullshit. You can't lie for toffee.'

Mearns turned to him. 'I don't want to drop him in the shit. If I tell you, you won't tell Eve?'

'Depends what it is.'

'What he said earlier is a lie. He's been searching for details surrounding the boy at the hospital.'

'What do you mean, searching?'

'Dredging through missing persons. Out asking homeless folk if they recognize him. The list goes on.'

'And Ron Miller is aware of this?'

She stared at him. 'Do you think Ron knows?'

Cooper didn't need to answer.

'Has he been working on Wellwood at all?'

'Not anything I know about. That's why I didn't have a clue about the little he reported back on it in the meeting. Stuff I guess he got from a simple Google search.'

'Mearns, that's not on.'

'Something's not adding up. It's like he's obsessed with this kid.'

'Any ideas why?'

'Nope. He keeps telling me it's because he was on the scene. Cooper, he's been on the scene of much worse.'

Cooper turned to her as he waited at the lights on

Victoria Road. 'You need to rein him in, before Eve gets wind of it. If you don't, then I will.'

Mearns nodded as she dug into her pocket as her phone rang. 'Mearns. OK. Thanks.' She hung up. 'That's the financials for Wellwood on their way through.'

Chapter 44

FERGUSON FELT THE FINGER twitch. The slightest of movements. So fleeting he might have dreamt it.

The finger twitched. Then again. Twice.

He looked down at the boy's, Archie's, hand in his. He squeezed, hoping the boy could feel it. That he knew someone was there.

He wanted to hear his story, needed to know how he had come to be on that road with no one to miss him, no way of anyone knowing who he was. He needed to find out who the guy was, the one from Summer Street in the CCTV, whether Archie had been running from him again that morning.

More than anything, he had to distract himself from the case they were working. He wasn't pulling his weight and after today he could no longer hide that fact. But he had to keep hiding the reason why. Those old mistakes coming back to haunt him. What he'd done plaguing him all these years. The not knowing what had happened. Now he did know, and whether he deserved his second chance at life would hang in the balance if the truth got out.

He squeezed the boy's hand tighter, watching as Archie's eyelid fluttered. Ferguson was on his feet, knocking his chair backwards. Shouting for the nurse. Hollering for anyone to come. To tell him what he was hoping for more than anything else. That the boy was waking and he'd soon know who he was.

Chapter 45

BLACK PRESSED AGAINST THE windowpanes of Eve's garden workshop. The place always made her feel that she could be anywhere. Her cottage was nestled down Loanhead Terrace, a quiet residential street off the bustle of Rosemount, a popular area of the city for singletons as it boasted rows of one-bedroom flats, with shops and pubs at their disposal.

She glanced up from the workbench and saw her reflection staring back at her, the light and warmth around her wrapping her in the escape and haven she craved and was hard to believe could be found in the middle of the city.

She ran a finger along the lipped edge of the dresser, not intending to work tonight, just needing to get back to basics, to feel the raw materials and to try and keep her mind from wandering back to Lucas's face in that body bag at Wellwood. To the X-ray in MacLean's hand.

MacLean had confirmed Lucas had died as a result of

smoke inhalation. So McCabe had been right; the boy had been alive when he was down there. Eve closed her eyes, which did nothing to black out the images in her mind.

There was no sign of foul play. No injuries on his body. Which didn't make things any easier because it still left room for the possibility that Lucas went down there of his own free will. A possibility that wasn't sitting well with Eve, not when a fire had ripped through the place whilst he was underground.

Eve's finger moved back and forth against the grain, her mind drawn to a place as dark as the night surrounding the shed – the inside of the barrel, an image she hadn't been able to shake since seeing that X-ray.

Even though she knew the child had been unborn, she could still hear its cries, crushed up in that drum, bones inside bone. That someone could've done that to the woman . . . Had they known about the child?

Did the woman dream of the little girl or boy within her and the kind of life she would give them?

Her own mother had. Not at first. Impossible to when her existence had come about brutally, from a man her mother hadn't known, other than through her pain down a dark alleyway.

As the truth had hit that she was pregnant her mother had done what others might not have. She had chosen to keep Eve, believing it wasn't her baby's fault and that the child deserved a shot at life. And Eve had been given the best life. Loved unconditionally by her mother and grandparents. Never made to feel different or unwanted.

Eve's issues with who that man had been and what he'd done in that alleyway – the monster whose genes she carried – were her own, never because her family made them so.

Had the baby in the drum been wanted by both its mother and its father? Did the father know? Had he been excited about becoming a father? Or had it been a one-night thing, two people who never set eyes on each other again?

Perhaps he hadn't noticed she'd disappeared. Maybe it was he who had made her disappear.

Eve wouldn't rest until she found out.

Then there was Lucas. Left underground. Forgotten. On purpose or because of some kind of prank gone wrong? Unlike with the body in the barrel, they could have the answers right in front of them.

Sitting in that youth hostel, both the staff and kids.

One of them had to know something. But no one was talking. Not a single one of them.

The question was whether the person who left Lucas to die, if that was what happened, was the same person who had started the fire. She needed to know; she had to figure out how.

Eve jumped as her phone rang. She snatched it from the workbench. *Mearns.*

'Hunter.'

'Those financials on Wellwood are back.'

'And?'

'And I can see why you said Stephen has the weight of the world on his shoulders.'

'Why?'

'There're loans out against the place. Red flags for late payments, the lot. If I was in this state, I'd be drinking too.'

Eve picked at the edge of the dresser. 'He said it was hard keeping themselves afloat. I didn't think it was that bad. How much are we talking?'

'The total figure, from what I can see, is in the region of two hundred and fifty grand.'

Eve whistled low. 'Shit. Tell Cooper and Ferguson I want them in the office first thing. We need to see where we're going with this. How did you get on with James Fyfe?'

Mearns relayed the events of earlier.

'I was hoping he may be the break we were looking for. Is CCTV being searched?'

'Yeah. Should have something by tomorrow. Scottish Water came back as well. The engineer was down the road on a job, an overnighter. He's due at a job near Market Street tomorrow afternoon. I said that Ferguson and I would meet him there.'

'Good. Speaking of Ferguson, are you going to tell me what's going on with him?'

There was silence on the other end, before: 'I don't know what you—'

'Cut the shit, Mearns.'

Mearns sighed. 'He's been looking into the boy from the hospital's story – not telling me what's going on, and not reporting back to Ron Miller.'

Eve stared out of the window, seeing herself again. 'What the hell is it with that kid?'

'I wish I knew. I'm struggling to see why he's invested.

I get he was there but it's not like they're not investigating. And I don't understand why Ferguson is letting it affect what we should be working on.'

Eve sighed. 'Let's see what happens when the boy wakes. In the meantime, tell him I want him there tomorrow. No excuses.'

Chapter 46

Thursday, 10 March

FERGUSON HADN'T BEEN PREPARED to see the boy propped up, watery blue eyes open. If what they said about eyes being the windows to the soul was true, Ferguson was guessing this soul was a damaged one.

According to the nurse, the boy had said very little since he'd fully come around overnight. That was normal, she'd said. Ferguson was hoping he'd be ready to say a little more now.

Ferguson lifted the water jug by the bed and filled a plastic cup before offering it to the boy. He gave a slight shift of his head to refuse it, and not without a scowl as his right arm shifted with the movement. The boy was yet to make eye contact, staring instead at his hoisted leg, or the ceiling.

Ferguson sipped at the water; then he rolled the cup back and forth between his hands, figuring out where to start. Did the boy recognize him at all?

'How're you feeling?' Stupid question although, given

the circumstances, it seemed like the obvious one to begin with.

'What do you think?'

The boy's voice was deep. An extended grunt. Taking Ferguson by surprise when it shouldn't have. This was more a man than a boy.

'Sore, I'd imagine. A little out of it.' Ferguson sipped again.

The boy turned, his glare hard. 'Listen, mate, who are you?' The look and the tone would've been like a slap if Ferguson had let them hit. He was used to kids like this. He'd mixed with them long enough – and had been one himself.

'I'm a copper. DC Scott Ferguson.'

'Great. Just what I need.'

'You're not in any trouble. Or at least you're not yet. I happened to be there when you got hit. I was sitting two cars behind on my way to work.'

'Lucky me.'

'You thought so at the time. Can you remember anything?'

'Can't remember shit.'

'Nothing?'

The boy shifted his attention to the bed.

'You were hit by a car. A van actually. A bakery van.'

The boy flexed his fingers, staring at them, as if seeing and using them for the first time. 'Guess the rolls were late that morning.'

Ferguson smiled; the boy was going to be OK. 'Your phone was wrecked, and you didn't have any ID on you. You've been a bit of a mystery.'

The boy's gaze stayed focused on the bed.

'At least you were. Am I right in saying your name's Archie?'

The boy looked at Ferguson, searching his face, perhaps weighing up whether he could be trusted. Ferguson's copper instincts were on high alert. Why had the boy been hesitant to confirm his name? Would whatever he was about to say be the truth?

'How did you get my name?'

'By asking around. That got me to the Aberdeen Cyrenians. They recognized my description of your tattoo.'

Archie flexed his forefinger and thumb.

'Are you homeless?'

Archie's jaw flexed. 'I doss on folks' sofas.'

'I heard you use the Cyrenians a fair bit. Or at least you have been the last couple of months.'

'Jesus. You've done your homework. I don't always have the money to get grub.'

'No shame in that. Things don't always go the way you hope they will. Why the last two months?'

Archie tutted. 'Situation changed. It happens.'

'Anything to do with the guy who was hassling you outside the Cyrenians?'

Archie glowered at Ferguson. 'What the fuck is this?'

'I told you I'm a copper. I'm a nosey sonofabitch by profession.'

'What makes me interesting to you?'

'You probably don't remember. You asked me not to leave you. When you were lying on the road and we were waiting on the ambulance.'

'I was obviously out of it.'

'Maybe. I told you I wouldn't, and I haven't. But I thought someone would miss you.'

Archie stared at the sheet partially covering him.

'There must be someone. Do you want me to contact anyone? Let them know you're here?'

'There isn't anyone.' He kept his gaze firmly downwards.

Ferguson swallowed, remembering what it was like to feel as though he had no one. How bad it felt day to day, let alone lying in a hospital bed with no one to know or care you were there. This boy had a story. Whether he would be willing to tell it was another matter.

'Where do you stay?'

'Here and there. I said that.'

'Before that?'

'Look, it's none of your business.'

Ferguson sipped at the water. He had been Archie, dossing on so-called mates' sofas, trying not to worry where breakfast would be coming from the next morning. He knew what deflection was; keeping his business to himself was about the only thing he did have. 'Fine, have it your way.'

'Are you going to leave me alone now?'

Ferguson stood. 'I am for now. Work calls. I'll be back tonight.'

'Jesus. Do you have to?'

'Call me a bad smell. Maybe if you open up a bit I'll disappear in time.'

196

Chapter 47

'How's the boy?' Eve stared at Ferguson at the back of the room.

'Good. Awake. His name's Archie.'

'Talking then?'

Ferguson smiled. 'With a whole load of attitude.'

'I take it your head will be back in the game now then?'

The smile disappeared from Ferguson's face.

Eve stared at him, aware of Mearns's own stare on her. 'I also assume you've updated Ron Miller?'

Ferguson slumped. 'If Ron's doing his job, he should already know. The hospital should've notified him anyway.'

'Never assume. Make sure you tell Ron anything you know and leave them to it from here on in.'

Ferguson glowered at Mearns before shifting his gaze to Eve. 'I haven't been doing anything but looking out for the boy.'

Eve motioned towards the empty seat where Cooper should've been sitting. 'Where's Cooper?'

Mearns shrugged. 'I told him to be here.'

'Fine, let's get on with it. What've we got?'

Mearns shuffled papers on her desk. 'As I said last night, the financials are shocking. Stephen is around two hundred and fifty grand in debt and it's secured against Wellwood.'

Eve saw Ferguson stare at Mearns, and figured he was as in the dark as Mearns had been yesterday with what he'd found out about Wellwood. 'And any news on the CCTV?'

Mearns's mouth turned down at the corners. 'Fyfe's story about being in Union Street at the time of the fire and fighting is legit.'

'Damn.' Eve rocked back on her soles. 'I reckon it's time for me and Cooper to pay our Stephen another visit.'

No sooner had she said it than Cooper was bursting through the door, a piece of paper flapping in his hand. Mearns jumped at the slam of the door.

Cooper didn't so much as glance in Eve's direction as he stormed up to Ferguson's desk.

'What the hell is this?'

Ferguson edged back from Cooper's wrath. 'A piece of paper?'

Cooper glared at Ferguson. 'Don't take the piss.'

Eve had to stop her mouth from hanging open. She'd never seen Cooper so angry.

Cooper waved the paper in front of Ferguson's face.

'Ron Miller stopped me in the corridor on the way here. All up in my face about you interfering with his case.'

'I wasn't interfering. I was there, for Christ's sake.'

'You gave them your statement.'

Ferguson was up now, reddening in the face. 'And they did bugger all to find out who that boy was. Do they even know he's awake?'

Cooper turned the piece of paper so Ferguson could see what was on it. 'And you have done nothing to make sure that they do. Including telling them about the little sideline you've been working when you should've been concentrating on Wellwood.'

Ferguson stared at the paper.

'Who the hell is this and why were you asking them to run a check on him?'

Ferguson glanced at Eve, cornered. 'I spoke to a few homeless guys, got a hit on Archie's tattoo. That led me to Aberdeen Cyrenians and they recognized him. Said they could look up some CCTV footage for me.' Ferguson pointed towards the picture. 'That guy was seen hassling Archie in the run-up to the accident.'

Eve's pulse throbbed in her neck. 'And you didn't pass this on to Ron?'

Ferguson remained silent.

'You don't like the guy but hampering his investigation? Jesus, Ferguson.'

Ferguson sat as petulant as a scolded kid. 'Well, it's not gone anywhere yet anyway. The kid wouldn't tell me who it was. Maybe it's not important. What's there to tell?'

The paper was shaking in Cooper's hand. 'What is there to tell? You slacking on the job and leaving Mearns to cover your arse is what there is to tell. Not updating the team on your findings about this boy is what there is to tell. More than that, not giving a shit about a dead eleven-year-old kid.'

'Of course I do! Archie is a kid too.'

Cooper was breathing hard; the Wellwood case was affecting him deeply, maybe more than any of them, being the only parent among them. Spittle flew from his mouth as he spoke. 'A kid who is still alive and nothing to do with you.'

Ferguson was beaten; he spoke more quietly now. 'I've done my bit.'

'What, starting with falling out with Lucas's father?'

Mearns felt the heat of Ferguson's stare on the back of Cooper's words.

Cooper thrust the paper closer to Ferguson's face. 'Ron Miller wants to know who this is. It took me all my time to keep him out of here.'

Ferguson held up both hands. 'Jeez. I'll go talk with him.'

Cooper let the paper drop. Mearns watched as it floated and landed on Ferguson's desk.

Cooper stepped back to let Ferguson past. 'You're lucky Mearns covered your arse as long as she did.'

Ferguson rounded on him. 'Following the boy through felt right to me.' He walked to the door.

Cooper followed him. 'What, at the expense of an eleven-year-old kid? At the cost of what else they found beneath that place?'

Ferguson charged on. 'Yes, as a matter of fact, and, while you're at it, I've been sitting with that same boy, and I'll continue to on my time until I figure out what the hell happened.'

Ferguson's voice cracked as he said the last word, stunning Cooper into silence. Eve stepped around the desk, blocking Ferguson's exit. 'Go speak to Miller; do what you need to do to make it right. Get your arse back here in time to go with Mearns this afternoon to interview the Scottish Water engineer.'

Ferguson scowled and marched towards the door.

Eve spoke low. 'Let him go, Cooper. I'll deal with him later. We need to go and see Stephen.'

She lifted her keys, leaving Mearns staring between the door Ferguson had left through and Cooper, knowing – as Eve did – that the two men were right in their own ways, and both were deeply affected by the fate of two kids.

Ferguson stomped along the corridor, people making way for him as he stormed through. He'd go and speak to Ron Miller all right.

He slowed as he got to the stairwell, taking time to breathe. The nerve of Cooper. He kicked the wall. Kicked it again. Deep down knowing he was this pissed off because Cooper was right.

He hadn't been as hands-on with Wellwood as he should've been. He had his reasons. Reasons he couldn't divulge.

Ferguson pulled open the stairwell door, stepping out of the corridor and into a space of his own, not able to forget the faces of his team as Cooper had torn into him. How could he put things right with Mearns? How could he give more to the case?

He peered over the bannister, saw the steps going down, down, down. He knew what he had to do. He just couldn't ever let anyone know it was him.

Chapter 48

'I NEED YOU TO start talking.'

Stephen looked up from the table they sat around. 'What do you mean?'

'Why don't we start with the reason you gave us for staying overnight at Wellwood sometimes?'

Stephen frowned. 'What's that got to do with anything?'

'Quite a bit, given you didn't tell us about being separated from your wife. Sleeping at Wellwood was a permanent thing.'

Stephen's face coloured. 'I don't see what my personal life has to do with this?'

'It's a pretty major thing not to tell us, considering you lied about why you were on the grounds of Wellwood on the night of the fire.'

Stephen sighed. 'Maybe I wasn't ready to speak about what's going on between me and my family. I still don't understand what it's got to do with the fire.'

Eve stared at him. 'It changes somewhat when you add it to Wellwood's financial position.'

Stephen froze. 'What? Why are you looking into that?'

Cooper placed the papers from Mearns on the table. 'Something you said about finding it hard to keep the place afloat. Obviously, we have to investigate all avenues, especially when there are no forthcoming answers.'

The colour drained from Stephen's face. 'You think I started the fire?'

Eve didn't take her eyes from him. 'Two hundred and fifty grand is a substantial debt, wouldn't you say? Enough for anyone to panic.'

Stephen was shaking his head, his mouth opening and closing.

'How did you manage to get into such debt?'

'It's been a difficult time. At first, I thought I could manage the repayments, but I kept getting hit with one thing after another.'

Eve leaned closer. 'Stephen, I need you to tell me the truth about what's going on here. The amount of debt, your marriage breakdown. What's to say this wasn't an attempt at an insurance job?'

Stephen was up on his feet. 'You think I would've set fire to the only thing I know? That I would've put the kids in danger?'

Eve glared up at him. 'Maybe you thought, with the way it started, there was every opportunity the kids would get out in time. You weren't to know Lucas was down in that basement.'

Tears were welling in Stephen's eyes. 'I promise you, I

had nothing to do with it.' He dragged a hand through his hair before banging back into his seat. 'I'm separated from my wife and I hate that it's happened. And I admit there've been times I've had a drink at nights at Wellwood – no different from if I'd been relaxing at home. I was living there because I had no other options.' He rubbed at his face.

Eve gave him a minute before speaking. 'You need to be honest with us. How did you get into debt? Was it a factor in you and your wife separating?'

'No. No, it's not. Like I said, times got tough. I fell behind with payments. With sorting out my own boys in the split. Audrey and I separated because of how much time I invested in Wellwood. You have to believe me: I'd never do anything to endanger Wellwood.'

'I've already highlighted that some of these kids have noticed a change in you – to the point that Matt and Lucas were scared of what it might mean.'

Stephen was crying now, staring at the table, obviously not wanting to see either Eve or Cooper. Eve stared over the top of his head at a shelf on the wall behind; something there, crammed between two thick books, caught her eye.

'What's that?' She pointed, Cooper following the direction of her finger.

Stephen coloured. 'It's a laptop.'

Eve glared at him. 'I don't recognize it as one handed over to us.'

'It's . . . it's a personal one.'

Cooper stepped around the desk and pulled the laptop free. 'We meant all technology. I'm sure the kids and staff viewed their phones as personal too when they gave them up.'

'I needed to be able to work.'

Eve dipped her head towards the computer in front of him that had been returned. 'And you can.'

Stephen stood. 'You can't . . .'

Cooper placed the laptop under his arm as Eve answered, 'We can and we are. If you have anything to tell us before we go, then I suggest you do it now.'

Stephen shook his head and dropped his gaze.

Was he telling the truth? Or was he afraid they'd see the lie in his eyes?

Chapter 49

Ferguson found Ron Miller in his office, bright red in the face – presumably from his encounter with Cooper.

'What the hell do you want?'

'Cooper said you wanted to see me.' Ferguson plonked himself in the seat opposite Ron.

'And because Cooper said, you came running here, yet you didn't think to do that beforehand?'

Ferguson raised his hands for the second time that morning. 'OK. I was wrong to get involved. I get it. I couldn't help it after being there. I felt responsible for the boy.' He slumped. 'I should've told you anything I did find out.'

Ron pushed back in his chair. 'Tell me now.'

'There's not much to tell. I took a punt on him perhaps being homeless and it paid off. One of the workers at Aberdeen Cyrenians recognized him and told me his name was Archie. Luckily they had CCTV footage of him, with a guy who appeared to be hassling him.'

'The guy in the picture I gave to Cooper.'

'At the end of the day, it's got nothing to do with the accident. So, I didn't see the need to tell you. It was my own curiosity about the boy. He didn't do anything wrong the day he was hit. He ran out. He wasn't committing any crime. More a case of wrong time, wrong place.'

Ron glared at Ferguson. 'I'm not sure I agree.'

Ferguson shifted forward. 'What do you mean?'

'Did you get anything on this guy?'

'No, I hadn't heard back. Cooper came in all macho spouting off about you.'

'The guy in that image is well known for being a loan shark. Brian Logan. Been preying on loads of poor buggers for years. It's catching him at it that's the problem – especially when he's got them all living in fear and refusing to talk.'

Ferguson remembered what Archie had said about not having enough money for grub some days. It didn't add up that he'd get tied up with a loan shark – not when he had no way of paying him back.

'Have you spoken with the boy?'

Ferguson nodded. 'This morning. I take it you knew he was awake.'

'I didn't, as a matter of fact. I've not long ripped the hospital a new arsehole for contacting you and not me.'

Ferguson said nothing.

'Did he speak?'

'I asked him about the guy, this Brian. He didn't give up anything.'

Ron shifted in his seat. 'I'm not happy about you being involved with my shit but maybe this kid will talk

208

to you. See what you can get from him about Logan. He might not have committed a crime being run over that morning, but he may be the key to another one.'

Ferguson stood. He'd planned on going to see Archie tonight regardless but now he had a reason to keep Eve and Cooper off his back.

Chapter 50

EVE SLAMMED THE DOOR of the car as Cooper got in beside her. 'I don't know what the hell to think after that.'

Cooper put the gear into first, crawling over the gravel to exit the youth hostel car park on to Great Western Road. 'Me neither. I want to believe what Stephen's saying but I'm not sure I—' He stopped as Eve's mobile rang.

MacLean.

'Hi. What've you got?'

'As friendly as ever. Got you an update on our body in the barrel.'

Eve was glad she was sitting for whatever MacLean was about to say. 'Shoot.'

'Extracting them from the drum was a lengthy process. Delicate. The girl's body was much better preserved than I thought it would be. Probably thanks to the barrel's seal being airtight and it being stored underground.'

Eve closed her eyes as she listened.

'From the skeletal and dental measurements I'd put

her between thirteen and fifteen years of age. Cause of death was one of two things.'

'Jesus. She was a kid.' She was aware of Cooper staring at her. 'Two things?'

'Yes. Her throat showed signs of being crushed. Likely caused by strangulation. Then there was blunt force trauma to the head. Something that packed a punch. A rock maybe. She had multiple comminuted depressed skull fractures.'

Eve closed her eyes. What had come first? Had the strangulation knocked her out but her killer wanted to be sure? Or did she see those blows coming? 'What else?'

'It appears she was wearing leggings. Pink. Still small patches of material on the legs. And something made of gauze around her waist.'

'Around her waist?'

'A skirt maybe.'

Eve pictured the fashion in the eighties, the things she'd worn herself. Loving Madonna on the *Like A Virgin* tour, who wore nothing but leggings, puffball skirts and denim jackets. Had their girl sung along to that song as Eve had?

'Looking at the skeletal remains of the foetus, I'd put it late on in the pregnancy. Around seven months perhaps. It was a boy.'

Eve couldn't answer. Seven months. At that age the baby could have survived an early delivery. She tried desperately to focus on what MacLean was telling her, rather than getting lost in thoughts about how long the baby might've survived after the mother was hit. Whether they'd both been alive when they were crushed into that barrel. 'How long do you reckon they were in there?'

'I'd say twenty years at a minimum, most probably a decade more.'

'Can you give me anything else?'

'There is something else but it's going to have to be sent off to be examined. To see if anything can be salvaged from it.'

'What is it?'

'A notebook of some kind. Almost like a pulp, the state it's in. Body fluids, I'd guess, but maybe something can be saved. Couple of drinks cans in there too.'

'Cans of what?'

'Cider. We might be able to tie a more definite date down to them.'

Eve saw the circular indent of the barrel in her mind, the room where the girl had been. Had she been drinking down there? Maybe she hadn't wanted the baby. If indeed it had been her drinking at all. It could've been whoever killed her and put her in the drum.

'Would we be able to do any DNA testing on those cans?'

'I'm there already. They've been sent off. Marked as a priority.'

'Thanks, MacLean.' Eve hung up and took a deep breath before turning to Cooper.

'We have something to work with now, something to bring to social services. That's got to get us further than Ferguson did.'

Chapter 51

MEARNS AND FERGUSON STOOD on the cobbled street of the Green, one of the oldest known parts of Aberdeen, tucked down off the main drag of Union Street. The long red locks of a young girl dominated the stone curve of Aberdeen Market. Street art that had crept through the city in the last five years, bringing new life into the old.

The girl's face overlooked them as they watched the water engineer's head appear above ground, through the manhole cover he'd been working under.

He smiled as he hauled himself out and on to the pavement. 'Can't say I don't know how to make an entrance. I'm Keith.'

Mearns smiled in return, not missing the dirt and grime covering the man's overalls. The fact he was working right outside a barber's shop called Hard Grind felt apt in that moment.

Keith got to his feet, wiping his hands with a rag before shaking hands with Mearns and Ferguson. 'Do you want to sit?' He motioned to the wooden bench outside the large square window of the barber's.

'We're fine, thanks.' Mearns let the man sit, the deep breath he took probably relief at being back out in the fresh air. 'Thanks for agreeing to see us.'

'No problem at all. That's some shit that's been going down at the kids' home.'

'Tragic.' Mearns gave nothing else. Ferguson was kicking at a cobble, letting Mearns take the lead. Much as he'd been doing throughout the whole case. 'We wanted to talk to you about the underground space you accessed around three weeks ago.'

'I saw that barrel, you know. Gives me the willies now after reading what I did in the papers.'

'What else can you tell us about the space as you found it?'

Keith looked between them. 'Not much. It was just the usual – loads of spaces like that up on Kincorth Hill. Can be a bit eerie the first time you go down into one of them. That little narrow hatch, a space as big as above ground, mapped out the same as the rooms above, wall divides, the lot. Quite something. If it were me, I'd have a games room and bar, no doubt about it.'

The red and white flower baskets hanging from the ornate Victorian street lamp by the bench swung lazily in the breeze, a world away from the grimness of the basement Mearns was picturing. 'Can't imagine people go down there much unless it's for repairs or maintenance.'

Keith fished in his pocket, pulled out a Lion bar and ripped the chocolate free of its wrapper. He held the bar out to Mearns and Ferguson, who declined. 'Sorry, love a bit of chocolate, me; work uniform's getting tighter every year. Anyway, you're right. Most folks don't venture down. What we usually get when we do open up the space is spider webs at the entrance, dusty steps and mouldy-smelling air.'

'And was it like that at Wellwood?'

Keith spoke through a mouthful of chocolate and caramel. 'You'll always get the spider webs but, no, this place wasn't bad. Kids were gathered around the ladder, excited to see what it was all about. I think the staff planned to take them down for a look.'

'I believe they did. When you say it wasn't bad . . . what do you mean?'

'The ladder was in good nick, not thick with dust. Floor was all rubble but the air in the place wasn't as cloying as usual. It's not going to be if it's accessed more regularly.'

Ferguson stopped kicking at the ground.

Mearns kept her features neutral. 'You think it was being accessed regularly?'

'Hard to tell but definitely recently. Said to the wife that I hoped it wasn't the kids. Made me wonder if their excitement was all for the staff not knowing they already knew about the space. Whoever it was, imagine being down there – then finding out what was in that drum? Doesn't bear thinking about.'

'Sorry, how did you know it had been accessed recently?'

Keith licked at his fingers. 'Like I said, I enjoy my chocolate. Was bloody starving when I was down in that basement, more so when I saw the Fizzing Cherry Dairy Milk wrapper.'

'And that made you believe access had been recent?'

'Had to be, that chocolate bar only came out a few months ago.'

216

Chapter 52

The Marischal College office was devoid of any character, designed to be functional, nothing more, light years away from the ornate granite building in the city centre that housed it. Eve and Cooper sat at the beige wooden table, opposite the data protection officer who was as wide as the blue-backed office chair he sat on.

Eve focused, clearing her mind of the call she'd taken from Mearns that appeared to be telling them either the staff, kids or both had been lying to them.

'I can't see any record of a call requesting information.' Martin Smith snorted, a deep guttural sound that made the ID badge on the lanyard hanging around his neck jump against the strained buttons of his cheap white shirt.

Eve glanced to her left as a female member of staff tottered past the glass-partitioned wall of the office on heels that were silent on the carpet-tiled corridor: another council worker, given the building was Aberdeen City Council's HQ, although plans were afoot to

217

move staff and the front desk of Queen Street Police Headquarters here too. Only a stone's throw away, but Eve was going to miss the old, decrepit building. 'Perhaps they didn't note the call, or my colleague left a message that hasn't been answered yet?'

Ferguson had definitely said he'd tried to access records but had been unsuccessful; however, given his lack of concentration on Wellwood to date, maybe that had been an embellishment to save his neck. 'Anyway, it was a more general background we were looking for then. Now we have something more specific. Something that may help us.'

Martin shifted his gaze from the screen, straightening in his chair as a glint crept into his eye.

Eve wasn't going to let the opportunity go to waste. 'You'll know about the recent goings-on at Wellwood?'

Martin nodded, his body tilting forward in the chair.

'Then you'll appreciate the confidential nature of this.'

Martin's head moved closer to Eve's as he glanced towards the partition, ready for his task; this was the most excitement he'd ever had in a work day.

'We need records for children who were homed there from the mid-eighties to the mid-nineties.' Going by MacLean's timeline, any further back would be too far and pointless – and the home had fallen empty upon the death of William Alderton in the mid-nineties. 'We're particularly interested in girls who were homed there, although anything you can give us would be much appreciated.'

Martin rolled his chair back to the computer screen,

the base squealing under the pressure. 'Do you have any specifics?'

It was Eve's turn to lean forward and talk in a hushed tone, making sure Martin remained engaged. 'Not as such but we are hoping you'll be able to help us with that.'

Martin's eyes were scanning the screen. 'The records are sparse. Given the rumoured background of the place, I figure the proprietors didn't always work in line with the local authority or provide records that were required. From what I can see, there may be paper files in archives.'

Eve glanced at Cooper. 'How long would it take to retrieve them?'

Martin's chest puffed out. 'I could reschedule my diary for this afternoon, go scope them out myself.'

Eve fished inside her jacket and handed Martin a card. 'I can't thank you enough; you have no idea what this may mean for the case. Please, if you find anything, anything at all, don't hesitate to call me on this number.'

Martin took the card between his chubby fingers and slipped it into his shirt pocket, peering out to the corridor as he did so. 'I'm on it.'

Eve walked out into the pedestrianized area outside Marischal College; grey clouds were gathering above the office and retail buildings of Marischal Square. She turned to Cooper. 'We won't have to wait long for information from our Mr Smith.'

Cooper smiled as Eve's phone rang.

'Hunter.' She listened while Cooper watched her.

She hung up. 'Talking about things not taking long, the findings of Stephen's laptop are back already. Didn't take much digging to unearth something. Let's go get that laptop and pay Stephen a little visit. I'll update you on the way.'

Chapter 53

EVE BANGED THE LAPTOP on Stephen's desk. He jumped as it landed. Eve pulled back the chair opposite him, Cooper pulling one over beside her, both of them hitting their backsides down at the same time.

Eve shoved the laptop across the desk. 'That didn't take long. You need to start talking. Big time.'

Stephen stared at the silver lid of the computer. 'I don't know what—'

'Spare us. Don't waste your time or ours. Let's start with the main stuff on that thing, shall we? The gambling sites?'

Stephen pulled at the neck of his polo shirt with a forefinger and thumb. 'It's personal, nothing to do with work.'

'I beg to differ. Given the debt you're in with Wellwood, I'm not believing this isn't linked. Some pretty eye-watering amounts in those gambling accounts of yours.'

Stephen swallowed, studying the door. 'This is an

invasion of privacy. What I choose to do in my spare time is my business. I'm allowed a life outside Wellwood.' Stephen backed away from the laptop as Eve pushed it closer to him, as if touching it might burn, branding his skin with evidence that would show his guilt.

Eve tucked a stray hair behind her ear. 'I'm not buying it. The thing is, you don't appear to have a life outside of these kids. In many ways that's commendable, but it's been at the expense of your marriage and family life, from what I can gather. And you may think what you're doing in your spare time is your business but it's not when you're living and breathing your work and it's affecting the kids.'

Stephen's head shot up.

'Again, I'll remind you of Matt and Lucas.'

Stephen slumped. 'I told you, everything I do is for those kids.'

'Maybe, but the way I see it, either the gambling got you into this mess, or the debt got you into the gambling. Which one is it?'

'You don't understand. The gambling isn't that bad.'

Said in the true voice of an addict. Eve had seen the figures.

Cooper edged closer. 'Stephen, you have to see it from our point of view. This debt is substantial. Maybe you couldn't see a way out.'

Stephen's gaze flickered between them before settling on Cooper. His voice cracked as he spoke. 'You do think I started that fire, don't you?' Fear crept into his eyes.

'Convince us you didn't.'

Stephen stood, raking a hand through his hair. 'I can't believe you're asking that. Like I would have put any of the kids in danger. Lucas . . .' His voice was hitting fever pitch.

Eve's voice was stern. 'Sit, Stephen.'

He didn't need asking twice.

'You told us those kids didn't know about the basement until three weeks before the fire.'

Stephen frowned. 'They didn't.'

'If that's the case then either you or one of your members of staff had been down in that space.'

Stephen's nose wrinkled. 'I swear to you, no one was ever down there.'

'The Scottish Water engineer says different. There was a chocolate wrapper down there. A new bar of chocolate only out a few months before. How do you explain that?'

Stephen's head was moving left to right in slow motion. 'I can't . . . I don't understand.'

'We need to speak to the other staff and the kids again. Someone is lying. Have a think about what we've found on that laptop. Decide whether you want to start telling the truth.'

Chapter 54

DÉJÀ VU. EVE AND Cooper sat side by side in the exact chairs and spot they had on the first day they'd met the kids in the dorm – even the kids were more or less on the same bunks they'd sat on that time too. Ben, Jake and Beth were by the lockers. They'd left Stephen downstairs staring at his laptop.

Cooper surveyed the room, his gaze resting on one kid before he moved to the next, making sure they were all focused on what he was about to say. 'We are going to ask you something. All of you.' He looked at Ben, Jake and Beth, whom they had kept in the dark. Eve wanted to see the reactions first hand. 'Our colleagues have spoken to the engineer who was down in the basement at Wellwood for those water repairs. We were led to believe that was the first time the hatch had been lifted in a long time, that you guys hadn't known about the space before then. It appears we were lied to.'

The kids' heads whipped between one another; Darren's expression was a warning, rather than shock.

'That same engineer told us he remembers seeing a chocolate-bar wrapper down there.'

It was Jake who spoke. 'Surely that doesn't mean anyone has lied. Chocolate has been around for a long time.'

Cooper glared, silencing him. 'Not this bar. This chocolate was a new edition, only out recently.'

The room was silent. 'Now I want all of you to think hard. Staff and kids. Someone was down there and that person has to be in this room, unless it was Lucas. Admitting it doesn't mean we are linking you to anything else that happened that night, it is only so we can get a true picture of what the hell is going on and eliminate things from our enquiries.'

Cooper and Eve both scanned the faces quickly before she spoke. 'Maybe you're scared to talk. Maybe whoever was down there hasn't told anyone else. You need to tell us. You can do that confidentially if you need to.' Eve took a card from her pocket, stood and placed it on the worn plastic seat. 'I'm going to leave this here. Don't be scared to use it. If you help us there's nothing to be afraid of but I can't promise things won't get frightening if that person continues to keep secrets.'

Eve made her way to the door and turned; every face was directed at hers. 'We have Lucas's funeral tomorrow. A day to say goodbye. Think about that. Help us find out what happened to him.'

Eve marched across the gravel driveway of the hostel and paused as her phone rang. Cooper stopped alongside her as she stared at the mobile phone display, not recognizing the number. She answered: 'Hunter.'

The voice was low, hushed. 'It's Martin Smith.'

Eve frowned before recalling the social work data protection officer who had promised to search for historical records for Wellwood. She imagined him in a raincoat and fedora in a call box down some alleyway near Marischal College.

'Thanks for getting back to me, Martin.'

'I'm not going to lie, what I could get my hands on was scarce. A lot of records were missing but one person did flag up, mainly because she's remained on our radar with aftercare. She's led a tough life. Been in and out of a lot of trouble since her years at Wellwood.'

Eve's heart quickened. 'Does she fit the time frame?'

'Yes. She was there.'

'Is she still in Aberdeen?'

'Yes, but I can't give you contact details. Not yet. I'd have to talk to management. See what they say. You'll appreciate my position.'

Eve's heart sank. 'Of course, but can you give me anything now?'

'I . . . I don't think I can. We'd have to approach her first, see if she was happy to talk to you. I'd imagine she's aware from the press what's been going on, yet she obviously hasn't chosen to come forward.'

Eve closed her eyes. 'Can you give me a name at least?'

There was silence on the other end.

Eve tried again. 'I won't do anything with it. You've

done us a huge favour. I won't forget that and I won't act unless you tell us if she's happy to meet.'

Martin sighed. 'I guess it can't hurt. Her name is Jane. Jane Henderson.'

She thanked him, pocketed her phone and turned to Cooper. 'It's a day for big reveals.'

Chapter 55

Then

SHE STAYS BESIDE HIM, both of them squashed shoulder to shoulder in the narrow corridor space, the beam of torchlight the only light down here with them.

'What is this place?' She knows to whisper, that Ms Fields and the others sleep above them. The bag she carries is now cradled against her chest in both arms.

'An underground basement of sorts.'

'How did you find it?'

'I read about them one time. Figured if this place had one it would be pretty impressive, given we're perched on a hill.'

'But when did you find it, with her always watching?'

'Covered a room at a time at nights when I could. Couldn't believe it when I found it, especially when I opened up the hatch. Was obvious the place hadn't been opened in years. Only thing down here was rubble, old dried-up paint pots and broken tools. I guess it's been accessed over the years for pipework or gas and electric

228

works but not any time since I came here. Doubt old Fields knows about it.'

'How often do you come down here?'

'Most nights. Good place to get away, to think.'

He thrusts the torch into the gap in the wall on the left, illuminating the largest of the rooms mirroring the day room upstairs: a space away from the bedrooms above where they don't have to be quiet.

She steps in, her head turning this way and that, following the torchlight and the space being revealed bit by bit.

He turns the torch on himself, shining it beneath his chin and up over his face. She giggles and comes close, placing the bag on the floor between them before taking the torch from him and shining it the same way as he has. Smiling, she bends forward, her nose almost touching his, and this time he lets himself be controlled, taking the kiss.

'I brought us a little something.' Her voice is breathy as she reaches down and takes two cans out of the bag. Super-strength cider. She holds one out to him.

'I don't drink.'

She laughs. 'Sure. Come on, live a little.'

He takes the can, watches as she lifts the ring pull on her own can, gas hissing into the darkness around them.

She raises the can. 'Cheers.'

And he tells himself that she is not his mother. That he is not one of those men. That the past is exactly that. She is good and she is his.

He smiles, cracks the can open and clinks it against hers before she reaches for him and he lets himself be pulled in by her. Wanting her, needing her – and whatever else she's offering.

Chapter 56

FERGUSON'S SHOES SQUEAKED ON the deserted hospital corridor floor as he made his way from the coffee machine. Most visitors been and gone by this time of night. His footsteps sped up when he spotted the doctor coming out of Archie's room up ahead.

'How's he been?'

'I want a word with you.' Her face was stern. 'I had an irate call this morning from one of your colleagues about updating you on Archie's progress before him. I was told not to entertain you.'

'Sorry about that. Ron's an abrupt guy, to say the least – I faced his wrath earlier and I can assure you that I'm here with his approval now.'

The doc looked unconvinced.

'I can call him if you'd like?'

She shook her head. 'I'm busy enough as it is and, to be fair, I'd take you over him any day.

Ferguson smiled. 'How is he?'

She glanced over her shoulder at the door Archie lay behind. 'Good. Full of attitude, as usual. Asking when he's getting out of this shithole. Excuse me, but you did ask.'

Ferguson smiled more widely. 'And were you able to give him an answer?'

She shook her head. 'Not anything definite. He's giving us very little about himself but that's a choice, nothing to do with loss of memory.'

'No word of family or friends?'

'Nothing.'

'Same. OK thanks.' Yet as Ferguson opened the door, he was hoping Archie might be ready to talk now.

When Ferguson walked into the room, Archie didn't shift his focus from the telly. God forbid the kid should be at all interested in his arrival.

'Brought you some chocolate, didn't think you'd be up for grapes.' Ferguson threw a bar on to the bed. Archie's gaze flickered towards it. Ferguson could tell it was taking him all his restraint not to pick it up, but he was probably already trying to figure out how to rip the wrapper from it with his one working hand.

'Miss me while I was gone?'

Archie screwed up his face.

'That much, eh?'

Ferguson made himself busy with the water jug, fighting a smile as he heard the rustle of the wrapper.

'Well, the doc reckons you're doing well. Had a nice chat with her before I came in here.'

'Her voice does my nut in.' Archie's words were a little strained as he fought to take the wrapper off with his teeth. There was no point in offering to help.

'Maybe, but she knows her stuff. Including the fact you're more than OK to chat and tell me a little more about yourself.'

Archie stopped short of taking a bite of the strip of chocolate he'd managed to expose.

Ferguson gulped at the cup of water in his hand before sitting. 'I figured maybe you could tell me about that guy I asked about.'

Archie put down the bar.

Ferguson was gripping the cup in both hands. 'Listen, I didn't plan to be there that day. At the time, whether you pretend not to remember or not, you wanted me there. I'm here and it would be good if you would talk.'

Archie was picking at the edge of the white sheet covering him. 'Am I supposed to feel I owe you something?'

Ferguson shook his head, staring into the cup. 'No. But since I've continued to be here for you, I figure you could at least try.'

Archie's head turned towards Ferguson. 'About what?'

'The guy from the CCTV footage. Come on, you're not stupid. I've figured that much out.'

'It was some guy. No idea who. Gave me a bit of hassle on the street. I figured he was out of it. I didn't read much into it.'

His mouth was tight as he turned his head back towards the TV.

'Did he say anything?'

'I can't remember what.'

'What if I tell you his name is Brian Logan. Ring any bells?'

Archie's fist clenched on top of the bedsheets.

'It should. Especially if you owed him money.'

Archie's eyes flickered towards Ferguson. 'What the hell are you on about?'

'Come on, Archie. I've been around the block. I was once much like you.'

'Aye, right. I doubt you were anything like me. Folk like me don't become a pig.'

Ferguson was sure he was supposed to be shocked at the word, or react, but these days, after years of being called that word by folk a lot worse than Archie, it didn't register. 'You'll have to take my word on that one then. I want to help. Let you know I'm here.'

'Why the fuck do you care?' It was said through clenched teeth.

Ferguson raised his voice a notch, wanting to make his point. 'I care because I remember being your age, as fucking angry at the world as you are.'

'And?' Archie spat the word.

'And I remember how it felt to think no one gave a shit.'

Archie sneered. 'So, what? You want to roll out the psychiatrist sofa and pick my brain?'

Ferguson attempted a smile. 'Not sure that brain of yours would be ready for it. Besides, I can't be arsed listening to all that psychobabble myself. Telling me what the guy Brian was hassling you about wouldn't be asking much.'

Archie stared but said nothing. Silent for a good five minutes before he picked the bar of chocolate back up off the bed.

'You aren't going to tell me?'

Archie bit into the bar and stared at the telly. 'I need to think about it but, if I do, he can't know you heard it from me.'

234

Chapter 57

Eve sat in the dark at the rustic dining table in her kitchen, her wet coat and shoes still on. The walk from the front door of her cottage to here had been a blur. In fact, the whole day had been a blur. The day had ended with a round-up of phone calls between her team, each of them with their own story to exchange. Even Ferguson had his own revelation, with Archie being mixed up with a loan shark.

She hadn't wanted to come home, keen to keep up the momentum, but tomorrow was Lucas's funeral and she wanted all of the team to be there. Fresh.

She shoogled out of her coat, throwing it over the stool next to her. *What a day.*

Revelations aside, Cooper and Ferguson had been at loggerheads, and Mearns had been covering Ferguson's backside when she shouldn't have been.

Her team were disjointed, but times had been a lot worse. Such as when Eve had returned to work after the loss of her colleague, DS Sanders, right into the wrath of

Mearns – the new girl on the block. Plus Ferguson with his anger towards her for things he believed she had or hadn't done and his doubt about her ability to do the job, both of which turned out to be about so much more. They'd come a long way, and one thing was for sure: only Cooper could ever be counted on to be a constant calming force throughout.

Eve hoped they'd be able to remember how far they'd come together and put on a united front at the funeral. Failing that, perhaps the reminder of what had kicked all this off would bring them back together. An eleven-year-old boy lost.

And a young woman and her unborn baby, murdered, left to rot. She could only pray Martin Smith would come through with the goods tomorrow, that Jane Henderson would be willing to talk and whatever she had to say would take them closer to answers that currently felt just out of reach.

Chapter 58

MARCIE WADE'S HEART RACED, gut instinct telling her there was a story here, and not just any story. The fact it had been handed to her was too good to be true. 'Thanks for seeing me.'

Jane Henderson looked frail, as if a strong wind would blow her away. The narrow armchair she sat in dwarfed her. She bit at the nail of her index finger. There was very little nail left on it, or on any of her other fingers, where the skin had come away and the cuticles shone red raw.

Jane lowered her hand. 'Excuse the state of the place. It's not much.'

'It's fine. You have a nice place.' Marcie did her best not to look at the magazines piled high, or the collection of used mugs adorning the table by her chair in the cramped bedsit off Linksfield Road.

'How did you find me?' She avoided eye contact with Marcie.

'I was given your name.'

Jane frowned. 'Who by?'

'To be honest, I don't know. It was a message left at reception and they didn't leave a name. Not that I'd usually reveal my sources but, on this occasion, it's true.'

The woman shifted in her chair, her collarbone jutting forward as she did. 'To be honest, that makes me feel uncomfortable.'

'Don't worry. I don't think there's any malice in it. With what's happened at Wellwood this week, they maybe thought you'd be the person to talk to.'

'Why, I don't know. I very rarely, if ever, talk about that place.'

Marcie rummaged inside her bag and took out a Dictaphone. 'Do you mind?'

Jane's gaze lowered to the machine. 'I guess not.'

'We won't speak about anything that makes you uncomfortable. If it does, tell me. I prefer to chat instead of scribbling notes.'

'Pah, it wouldn't be much of a chat if I left out everything uncomfortable.'

Marcie pressed record and placed the gadget on the table. 'Why don't we start with when you were a resident at Wellwood?'

Jane cleared her throat. 'I was put there in the late eighties.'

'How long did you stay there for?'

'Six, seven years.'

'Who ran it back then?'

Jane tilted her head to the side and rubbed her cheek against her shoulder. 'Sally and William.'

'What were they like?'

Jane's upper lip curled. 'Now there's a loaded question. Put it like this, I've never been so glad to hear of two people's deaths.'

Marcie's toes curled inside her shoes in anticipation. She nudged the Dictaphone closer to Jane, taking no chances of the mic not picking up what she was about to say. 'I'm all ears.'

Jane bit at her nail again. 'I never liked either of them, right from the off. I arrived there alone and scared, and they did nothing to make me feel welcome. I could see from the first day there how they treated their staff, never mind the kids.'

'How did they treat them?'

'The staff – with an iron fist. From what I learned from the other kids later, the ones that had been there a while, some of the staff tried to retaliate but they learned to pipe down pretty quickly or lose their job.'

'They were tough on them?'

Jane pulled a leg up and under her. 'Yes. Abrupt. Threatening. I think the staff worried for their jobs but more about us. We had no options.'

'In what way did they worry about you?'

Jane pulled at her thin, brittle hair. 'As much as anyone would, given what started to happen.'

'Which was?'

The woman inhaled deeply, blowing back out fast through her lips, her cheeks expanding. 'Sorry. This is still bloody difficult to talk about after all these years. It's affected me in ways you can't imagine. Brought so much trouble into my life.'

'I understand. Take your time.'

Jane moved her leg out from beneath her, bending it up in front of her, creating a barrier between her and Marcie as she hugged her knee. 'We were punished unfairly. Privileges removed and so on. I sometimes thought when it was Sally . . .' Jane paused. 'Ms Fields, we had to call her. Either name too nice for her. Anyway, when it was her doing those things, it was more to do with the staff. She saw it as leverage to keep everyone in line. It only got worse from there.'

'Being unfair to the kids?'

'Not only that. She, they, could be cruel too. Bad. The worst thing is they got enjoyment from it. William especially.'

'Physical stuff?'

'Yes. A lot more went on in that place than the kids ever spoke about. The harder stuff was done behind closed doors. I don't know some of the stuff that went on and I lived there. But you could see the pain.'

'Didn't other members of staff try to protect you? To do something?'

Jane shrugged. 'I guess they did in their own way. Maybe people were scared they wouldn't be heard. Frightened for their jobs. There was a caretaker who tried to change things.'

'How did he do that?'

'He went to the powers that be above her and they listened. I remember us feeling hopeful something would be done – that things would change. There was an investigation of sorts. Some big meetings. The next we knew, not one damn thing had changed. Never did before she died. William was lost without his sidekick

240

and we all got shipped off not long after. I heard he got ill.'

'Are you able to give me details of some of the stuff that went on there? What do you believe was going on?'

Jane was rubbing at her shin, staring at the table. 'We were in need of love. Care. Safety. What they gave us . . . it was nothing short of abuse. Physical and mental. Degrading us, stripping us of any dignity, of any belief we previously held in ourselves.'

Marcie was already seeing tomorrow's headline. 'Can you give me examples, as hard as I know that is?'

Jane closed her eyes for the briefest of moments. 'They'd hit us. Belts, canes, sticks, shoes sometimes.'

Marcie was drinking in every word. 'And you saw this?'

'A couple of times through the window of her office. Sometimes we'd talk to one another when it was safe.'

'And staff let this happen?'

'They were clever. Manipulative. The staff were as scared of them as we were.'

Marcie shuffled forward on the small sofa. 'Jane, was there sexual abuse?'

Jane hugged her leg closer. 'I can't be sure but . . . I never experienced that.'

'Didn't any of the kids try to run from it?'

'Yes, but they were always found and brought back – and beaten when they were. I was never that brave.'

'Was that the worst of it – the beatings and the hitting?'

Jane bit at her top lip. 'I wish it had been.'

'What else went on?'

241

'Christ, I haven't thought about this in such a long time. I guess I've tried to block it out. Not that it's got me anywhere. I blame Wellwood for how my life's turned out. Alone, with dead-end jobs.'

'It doesn't have to be that way. Perhaps talking will help you move forward?' Marcie wanted all the details.

Jane closed her eyes again. 'I remember being made to kneel in the corner for hours at a time; sometimes I was locked in cupboards. One of the kids was a bed-wetter. They'd make them take a cold bath. Ice cold. They once made him wear his wet sheets to breakfast.'

'Jesus.' Marcie's name would be up in lights with this story.

'We were scared. Sometimes of what was being done to others. The threat of what could come our way. Conditioned by them. One or two stood up to be counted but it was the more bolshy lads.' Jane opened her eyes. 'It wasn't right, and it shouldn't happen. But it does. Every day.'

'Jane, do you think they would've been capable of being involved with what was found down in that basement?'

Jane stared at her, making eye contact for the first time. 'Who else would it have been? It had to be them and, the thing is, I think I know who the girl in that barrel might've been.'

Marcie had to stop herself from jumping out of her chair. 'Who?' She whispered the word, as on the edge of her seat as she hoped the readers would be.

'There was a girl there at the time. During the worst of what I told you. Danny. Her name was Danny. She was about fourteen. Wild. Tough background. Into stuff she shouldn't have been at that age. Drink more than drugs.'

'Were you friendly with her?'

'She kept herself to herself mainly. Not a girl's girl. I don't know if that was because of whatever had happened in her past.'

'Protecting herself?'

'We all did that. But it was there, raw on our faces, if you knew what to look for. A lot of our behaviour was about kicking back against our past. About what we were living in at Wellwood. I think drinking was an attempt at escape for her.'

'From what you've told me, I guess Danny would've been a target of Sally's?'

'For sure. But the more Sally came down on Danny, the harder Danny kicked back.'

'Were there boys on the scene with her?'

'Not boys. A boy.'

Marcie straightened. 'Tell me about him.'

Jane sighed. 'I don't know . . . he was a quiet lad. Pretty much kept himself to himself. At least he did before Danny arrived. That girl came through the front door and from that day on John could never see past her.'

'Was it reciprocated?'

Jane smiled at the memory. It changed her whole face. 'For sure. As I say, she was wild. I think she was attracted to his calmness. To her opposite.'

'They got together?'

'It was no secret.'

'Surprising given what went on in that place.'

'Oh, Sally hated it. She would've been against anyone

being happy, but I think it was more the thought of two heads together. That two kids might stand stronger together against her than one. She liked to keep the kids separate, to try and drive them apart.'

'Did the other kids have a problem with Danny and John being together?'

Jane shifted in the chair. 'Not that I ever saw. They weren't ones for fawning all over each other in company. Perhaps there was a little jealousy that they both had someone, but I never saw any fallouts over it. Sally tried to stop it though. Any way she could.'

'By doing what?'

'She'd separate them. At mealtimes, free time, whatever. Punish them if they tried to be together.'

'Did it work?'

Jane scratched at her head. 'I guess that question is the one I asked myself back then, and a thousand times since. Especially after the papers this week.'

'Why? What happened?'

Jane's gaze was intense. 'I don't know. That's the honest truth. I can tell you things took a turn for the worse. There were a couple of times John and Danny were caught together in, shall we say, compromising positions. A rumour eventually spread between the kids that Danny was pregnant.'

Marcie almost whooped. 'Was she?'

'I never found out. Round about then both she and John disappeared from the home. Took what little they had with them.'

Marcie was finding it hard to hide her excitement. 'And went where?'

Jane looked at the floor, lost in memories. 'They never told anyone. I assumed they ran. They were never found.'

'But were reported missing, I take it?'

'Sometimes runaways would come back or were returned, like the ones I told you about who were beaten. Other times they just disappeared. Poof. Like they never were there. Maybe kipping in a sleeping bag in a doorway somewhere. Maybe no longer with us.'

Marcie couldn't get enough. 'What happened after that?'

Jane sighed, a deep, resigned sound. 'Nothing. I think Sally was glad to be rid of them. Especially if the rumoured pregnancy was true. Wouldn't have been too good under her roof and reign. Maybe they simply wanted to be together. I liked to believe for a long time that they were somewhere safe. Somewhere better. Three of them. A family. Something they'd never known themselves.'

'But you never did find out?'

'No. And then I read the paper.'

Marcie watched Jane, lost in old memories. 'And now?'

Her eyes watered. 'And now? Well, it's whether Danny ever left that building.'

Marcie was writing the article in her head already, starting with the fact that the body in the barrel might not have been alone.

Chapter 59

Friday, 11 March

Six a.m. Eve lifted her collar against the early-morning chill as she exited Loanhead Terrace and crossed the deserted street. The Queen Vic was in darkness for now but would be full of revellers by lunchtime. She made her way down Rosemount Place, passing letting agents and sunbed posters, unaware of them all as she imagined the strong coffee and croissant awaiting her arrival at the Sainsbury's Local. She was in dire need of the caffeine hit after a night where sleep had escaped her – questions gnawing away at her, eventually driving her to work in the shed.

The overhead heating was welcome as she stepped through the sliding doors of the store, wasting no time in heading to the bakery shelves and the coffee machine. She marched down the aisle, the smell of warm pastry wafting up to her nose, the warm cup in her hand a comfort as she thought about what lay ahead today. She joined the queue behind another early riser and glanced to her right, to the news-stand, copies of the local

Aberdeen Enquirer and the nationals standing upright. Her gaze darted along them, catching on the *Enquirer*'s front page. Her grip tightened on the items in her hand. Her heart thumped as she lifted a copy before throwing down change at the cashier, needing to get out of there, white-hot anger driving every step home.

Chapter 60

'JESUS CHRIST, THAT WOMAN is missing a heart.' Cooper slammed the morning newspaper on Eve's dining table.

'Told you it was bad. How the hell did Marcie get to her before we did? That only leaves one person in the frame.' Eve slouched back in her chair.

'Of all the days . . .' Mearns's voice reflected how they all felt.

Ferguson was standing against the Aga; all of them looked different in the black suits they wore. 'Have you tried to get hold of the data protection guy?'

Eve sipped at the mug of coffee Cooper had made, the croissant bought earlier still lying in the paper bag on the worktop. 'I don't have a number for him out of hours, but he'll get a piece of my mind as soon as I can get hold of him.'

Eve closed her eyes as she inhaled the coffee aroma, Marcie Wade's front page swimming in her head, making her feel sick. Not only because of what Jane Henderson had revealed about Wellwood's history, but because they had been close to getting to her first.

'Ferguson, when you said you were coming up against brick walls with getting access to historical records, did you definitely leave a message?'

Ferguson straightened. 'Of course I did.'

Eve said nothing, knowing he would read criticism into her silence. He had been tasked with investigating Wellwood's history, but it had taken her and Cooper's involvement for them to get anywhere with it. Because Ferguson was too busy seeing to Archie. That fact had lost them time, mere hours which Marcie had gained.

Regardless, Eve couldn't forget what Jane Henderson had been through, the events she'd described that had taken place under that roof. Under Stephen Alderton's father's care.

Was Stephen like his father? Had she been blind? Was that why the kids hadn't said a word? If that was the case, could one of them have been capable of burning down Wellwood to make it stop, or was Stephen innocent of abuse but simply in great debt and desperate to make it all go away?

What she'd read in the paper, together with the information that Stephen's father and Sally Fields had been responsible at the time, now made her question if Stephen had known about that drum all along.

But the fact was Marcie Wade now knew, or at least had strong evidence, that the woman had been pregnant. And all of this had been released on the day of Lucas's funeral.

She couldn't bring herself to call Stephen to check if the staff or kids had seen the papers. The press would be there today, baying for blood.

She looked back down at the newspaper on the table. Marcie had really gone for it, filling column inches with sensationalism, speculation and shit. Shit too close to home. Scandal flying off the shelves on a day when it should be about Lucas. She was surprised Hastings hadn't been on the warpath yet, but it wouldn't be long.

Eve's anger was barely contained. She'd wanted to call the *Aberdeen Enquirer* and talk directly to Marcie, but it was a pointless exercise and would make no difference. Marcie would be at the crematorium. She'd have to trust herself to remain calm, not to react to any goading that might come their way. Some chance. It was taking all her energy not to lose her rag with Ferguson, who stood just inches from her, unaware that if he'd done his job more thoroughly . . . But maybe that anger was misguided. Maybe even if he had done everything by the book, he still might not have got to Jane Henderson before Marcie. What's to say Jane Henderson hadn't gone to Marcie herself?

She checked her watch, grimacing as she saw the time. 'We have a funeral to go to.'

Chapter 61

Eve looked around the Aberdeen Crematorium chapel, unsurprised to see no new faces except the minister's, not at all shocked to see Lucas's grandmother and father there, albeit rows apart. The woman had miraculously stopped dabbing at her eyes as soon as the crematorium door had closed and the press had been shooed away, Marcie Wade included. James Fyfe was still pretending.

Now more than ever, it was obvious Lucas had known very few people in life and, apart from a woman and man who had been a grandmother and father by blood only and never in any other way, it was the Wellwood kids who were there for him. They and the staff.

Eve turned as the back doors opened. Stephen and Ben were standing there in sharp black suits that only made the white coffin they carried all the more jarring. She watched, unable to take her gaze from the too-small wooden box on their shoulders – Jake and Beth taking a shoulder each at the back.

Eve forced herself to study the four who carried Lucas.

Staring at Ben first but then each of them in turn, hoping for a sign, the slightest of twitches that might unmask a burning guilt for what had happened to the boy. She could see nothing as they made their way down the aisle in measured, sombre steps.

Eve turned her head towards the front as they came near, staring at the backs of the kids' heads before her. Wishing she could see their faces. If being here would stir anything within them – *if* one of them were responsible.

For starting the fire or perhaps for closing that hatch, knowing or not knowing what was to come.

If any one of them – the staff or the kids – had been responsible, it scared the hell out of her. Not only because of what they'd done, but because they'd made it this far without breaking. Which begged the question: what could that person be capable of next?

The doors of the chapel opened to sunshine – uninterrupted for a moment before Eve spotted Marcie Wade and the day darkened. Eve's fists clenched at the sight of the woman, but she was surprised to see only Marcie waiting, expecting the morning's front page to have attracted the nationals by now. Maybe they had a little more respect. More likely they'd be waiting at the hostel for the Wellwood staff and children to return.

She walked alongside Cooper, Mearns and Ferguson, pretending to listen to small talk, watching the staff and kids being huddled across the car park to the Wellwood minibus. She clocked Stephen walking round to the driver's door, stopping – no, freezing as someone stepped in his way.

Eve stopped walking and nudged Cooper, who followed her eyeline. The man was dressed all in black, heavy set and with a face that had seen many a fight.

'Shit.' Cooper hissed the word beside her.

'Wouldn't mess with him.' Eve was fixed on the two men; Mearns and Ferguson were staring alongside her now too.

Cooper was straining his neck, trying to get a clearer view. 'No, it's not that. I know that guy.'

Ferguson was frowning. 'So do I. That's Brian Logan. The guy in the CCTV image. The one who was hassling Archie outside the Aberdeen Cyrenians. The loan shark.'

253

Chapter 62

EVE, STILL DRESSED IN black, turned on her mobile as Cooper drove them the short distance from the crematorium to the hostel. The phone bleeped within seconds. She turned to Cooper. 'Seems I won't have to go hunting for our data protection officer, Martin Smith, about how Marcie Wade got her story. He's left a message.'

She listened to Martin rambling, the concern in his voice and his fears for his job after helping them, making it clear that he had not been Marcie's source and that the story had hit him as hard as it had them. She hung up. 'Martin isn't the one who gave Marcie Jane Henderson's name, which leaves me clueless as to who did.'

Eve pressed to return the call, tutting as it went to answerphone. 'Martin, it's me. I'm relieved to hear you were as unaware as us. On a positive note, it's given us clear names to look up records for. I'd appreciate if you could still help us and search records for Danny and John in the time frame mentioned.' She paused. 'I can assure you that your job will not be under threat and if you need authorization to look into this, then let me know.'

Cooper pulled into the hostel car park. Eve stiffened as she saw the scrum of reporters gathering at the foot of the youth hostel's stairwell. It was time to go to work.

Stephen stood by the window – where he'd been since they'd shifted the reporters and got the staff and kids safely inside.

Cooper sat by Eve's side.

Stephen turned from the window, his face ashen, the black tie around his neck hanging undone. 'What do you want to talk to me about now? I can't take much more today.'

'Who was the guy you were talking to?' Eve didn't take her gaze from him.

'What guy?'

'The one who stopped you by the minibus.'

Stephen swallowed. 'Someone I'd hoped I wouldn't see any time soon. Nothing to do with Lucas. Why?'

Eve clasped her fingers together and placed them on the desk. 'Because we happen to know he's a loan shark, operating in the area. Strange he'd approach you at a funeral, don't you think? But, then again, given your debts, perhaps it's not so strange.'

Stephen pulled out the seat opposite them, standing clearly not an option any longer as his face paled further still. 'It's not what you think . . . It's . . .'

Eve gripped her hands even more tightly together. 'Tell us what it's about then; tell us why Brian Logan was trying to speak to you. He didn't seem happy, that's for sure.'

255

Stephen sighed, long and deep, pulling the tie free of his shirt collar and rolling it between his fingers, not looking at Eve or Cooper. 'I got in some trouble.'

'We know. We've seen the financials.'

'This was getting too close for comfort. They were talking about closing Wellwood. I had to act. I couldn't get a loan anywhere because of the credit history. I was desperate.'

'How much do you owe him?'

Stephen unravelled the tie. 'I've lost track.'

'You've lost track?' The disbelief was clear in Cooper's voice.

'What with the separation from my wife and the debts and now all this, I can't get my head straight.'

Stephen looked pathetic. Eve might've felt sorry for him if it wasn't self-pity he was wallowing in. 'Stephen, by the sound of things, your head hasn't been straight for a long time.'

Chapter 63

Ferguson didn't bother to bring Archie anything this time. This afternoon wasn't about giving, it was about getting. Getting answers from Archie even if he had to prise them from him. His footsteps echoed off the walls as he marched down the corridor. Determined both in mind and body that he wouldn't leave here without knowing what the hell was going on.

Archie jumped as he entered the room, grimacing as his hoisted leg moved; there was none of the attitude he'd displayed before when he saw Ferguson's face.

'How do you know Brian Logan and why the hell was he up in your face in Summer Street?'

'Jesus, you're like a dog with a—'

'Now.' Archie shut up as Ferguson lifted the remote to turn off the telly. 'The whole story.'

Archie glowered at him. 'I've put some folk his way. No big deal. Folk have been glad of the option. He sometimes gave me a little something for finding him the business.'

'And the other day?'

'One of the clients wasn't paying up. Logan was getting pissed off. I don't know why but he thought putting pressure on me would change that.'

'And what was this client's name?'

'Like I'm going to tell you.'

Ferguson leaned over the bed. 'This is serious, Archie. It's to do with another case we're working. An eleven-year-old kid. Dead. In a fire. That guy was at his funeral today.'

'What fire? Where?'

'Wellwood kids' home.'

Archie's face went as white as the sheet he was lying beneath. 'A kid died?'

'Yeah, and this guy might be connected. I want the name. Now.'

Archie's mouth was opening and closing.

'NOW.'

'Stephen Alderton.'

Ferguson froze for the briefest of moments. He rubbed at his face. 'Jesus, Archie.' Ferguson's mobile was out and dialling Eve's number before the boy could say anything else.

Chapter 64

Eve had left the room to take the call and now she was pushing the door open again forcefully, Cooper and Stephen's heads snapping round as she thundered back into the room. 'Archie. What can you tell me about the boy called Archie?'

Stephen appeared confused for a second. 'What?'

Eve glared at him, no patience for mucking about. 'You heard me.'

Stephen lifted the tie from the table. Eve would've happily strangled him with it. 'I don't understand . . . what is it you want to know?'

'How about we start with why you never mentioned him when we spoke about Brian Logan?'

Stephen ran a hand through his hair, the strands as red as his face. 'Why would I?'

Eve wanted to shake him. 'Because he introduced you to Logan.'

Stephen sat back, trying for casual. 'He did, and I've never said he didn't. I didn't see the importance.'

'You didn't see the importance? How do you know Archie?'

Stephen was looking at the door, as if measuring up his chances of escape.

'How did you know him?' Eve wasn't taking any shit.

'He was one of the kids here until about six months ago.'

Eve hoped she was hearing things. 'You are joking, aren't you?'

Stephen bowed his head to the floor. 'I'm not proud but it's not what you think.'

Eve's hairs were up on the back of her neck. 'Not what I think? What? That you used one of your kids, someone who you are supposed to protect and care for, to arrange a dodgy loan for you?'

'No, the loan was arranged after he left Wellwood.'

'Oh, and that makes it so much better?' Eve sat down next to Cooper, not trusting herself to be standing anywhere near where Stephen sat.

Stephen had dropped the tie and was wringing his hands together. 'It's not how it sounds. I was desperate. I was aware from trouble we had had with Archie in the past that he knew people, that he was involved in stuff we couldn't get a grip on. He'd left as he was of age – that and the fact he didn't want to be reined in by us, no matter how hard we tried. There was nothing we could do to stop him. But I kept up with him. Checked in weekly. It kind of came about on one of those calls.'

Eve couldn't speak.

Cooper took over. 'You didn't think to tell us that one of your kids had left six months before the fire?'

'No. Why would I? I don't see what it would have to do with something that happened after he left us.'

Eve couldn't believe the stupidity of the man in front of her. 'You can't see why we might've been interested in the departure of a teenage boy from Wellwood in the last few months? Not a thought about it when we asked you to tell us about the set-up, about all the kids?'

Stephen was shaking his head. 'No. He wasn't with us any more. He was the only one that left in that time. You don't think Arch—'

Eve had to be careful. 'All I know is you are up to your neck in debt, and a fire all but destroyed Wellwood. We find out you're in hock to a loan shark who may have his own motives for that fire, never mind that you may have your *own* motives for the fire, and there's a link to a kid you homed. We have to be given ALL the facts. You and the other members of staff were asked extensively about the kids and the set-up at Wellwood. What, you all just decided to forget about one of them?' Eve was struggling to keep her voice steady.

Stephen sat with his palms upwards on his lap. 'It wasn't like that. Not at all. I've never forgotten about any of the kids who have gone through Wellwood in all the years I've worked there. Not one.'

Eve wasn't about to give him any medals.

'I honestly didn't think about it, let alone think it was important.'

Eve could've screamed.

Stephen's face was scrunched up, as if he was trying to make sense of what was being asked of him. 'These kids can be emotionally and mentally scarred. Some of them

261

are happy to fit into our structure, routine and way of life, but others are unable to. Archie was one of the ones who couldn't.'

'Couldn't as in . . .?' Eve wanted to know everything after being told nothing.

'As in bunking off school, refusing to do rota, sneaking out after dark, bullying some of the other kids, stealing stuff.'

'What did you do about all of that?'

'Kept everything as it was. Showed him that was the way Wellwood worked. The only way we'd make it work. He had to want to buy into it.'

Obviously, he didn't. 'Did you ever ask him what the problem was?'

'Of course we did but these kids aren't like the ones in the storybooks – all open and approachable. They keep things inside. Like I say, sometimes they feel that's all they've got.'

Eve needed more. 'Did you ever try to bring him back to Wellwood?'

Stephen looked offended, as if he was being judged again – this time by Eve instead of the press. 'Like I said, I checked in weekly, hoped he'd see sense. But he was of age. He chose to leave. He told me he was kipping on someone's sofa. Sorting out what he wanted to do. Not in some doorway.'

Eve listened, but it didn't change anything. 'Unfortunately, that wasn't the case.'

Confusion followed by fear flitted across Stephen's features. 'He's OK . . . isn't he?'

'He is, or at least, he will be. But he came close to

being far from OK. He was knocked down in Crown Street a few days ago. Ended up in intensive care with broken bones and a head injury. He's not long been brought round from an induced coma. One of my colleagues was nearby when the accident happened and has been there for him since. We had no ID for him, and no one had come looking. A John Doe.'

Stephen slouched. 'Jesus. Is he going to be OK?'

'They say he'll make a good recovery but not without time in hospital.'

Stephen's eyes were haunted. 'And if I'd mentioned him before now . . .'

Eve felt a sliver of compassion for Stephen amongst her anger and frustration, but only a sliver. 'We might have known sooner instead of my colleague having to trawl homeless shelters. Someone recognized the description of Archie's tattoo, which led to CCTV showing Brian Logan hassling him outside one of those shelters.'

Stephen stared at Eve, his hands still rubbing at one another. 'He was hassling him because of me.'

'Looks like it – especially with Logan turning up. But that's not what I'm most interested in.'

Stephen paled. 'What is it? What?'

'Archie was hit by a van the morning after the fire. Ran out on to the road. The old guy driving didn't see him coming until it was too late. What was he running from? Logan? Or had he started that fire because he was put up to it?'

Chapter 65

'WERE YOU THERE THAT night?' Ferguson had burst back into the hospital room after taking Eve's return call.

Archie's head shot up. 'Where?'

'Wellwood. Were you at Wellwood that night?' He needed to hear it from Archie, praying it wouldn't be the answer he was expecting.

Archie frowned. 'You think I started the fire?'

Ferguson's heart lurched. 'I'm not saying that; I'm asking you to tell me what you know. I've been on the phone to my boss. She's told me what Stephen told her.'

Archie bit at the hospital band on his wrist, turning it. 'Say I did know something. Then what? I go down as the snitch and get other folk in the shit?'

Ferguson was growing impatient. 'Depends what you have to tell me. Telling me will be better than what might happen if you don't and we find out the truth later.'

Archie stopped playing with the band and stared at the ceiling, his jaw tight. He looked at Ferguson several times, turning back to the ceiling every time, his lips tight as if holding his breath and his truth. He gave a long sigh. 'Fine. I was there.'

Ferguson tensed, bracing himself for what was to come. 'Tell me. Everything.'

Archie's gaze remained on Ferguson. 'I was there but I didn't start the fire.' Attitude was rolling off him. Protection.

'Who did?'

Archie sniffed. 'The truth?'

Ferguson's blood pressure was rising. 'Of course the bloody truth.'

'I don't know.'

Ferguson screwed up his face. 'What do you mean you don't know? You said you were there.'

'I was. By chance. About something else.'

'To do with Brian Logan?'

'I figured I'd go and talk to Stephen, see if he could afford to pay something, get the guy off my back. When I got there, the place was already going up in flames. I didn't see anyone, other than the staff and kids spilling out into the car park. I thought they'd all got out.' Archie fell silent. 'Was it Lucas?'

'Yeah.'

'I'm sorry. Makes me feel worse.'

'What do you mean?'

'Watching the fire, right up until the fire engines arrived. Enjoying it.'

'Enjoying it?' Ferguson was struggling to keep the disgust from his voice.

'Sounds bad, I know. I can't explain it, but I have a

thing about it. Matches, lighters, small fires, bigger fires. Nothing serious. Nothing where anyone has ever got hurt. Damage to property, maybe, but not folk.'

'And everyone at Wellwood knew about this?'

'Jesus, no. It started before I moved there and I've been doing it secretly since. I read somewhere there's others like me. Fascinated by fire. Usually it's folk with as fucked up an upbringing as me.' Archie glanced at Ferguson. 'Hey, you said you wanted me to open up.'

Ferguson was still adjusting to who this kid was after all the hours sitting waiting for him to wake. To judge wouldn't get him anywhere. He knew that from his own childhood and from his job. The blasé statement of facts shouldn't surprise him. He wished for Lucas's sake that it had only been property that had been damaged this time.

'Do you think Logan had anything to do with it?'

Archie shrugged. 'I wouldn't put anything past the guy.'

'What about Stephen? Do you reckon he could've done it as an insurance job?'

Archie was already shaking his head. 'Nah, that place was his life.'

They both sat in silence a moment before Archie broke it. 'Why did Lucas not make it out?'

Ferguson could see the kid's pain, clear that there was a heart in there. 'They found him underground.'

Archie's eyes widened. 'What do you mean – underground?'

'In the basement. I doubt you knew of it. The kids only found out three weeks ago, when maintenance works were being carried out. There was a hatch and a ladder leading down to a huge space you can stand up in. Somehow Lucas had got down there before the fire started.'

'I didn't know. I couldn't have. But I was there before the fire had spread. If I'd been the one to make the 999 call, instead of one of the neighbours once they saw the smoke, they could've got to him in time.' There were tears welling in Archie's eyes.

'No, you couldn't have known, but he either got down there himself or someone put him down there.'

'No, they wouldn't have, they—'

'You don't know that. And if someone did put him down there deliberately, the question is whether it was the same person who started the fire or whether it was unrelated.'

Archie was struggling not to let the tears fall. 'But he was a kid.'

Ferguson didn't say that Archie was a mere kid himself. 'You'd be surprised at some of the evil things that go on in the world.'

And they both fell silent again.

Chapter 66

Costa at Marischal Square was quiet at this time of day. Something Mearns was sure Ferguson was glad of, given the look on his face. 'So, what brings us here?' she asked.

'Thought we could do with the caffeine hit after everything that's happened today.'

'It's been a shitstorm. Sounds like you didn't get much more out of Archie than Eve got out of Stephen.'

'Nope. Any luck on tracking down Brian Logan?'

'No. The guy has the brass neck to turn up at the funeral before disappearing off the face of the earth.'

'Did you try that number I got from Archie?'

'It's bouncing to answerphone. I've got someone trying to put a trace on it.'

Mearns sipped at her latte, watching Ferguson over the brim of her mug. 'Come on then, what are we here for?'

Ferguson picked at the Danish he hadn't taken a bite of since sitting down.

'Ferguson? You might as well spit it out.'

'What?'

'Whatever's making you sit here with your bottom lip tripping you up. Whatever made you ask me here. I get the feeling it's not just about today.'

Ferguson said nothing, avoiding eye contact.

'Let me start. Now it looks like Archie's going to be OK, and we know about the connection to Wellwood, what is it with this boy? You told me it's about you being there at the crash, about him talking to you, but that's not cutting it. I think there's more.'

Ferguson stopped picking. 'Does it matter?'

'It kind of does when I've been covering your arse at work.'

Ferguson took a gulp of his coffee. 'I guess that's what this is about. I wanted to apologize for letting you take up the slack. For not being there doing what I should've been.'

'Wow, can I have that in writing?'

Ferguson balled his napkin and threw it at Mearns. 'Don't push it, but thank you.'

Mearns scrunched the napkin in her hand before placing it between them. 'What else?'

Ferguson stared at her. 'And it's usually me that you say is a pain in the arse.'

'Something I guess we have in common.'

Ferguson sat for a moment, weighing something up. 'If I tell you, will it remain between us?'

'Of course. Who have I got to tell?' Mearns sipped at her coffee. Where was this going?

'He reminds me of me when I was a kid.' Ferguson set down his mug.

'That's it? That's all I'm getting?'

He picked up the pastry and put it down again. 'I saw him on that road, the way he was dressed, the fact he had nothing on him, and I saw myself.'

'Meaning?'

'Meaning I had a less-than-perfect start. I was a bit of a loner. A drifter, if you like.'

'I never would've thought it, not as anal as you are about that hair of yours – and those guns.' Mearns poked at his arm.

Ferguson managed a smile. 'Well, I changed things, didn't I?'

Mearns ran a finger around the lip of her mug. 'I remember talking to you one time. Whilst we were working that trafficking case. We were staking out the barman, and I happened to mention your dad.'

'I remember.'

'You spoke about not having folks.'

'Yeah.'

Mearns didn't push, leaving Ferguson to guide the conversation.

'I did things I'm not proud of. Things that could've seen me in a different place now – and not a good one. I stopped that from happening. Joined the force.'

'You think Archie's in trouble?'

'He might be. It sounds stupid but he's around the age I sorted myself out. If I can do that for someone else, then it would mean something.'

'I get that.'

'Do you?'

'Yes, and I say you should try. That's all you can do.'

Ferguson was staring at his hands. 'Archie wasn't the only reason I wasn't pulling my weight on the case.'

'Yeah?' She said it with caution, not sure where this was going.

'There're things I didn't want to remember about my past. Stuff I've worked hard to erase.' He wouldn't look at her.

'Like what?'

'Where I was brought up. Things that happened. People who did things that shouldn't have been allowed. Things I did that I've never forgiven myself for. Bad shit.'

Mearns didn't speak for a moment, struggling whether to ask for more detail, opting instead to stay safe. 'And what does that have to do with Archie?'

'Everything.' Ferguson dropped his head into his hands.

'How?'

He closed his eyes.

Mearns's voice was soft. 'I don't follow, Ferguson.'

Ferguson straightened, attempting eye contact. 'At first Archie reminded me of myself as a kid, but I guess I was also trying for an excuse to distance myself from Wellwood and the investigation.'

'But why?'

'Because of my past. But it turns out he's also from the same place as I was.'

Mearns stared at him, her mouth slack. 'What do you mean, the same place?'

Ferguson was trying to keep the emotion from his voice. 'A home, Mearns. A kids' home.' Ferguson looked away, anywhere but at Mearns's face. 'We're both from Wellwood.' It was little more than a whisper.

271

'Wellwood?' Mearns's voice was high.

Ferguson gulped.

'That's why you've been acting so off.' Mearns's eyes were wide.

'I was there, Mearns.' Ferguson's eyes were haunted as they met hers. 'I know who's in that barrel. I might be responsible for her being in there.'

Mearns's brow creased, her body tensing. 'Jesus, Ferguson. You have to tell the boss.' She reached for his hand. 'Shit. I don't know what to say but you must know I can't cover you on this one.'

Ferguson nodded once, grasping Mearns's hand, needing to hold on to something whilst everything around him fell apart.

Chapter 67

Then

SHE LOVES BEING DOWN here as much as I'd hoped. It's dark and it's dirty but it's ours and something we both need badly to escape what goes on above. I live for the nights.

We've made the space beneath the day room into a den of sorts. Laid cardboard on an area of the floor and brought blankets down for warmth. Things we knew wouldn't be missed. We sit by the chimney breast that stretches upwards to a real fire above and we pretend it's our own room, our own home. We fantasize that we go to bed together, like any other couple, and she lets me do things I never thought I would, and I'm surprised to find that it doesn't feel like all those things I watched them do to my mother. Those things they did to me. This is different. This is good.

Her face is illuminated in the torchlight shining on us, the torch itself propped and balanced on the edge of an old oil drum. She sips from her cider can, pulling a little notebook from the same bag she carried the cider in, and turns to me. 'You're staring at me again.'

I smile, really smile, and take a gulp from my own can. 'What's that you've got?'

'My diary.'

'I didn't know you kept a diary.'

'I didn't but things are different now. I feel I have a life. I have you.' She pressed against his side. 'I have something to write about.'

And I smile again. So many nights here together and I've come to enjoy not only the escapism that Danny and being down here give me, but the warm, fuzzy feeling that comes from the cider. Making everything blur at the edges, softening the reality above ground. It's like I want more of it each and every time I come down here. She laughs and says I'm getting worse than her. I say we're the same, in every way.

I say it again now as I move over and pull her to me, needing to get lost in her again.

Chapter 68

'WHY DIDN'T YOU TELL me?' Eve was pacing behind her desk, unable to sit, her tone as hard as her hazel-green eyes.

'Spent a lifetime hiding it so why would I?' Ferguson sounded like a spoilt kid, attitude dripping off him, which Eve took as an attempt to protect himself.

'You and I both know why, Ferguson.' Eve sat, her stare fixed on him.

'Sorry. OK?' Ferguson barked the words at her before stopping, perhaps forcing himself to calm down. He spoke more gently once he had. 'I fucked up. I should've said something, but my mind was on the boy. On Archie. I didn't want to think about Wellwood. About what letting that place back in my head might do. Little did I know Archie would be bringing me back there anyway.'

Eve waited, leaving him struggling with his thoughts, seeing something in his slouched frame and his slackened features she'd never seen before. Defeat. Not because he'd been keeping something from her. This was more than that. This was about what had happened at that place. She thought back to Marcie Wade's interview with Jane Henderson. The sheer horror of what the kids had been through at Wellwood in the past.

She let the silence stretch between them, deciding how to approach this. Her voice was softer when she spoke. 'I'm not going to pretend that I know what you've been through. I wouldn't dare. You've had a lot to deal with and face. The things that went on at that home. Stuff that was allowed, even encouraged, under Sally Fields.'

Ferguson flinched as though he'd been slapped. 'Sorry. You'd think after all this time I could hear that name without reacting.'

'Ferguson, you don't have to be some hard man in front of me. I can't imagine what she was like. Her name just makes me picture the actress who starred in *Sybil*.'

Ferguson grunted. 'Try the psycho mother in that film who abused her. You'll get the picture.' He wouldn't look up. 'I'm not trying to be . . . I . . . Well, maybe I am. I've spent years trying to be stronger, putting on a front.'

'You do it well. To the extent of being a right pain in the arse.' Eve's tone was friendly, gentle. 'Do you remember Jane Henderson who gave the interview to Marcie Wade?'

Ferguson coloured and dropped his chin to his chest. 'Ferguson?'

'Yes. It was me who gave her name to Marcie Wade.'

Eve froze, staring at the stop of his head. 'What the hell? Jesus, why would you do that? To the team? To the investigation? To bloody Wellwood?'

Ferguson was picking at his cuticle. 'I was angry. It was after Cooper called me out about the CCTV image, about slacking. I wasn't thinking straight. I didn't know how to bring Jane Henderson to you without telling you about my background. I thought . . . and I know how wrong I was . . . that if I gave an anonymous tip-off to Marcie then it would be exposing the truth, that I would be doing something.'

Blood was coursing in Eve's veins. 'You didn't call the social work department to request records, did you?'

Ferguson shook his head. 'No.'

'Because you were scared your name would come up.'

Ferguson didn't argue. His face crumbled as he inhaled deeply and blew out. And again. 'If I'd known you were going to find her, then . . .'

Eve let it go, for now. 'Do you agree with Jane as to who might be in that barrel? We have social services trying to pin down records for her.'

Ferguson's face said it all.

'Do you know how they got in there?'

Ferguson squeezed his hands together.

'Listen, I get why you distanced yourself. In some sense I understand why you did what you did. I do. Now is the time to set things right. Who knows, maybe you'll get some small piece of closure being a part of bringing all of it to light?'

Ferguson was still, his eyes boring into the desk, taking measured breaths. Eve was about to apologize and tell him she was wrong to try to push him when he spoke.

'There's something in us kids, you know.'

Eve didn't move or say a word, sensing Ferguson needed to get out whatever he was trying to say.

'It's like we're drawn to each other, that we somehow sense what each of us has been through. I've felt it a couple of times in my life and been proven right, and I felt it that day holding Archie's hand as he lay on the road.'

Eve was beginning to understand Ferguson's need to be there for the boy. Beginning to make sense of what she'd seen as an obsession.

'He reminded me so much of myself. Before he came around from the coma. Maybe it was supposed to be me who found him. Me who was supposed to confront all this.'

'Maybe.' Ferguson's head was still bowed. Eve went on: 'It says a lot for what you did for him.'

His head shook side to side. 'I don't mean that. I'm not after some kind of praise. What I mean is I've spent my life keeping secrets; maybe it's time for me to tell some of my truths, or at least do as you've asked and try to make a little peace with the past.'

Eve could see Ferguson battling with the decision. 'I'm not going to force you to do anything. It has to come from you, and I'll respect whatever decision you make.'

Ferguson took a deep breath. 'It's much more than me agreeing with Jane as to who was in that barrel.'

Eve waited, her heart racing.

'I might've been responsible for her ending up in there.'

The hairs on the back of Eve's neck prickled. 'What . . . what do you mean?'

'I told that bitch, Ms Fields, that I thought Danny might be pregnant.'

'And you think Fields acted on that?'

Ferguson pushed back against the chair. 'What else am I supposed to think, now that I know what I do?'

'What about John? Do you know what happened to him? Social services are also tracking records for him.'

'No. I didn't even know what had happened to Danny before all of this.'

'Then that makes him a person of interest but, that aside, none of this makes you responsible for what happened to them. You can't blame yourself for that. You were a kid, for God's sake.'

Eve could only hope he'd take her words to heart. She'd spent her life blaming herself for being born. A baby. An innocent kid. 'I'm going to say something. Something that'll surprise you and doesn't need to go further than these four walls.'

Ferguson's eyes were dark.

'You and I are more alike than you know. As strong-willed and determined as each other but a lot of that is born out of our life experiences.'

Ferguson frowned. 'I always figured you had a great upbringing with your mum and grandparents. Not that we've ever spoken about it in great detail, but I got that impression from the few times you have spoken about them.'

'I did. No doubt about it. What you were saying about finding Archie, about how maybe it was supposed to be you, well, there was a reason my mum was my mum. That I was supposed to be with her.'

'How?'

It was Eve who dropped her attention to the desk now, fidgeting with the piece of paper closest to her. 'Like yourself, my life is full of secrets. My mum was raped. I was the result. She never knew my father and therefore neither do I.'

Ferguson was staring at her, open-mouthed.

Eve stood, pulling more paper towards her, shuffling sheets that had already been straightened. ' "Father" is not a word I'll ever associate with him.' She laid the papers back down, her gaze fixed on them. 'Next to no one knows about that. I can't dictate to you what decision to make about whether to help us, but I'm always searching and hoping that closure will come my way.'

Ferguson sat silent, staring, his features soft.

Eve looked at the desk as her phone rang. *MacLean.* She lifted the mobile, her focus on Ferguson. 'Think about it. I need to take this.'

Chapter 69

EVE STOOD AT THE front of the incident room, ready to whip up her team. 'As you all know, there have been significant developments in the Wellwood case. We now have a link to Archie through Stephen and Brian Logan.' She looked at Mearns. 'Any luck with Logan?'

Mearns shook her head.

'Finding him is our priority. After being seen approaching Archie and again at the funeral, and knowing what we know about the debts and Stephen's unpaid loan, there's nothing to say he's not involved in the fire and therefore Lucas's death.'

The room was silent.

'I plan to bring Stephen in. He's not telling us the full story.'

Cooper spoke up. 'But we have nothing tying him to the fire.'

'We have nothing tying anyone to that fire, but he has continued to keep secrets. I want to know what else he's hiding.'

Eve straightened, commanding attention from the room. 'The identification of the girl in the barrel has also been confirmed, half an hour ago.' This was for Mearns's and Cooper's benefit – Ferguson had had the right to be told first. 'Dental records and DNA sampling have given us a match for Danny Watt, as reported in the press by Jane Henderson.'

Eve stayed silent a moment, out of respect for the girl.

'Obviously, Sally Fields and William Alderton are no longer alive, so determining whether they had anything to do with Danny and the baby's deaths is going to be hard, so we also need to be looking at what became of Danny's boyfriend, John Findlay. From there it'll be a process, a long painful one given the time that has passed, of attempting to expand on the few facts we have to go on, in the hope we can uncover the truth.'

Eve avoided eye contact with Ferguson. They should be leaning on his connection to Wellwood – his memories – using him to get whatever they could from that. She could only hope he'd be willing to let them.

Eve turned as her phone rang, the number for the youth hostel flashing up on the screen. She put the phone on loudspeaker as she answered. 'Hunter.'

'Stephen's gone.'

Eve stared at her colleagues as she processed what Jake was saying. 'What do you mean, gone?'

'I've been here since we got back from the funeral. He told me he was going for a nap; said he was shattered after everything that's happened today. I went in to ask if he needed anything and he's not there.'

'Could he have gone out?'

'Not without saying. I've tried phoning him but he's not picking up. He always answers his phone.'

Eve closed her eyes. 'When did you last see him?'

'About four hours ago. I assumed he was in the office.'

'Any ideas where he might have gone?'

'Stephen doesn't have a social life. The home is his life. The only place I can think of is his wife's house, but that's a long shot.'

Eve opened her eyes; the whole team was staring at her. 'Do you have an address for her?' She picked up a pen and scribbled down the details. 'Thanks. I'll see if we can track his phone.' She hung up. 'Ferguson, get me a trace on Stephen's number. Mearns, check out CCTV around the hostel in the last five hours. Cooper, you're with me.

Chapter 70

THE SEMI-DETACHED GRANITE HOUSE in Braeside Place was like any other home in the street. Ample in size, wooden blinds at the windows, a neatly kept patch of grass out front and a gravel driveway big enough for three cars.

Eve walked up the drive, Cooper by her side, pink stones crunching beneath their feet. A bright white sensor light clicked on above the door as they approached, alerting those inside to their arrival. Eve heard a key turning in the lock before they had reached the doorstep.

The woman who answered was slender, the yoga pants and vest top she wore showing toned limbs. Her thin, mousey-brown hair was scraped back from her face, which was make-up free and fresh, no obvious hint at the stress she was bound to have been living under.

'Audrey Alderton?' Eve held up her ID.

'Yes. What's this about?'

'It's about your husband, Stephen. Is he here?'

Audrey frowned. 'Here? No.'

'Can we come in?'

Audrey stepped back, as if she'd been expecting this.

The conservatory was stylish and warm; underfloor heating to thank for that, Eve guessed. 'You have a lovely home.'

'Thank you. What's happened? I know about the fire. I saw the awful stuff in the papers this week. I haven't been able to get hold of Stephen.'

'Is it unusual for him not to answer your calls?'

'No. I don't call him much. You do know we're separated?'

'Yes. One of the staff members told us.'

'It's not exactly amicable but after the papers, the funeral . . .'

'Do you mind if we ask why that's the case? The separation not being amicable?'

Audrey crossed her legs. 'Can I ask first what this is about? Why you're here?'

'Stephen is missing.'

'Missing?' Audrey's hand flew to her throat.

'It's only been a few hours but it's out of character according to staff at the hostel and, in light of recent events, we're concerned about his whereabouts.'

'I can't imagine what he's been going through.'

Eve could see there was still genuine affection there, regardless of the state of their relationship. 'In the course of our investigations into the fire, we've uncovered some financial information about Wellwood that could be relevant.'

'Let me guess. Debts?'

Eve was glad it wasn't coming as a surprise to Audrey. 'Yes. Substantial ones.'

Audrey swept an arm around the room. 'This lovely home is in danger of being taken away from us. From me and the kids. Stephen remortgaged it without me knowing.'

Eve was taken aback. She knew the debts were bad, but she had no idea it had seeped into his personal life too. 'How did he manage that without your consent?'

'Don't ask me, but he did.'

'How old are your kids?'

Audrey pointed to a framed picture on the sill, two boys standing together in football kit. 'That's an old one. Daniel is away in Edinburgh now at uni. He's eighteen. Craig's sixteen and still stays with me.'

'Is he here?'

'She shook her head. 'No, he's working. Got a part-time job at Pizza Hut three nights a week around school. He's in fifth year. Don't know where he gets the energy.'

'If you know about Stephen's debts, it may come as no shock to you to hear that we believe a loan shark made a visit to him after the funeral.'

'Doesn't surprise me at all. Gambling is an idiot's game.'

Eve wished they'd come here days ago, but there had been no valid reason at the time.

Audrey looked out of the window to where a cat was slinking through her garden. 'It's been spiralling out of control for a long time. There was a time I believed

Wellwood was our only problem. That he was married to the place instead of me.'

'He didn't use to gamble?'

'I have no idea. What I will say is Stephen is not a bad man. Sitting here, I find it hard to believe I'm speaking about the man I married.' Audrey rested her arm on the bamboo rest of the conservatory chair. 'It's complicated. He's complicated. A man with such a good heart, but he had a difficult childhood that's left him with scars.'

Eve glanced at Cooper. 'He had a tough childhood?'

'Worse than a lot of the kids he takes in. You did see the papers? You do know who his father was?'

'Yes, but he told us his father was only in his life until he was six.'

'Believe me, that was long enough, and the abuse didn't stop when his father left.'

'His mother?' Eve heard the surprise in her own voice.

'From the little he told me, she could be even worse than his father. It made him determined to be better. To be there to help others.'

Eve couldn't deny seeing herself, and Ferguson, in that statement.

'He got a job as a youth worker. His father died and Wellwood was left to him. And he embraced that. I can assure you, from the bottom of my heart, he loves those kids. He'd never do anything to harm them. I know that.'

'So why the gambling and the financial mess?'

Audrey stared at Eve. 'Have you ever heard of compassion fatigue?'

They both shook their heads.

'It can happen in carers, especially those under

287

pressure. It's common in those who have suffered trauma themselves. Living through the trauma of others can cause old memories to resurface.'

'That's what happened to Stephen?'

Audrey's voice was soft. 'I read everything I could get my hands on to try and understand what was happening to him. It's described as . . . I remember this word for word . . . "a state of significant depletion or exhaustion of the person's store of compassion, resulting from repeated activation over time of empathic and sympathetic responses".'

'Have you ever spoken to him about this?'

'Tirelessly, when I still thought our relationship could be saved. He didn't want to listen. He displayed all the classic symptoms – isolation from others, insomnia, lack of motivation, physical pain, the list goes on. But it's the coping behaviours he adopted that were the confirmation for me.'

'Gambling?'

'Yes.'

They sat silent for a moment before Audrey spoke again. 'Have you found the person responsible for the fire?'

Eve shook her head.

'I can't believe anyone could do such a thing.' She stared at them. 'You don't think he had anything to do with that?' She was clutching at her necklace.

'At the moment, we can't be sure of anything.'

Audrey shook her head. 'It all sounds bad, but I know, as clearly as I know I love my kids, that Stephen would never do anything to harm anyone.'

Eve said nothing, wanting to believe it. But she couldn't rule out the possibility that gambling and debt had driven Stephen to do something stupid, not thinking for one moment that anyone would be in danger of harm. And now he was on the run.

Chapter 71

'I want to help.'

Eve, only moments back from Audrey Alderton's, looked up to see Ferguson standing at her office door, one shoulder propped against the door frame.

'Then I guess you'd better come in.'

Ferguson pushed himself away from the jamb and straightened, taking slow steps towards Eve's desk before sitting. His back was rigid in the chair.

'I realize how hard this is for you and I appreciate you doing it.'

Ferguson dipped his chin in acknowledgement.

'I'm heading up to the hostel after this.' Eve updated Ferguson on their visit with Audrey. 'This may be a little extreme, but I want the kids and staff moved out. I've no idea where Stephen's head is at. I've phoned Jake to get things in motion. I said I'd see him there. Any luck on the phone trace or CCTV?'

Ferguson shook his head. 'The phone's been switched off. The CCTV is still ongoing, but Mearns is on it.'

Ferguson paused. 'Boss, I'd like to be the one who comes with you. To the hostel.'

Eve stared at Ferguson, unsure whether it was the right thing to do, considering how close he was to the case. 'I'm not sure that's a good idea.'

'Please. It's not the Wellwood I knew. That place was destroyed in the fire. It's not the staff or kids either. I can do this. Please let me. I'd like to help.'

'How about we start with how you planned to help me when you walked in here?'

Ferguson rubbed at his forehead, steeling himself. 'I told you I knew Danny. It's been a long time since I let myself think about her. About any of them. I remember everything about them. Everything. Every stray hair, every bitten fingernail, every cry, every laugh. I remember it all.'

A lump rose in Eve's throat. 'You remember all their names?'

'Especially the names. I made sure I remembered every one of the kids who came through that place during my time there. As if by simply remembering them it ensured that they were someone to somebody else, that they were important.' Ferguson was struggling to keep his voice level. 'There were six of us. Danny and John, I never knew what happened to them. Michael died of an overdose two years after Wellwood closed. Alana became a prostitute down south. She was raped and murdered eight years ago. Then there's Jane. I've never tried to contact her, but she's crossed my radar from time to time. She fell in and out of trouble.'

'Jesus.' Eve didn't know what to say, but this man in front of her had achieved what the others hadn't been able to. He'd survived and he'd become a damn fine officer. Every spat between them, the attitude that had rolled off him over the years, his dogged determination to do the job . . . all of that was in crystal-clear focus now. 'I have no idea what you went through in that place and I don't expect you to tell me.' Her voice was soft as she spoke. 'Unless you want to.'

Ferguson's jaw tightened, his frame still poker straight. 'That's a step too far for now, maybe one I'll never take, but let's start with me taking one step at a time.' Ferguson groaned. 'Jesus, I sound like one of those newfangled counsellors.'

Eve smiled, glad of the mood shift. 'Hey, you don't have to talk to me about counsellors.'

Ferguson's shoulders dropped as he reached inside his jacket and took out what appeared to be a folded newspaper page. He said nothing as he unfolded it and placed it on the table between them, flattening the page at its edges before turning it round to face Eve.

It was a photo. Black and white, blurred, the faces of six kids staring out at them. They were standing in a huddle of varying heights and sizes, flanked by a stern-looking woman and a man who appeared as wary of her as the kids did.

'What's this?' Eve had read the caption under the photograph, but she wanted to hear Ferguson say it.

'Let's call it my past. One I tried to forget, but it doesn't want to let go. Clearly.'

Eve scanned the faces, expecting to recognize Ferguson somewhere there, but nothing familiar jumping out at her. 'Are you in this photo?'

Ferguson turned the piece of paper around, placed a forefinger on one of the faces before turning it back to Eve. 'That's me right there.'

She peered at it, not seeing Ferguson in the child at all. 'Are you shitting me?'

'I wish I was.'

Eve peered at the image, trying to make out something of the Ferguson of today, but all she saw was a short, painfully skinny boy with a bad haircut. She wanted to lighten the mood further – needed to, for Ferguson's sake. 'Nice hair.'

'Now you might get why I'm anal about my hair.'

The hint of a smile was there. Eve thought about Ferguson's extreme exercise routine. Taking care of himself when it hadn't always been within his control to do so, becoming stronger than he had been as a child when he was unable to fight back or protect himself from harm. A need to be anything else but the kid in the photo.

Ferguson pointed to a girl in the picture who stood two along from him. Her hair in the black-and-white image looked fair. It was past her shoulders and her face shone out from the photo. She was beautiful, a mischievous grin on her face and a tilt to her hip showing confidence despite her young age, and that she'd been in touch with being a woman. But it was the clothes Eve stared at more than anything. Her gaze flickered as Ferguson spoke.

'That's Danny.'

Eve was remembering what MacLean had said about what little clothing had been left on the girl's body. 'It

293

appears she was wearing leggings. Pink. Still small patches of material on the legs. And something made of gauze around her waist.'

Eve met Ferguson's gaze as he looked up from the page. She cleared her throat. 'Which one is John?'

Ferguson's finger skimmed the page, stopping on a serious-faced boy who scowled at the camera instead of smiling.

Eve could see, even with the attitude, he was an attractive kid. Tall for his age and more filled out than Ferguson had been.

'And that's Jane.' He pointed at a skinny kid, sadness clear in her eyes.

'Tell me what you remember about Danny and John.'

Ferguson lifted his hand from the paper and sat back, adopting his usual slouched position this time, as if saying their names out loud had lifted something from him. 'John was at Wellwood first. Quiet kid. We all were. We were conditioned to be that way with her around.'

Ferguson made no move to point out the woman who flanked one side of the children in the picture, and Eve was already sure it was Sally Fields. 'He kept himself to himself. I guess you might say he was a bit of a strange one, but your average Joe would've probably said that about all of us. Anyway, he was different after Danny arrived.'

'Different how?'

'I still remember the first day she came. It was like life rushing into the room. She had this thing about her. She was pretty, but it was more than that.'

Eve stared at the image again, seeing the life in Danny's eyes, evident despite the black-and-white still image.

'She made a beeline for John that day. Maybe it was the dark, brooding thing, but it was like she knew what she wanted. He was it.'

'I bet they made a good-looking couple.'

'For sure. He was the same though. It wasn't your typical movie-star looks. His background had seen to that. Like her, he had something.'

'What do you mean, his background had seen to that?'

'I saw him with his top off once. There were marks all over him.'

'What were they?'

'Scars. All shapes and sizes. Now I'm older, I know they were cigarette burns, amongst other things.'

'Jesus.'

'I'm not going to lie, I used to watch them going about the place, their little looks and exchanges, and I did feel a bit jealous they had that. That they had each other in there.'

'How did that go down with the others? The kids?'

'The kids didn't care either way. It wasn't like any of them were losing a friendship. As I said, John didn't mix. And Danny was new. I think, if anything, they were in awe of Danny and how she wouldn't let the place bring her down.'

'And did they try to bring her down?'

Ferguson's eyes darkened. 'Try? That bitch Fields was hell-bent on bringing everyone down and, before that girl arrived, she'd done a pretty good job of it. Her and her sidekick. I sometimes used to think Danny possessed something. Knowledge or a vibe or whatever, but it was like she was untouchable, like she knew Ms Fields wouldn't win with her. Because of that she and John were left to get on with it.'

'Staff never commented on their relationship?'

'Don't get me wrong, Fields and Alderton did things to keep them apart. Plenty of things. Some as fucked up as the stuff they pulled with the rest of us. But none of it worked. In time, they realized there was no keeping them apart. That together they couldn't or wouldn't be broken.'

'What happened?'

'I don't know. Nobody did. Woke up one day and they were gone.'

'Gone? No warning?'

Ferguson swallowed, dry lips parting, his gaze flitting between Eve and the floor. 'Other than what I told you I told Ms Fields.'

'That Danny might be pregnant?' Eve could see why he'd blamed himself.

Ferguson closed his eyes. 'She was beating me, and I couldn't take any more. I was angry, hurt, and I blurted it out. Shouted at her for always targeting me when Danny and John were doing what they were doing.' Ferguson's voice cracked. 'I'd seen her stomach, one day when she lifted her top in the kitchen and didn't realize I was there.'

A bubble caught in Eve's throat as she spoke. 'Did you say anything to her?'

'Yes. But it came from a good place. I said she had to

see a doctor. That she couldn't hide it forever, or go through it alone.'

'What did she say?'

'That they were going to be doing something that would mean no one would have to know.' Tears welled in Ferguson's eyes. He wiped at them as he continued. 'I didn't mean to say it that day. I swear I didn't. The next day they were gone.'

'Oh my God, Ferguson.' Eve wanted to comfort him but didn't know how.

'I wanted to believe that what she'd said was true. That they'd run off somewhere and they were happy. But what if I'd caused them to come to harm? If Fields and Alderton had hurt them in some way? But I never imagined what we know now.'

Eve didn't move. 'What did they say when they disappeared?'

'I remember Fields and Alderton huffing and puffing about them running away, said they were welcome to one another and had better not come back. It was like they didn't care, and I'm sure they didn't – except maybe in the sense they were angry that Danny and John had got one up on them. Put it like this: all of us paid for it in one way or another for a good while after that. Or at least, we paid for it more than normal. I was never sure if it was all an act – to cover up what they had done.'

'Did any of you ever question them leaving?'

Ferguson shook his head. 'There was no reason to. Of course I had my fears. And now, now that barrel has been found . . .' Ferguson cradled his head in his hands.

'Jesus, Eve, all these years I worried. Was I the reason they were killed?'

Eve stretched across the table, offering a hand which Ferguson grabbed. 'You were a kid. A kid in pain who was hurting, and you said something. You are not responsible for whatever happened after that.'

Tears rolled down Ferguson's face.

Chapter 72

Then

'I'M PREGNANT.'

Cider spills down my chin as I cough up the gulp I've taken. I wipe it away with the back of my hand, more cider spilling from the lopsided can. She's staring at me in the torchlight, waiting, and I can't find any words.

She raises her own can and gulps greedily from it, squashing the empty can in her hands when she's done and tossing it towards our fake fireplace.

'Are you sure? Are you not too young for that?'

She laughs, but not her usual laugh. A low guttural sound. 'Not too young to have periods and definitely not too young to have sex, so . . .'

'How do you know?'

She brings her knees up, clasps them with both hands. 'No period.'

'Maybe it's late for another reason.'

'Missed twice now but maybe, and maybe Sally Fields up there is an angel.'

'Twice? And you didn't tell me before this?'

She says nothing, only stares at the floor.

'What do we do now?'

She turns to me, tears glinting in her eyes. Did she want something different from me? 'I guess you need to tell me how you feel about it.'

'Shocked.'

'No shit. What else?'

The way she says it, all quiet, like she's hoping for something.

'You're not thinking about keeping it?'

She starts to sob, her face crumpling up.

'I mean . . . we're so young. We live in a home, for fuck's sake. With her. What do you think she's going to do about it?'

'But what if we didn't stay here?'

'And go where?'

'Anywhere. We could get help to find somewhere to live. With the baby, people would have to help us. We could make what we have down here real. Up there.'

I stare at her, something bubbling in my throat. Thinking about when I was a kid 'up there'. That 'up there' made no difference. That I had a mother who loved the bottom of a bottle more. That the person I was because of her couldn't ever be a father to any kid. 'Is that why you've done this?'

She looks as if she's been slapped but I want to know. Now.

She stands, rigid. 'I've done this? *We've* done this.' She goes to the bag by the drum and pulls another can from

it, tugging at the ring pull and knocking her head back
as she pours it down her throat.

'Should you be having that?'

She laughs, glowering at me. A low, nasty laugh as she
bends for a third can.

Chapter 73

FERGUSON PAUSED FOR THE briefest of moments on the top step of the main entrance to the hostel, perhaps steeling himself for walking into a set-up that he never thought he'd have to confront again.

Eve pulled open the door, making it easy for him to follow her in.

Jake was padding about in the entrance hall, waiting for them; Eve had called from the car on the way there. Worry creased his forehead. 'Do you think he'll come here?'

'It's purely a precaution. He's clearly not in sound mind and no one has seen or heard from him. Given the fact that he's currently unaccounted for . . .'

Jake's voice shook when he spoke. 'But you don't seriously think he'd try and hurt them, do you?' He looked towards Ferguson.

Eve realized they hadn't met. 'Sorry, this is my colleague, DC Scott Ferguson.' They shook hands. 'As I say, it's hard to know what he's capable of.'

Jake's hands were opening and closing by his sides as he stared at Ferguson. 'I guess his life must appear to be crumbling in front of his eyes.'

A shuffling noise made Eve look up. Matt was crouched and peering through the bannisters at the top of the stairs. Ferguson ushered Jake into the day room as Matt stood and scurried away. Eve could only imagine what the kids were going through, but there were more pressing matters at hand.

She walked into the day room, too wired to sit. Beth sat there, pale and trembling. Eve looked at Jake. 'Is the place set up for you and the kids to leave?'

He nodded. 'They're letting us use the church hall up the road.'

'Mannofield Church?'

'Yes.'

'Hopefully it won't be for long.'

Ferguson stepped forward, his voice firm. 'Go and round up the kids. We'll wait until you've done that.'

Jake left the room.

Beth watched him go, lost. 'I can't believe this is happening.'

Neither could Eve.

They turned as the door opened again and Darren's frame filled the doorway. The eldest of the kids, almost a man really. His brown eyes bored into Eve. 'Can I talk to you?'

'Now?'

'Yes.'

Chapter 74

DARREN SEEMED YOUNGER THAN his years as he faced Eve, the nerves written all over his features.

'What is it you want to talk about?'

Darren shifted in the hard-backed chair. 'I wanted to be honest with you. Now that certain things are out in the open.' He looked at the window. 'Now that Stephen is missing.'

Eve could hear the doubt in Darren's voice. 'Take your time.'

'We knew about Stephen's . . . problems.'

'You knew about the debt and the gambling?'

Darren stared at his hands.

'How did you find out?'

'A couple of ways.' Darren scratched at the dark stubble on his chin.

'Why don't you talk me through them.'

Darren's hands dropped back to his lap. 'The first time I saw him, I had to look twice. Not because he looked any different away from Wellwood. Not that I

304

thought he would.' He held eye contact with Eve. 'But you know what I mean. That way you're shocked if you see a teacher out of school, like they don't exist outside the classroom.'

Eve knew exactly what he meant.

'It wasn't that, though. An amusement arcade was never a place I expected to see him.'

'An amusement arcade?' It wasn't what Eve had been expecting.

'As I watched him, I told myself it wasn't all that weird. I knew he had kids. Snatched info given to me by the other kids back then, some of it true, as much of it bullshit. But the bit about him having kids I believed. I figured I'd see some snotty-nosed boy or girl run up to him at any moment, tugging on his leg, begging for more money for the slot machines.'

'Were you on your own there?'

'No, I was with my father. One of our measly two hours every fortnight.' Darren's gaze never wavered from hers. 'I tried not to lose sight of him, and I never saw any kid going within a foot of him, and he didn't see me. All his concentration was on the machine and it did a good job of taking his money.'

'What did you think?'

'Nothing at first. I figured he was maybe a big kid when not working, that he liked to go and play for fun. I didn't think about the money side but, after a while watching, I figured he did look different out of Wellwood. Angry. Frustrated. I got a shock when he started banging his head on the bandit machine that he'd not moved from in over an hour.'

Eve scowled. 'He was banging his head?'

'One of the security guys came over and removed him. Anyway, I still thought it was a bit of a funny story. I came back and told the others. Archie wasn't surprised. He told us Stephen was heavy into gambling and that he'd seen him on some of the betting-shop machines known to be addictive that take a fortune off you.'

'What did you guys think at that point?'

'Not too much – until the separation from his wife. He changed. Suddenly he was unshaven, smelly, snapping at everyone. I heard him one night in the office pleading for more time. Saying that he would pay up.'

'That must've been scary.'

'It was. Wellwood was all me and the other kids knew. Like a family. The thought of losing the place, it was unthinkable.'

Eve remembered the texts between Matt and Lucas. 'What did you do?'

Darren rocked back on the chair. 'What could we do? We hoped. Then, when the fire happened . . . I'm not going to lie, I thought maybe it was an insurance job.'

'You did?'

'Yeah. And I feel terrible saying it, but I wanted to tell you that Stephen would never have done anything to harm us. I know he's not thinking right but there's no way he would've known Lucas was down there.'

Eve leaned forward. 'Darren, do you know why he was down there?'

Darren shook his head. 'I swear I don't, but we did lie. Some of us had been down there since the works had been done. Not doing anything dodgy – hanging out,

306

having a laugh. Nothing bad. But none of the staff knew and we didn't want to tell you because we were scared what that would mean. What you might think had happened to Lucas. And I promise that chocolate wrapper wasn't any of ours.'

'Do you think it's possible Lucas went down there alone?'

Darren looked straight at her. 'No, and I'm as sure of that as I am about Stephen not being capable of hurting anyone.'

Chapter 75

AN HOUR LATER AND they were out in the hostel's car park, Jake and Beth loading the kids into the minivan whilst Eve and Ferguson watched on high alert.

Eve stepped forward to the open bus door as Beth got in. 'We'll let you know as soon as we have any developments. In the meantime, I'll get an officer stationed outside the church.'

Beth's hand flew to her necklace. 'Is there a need for that?'

'Let's err on the safe side.'

Ferguson came up alongside her. 'If it helps, and if it's OK with the boss here, I'd be happy to do it.'

Beth turned to him. 'I've just met you, but it would be nice to know the face.'

Eve nodded.

Jake was loitering on the gravel beside the bus, not looking any better than he had in the day room. 'Ben is meeting us at the church. I feel helpless, like I should be doing something.'

Eve could understand that. 'You'll be no use to the kids if you don't get some sleep.'

'I guess.' It was said with hesitation.

Eve looked at the bus, willing him to get on it.

Jake didn't move. 'I want to help, if you'll let me.'

'How do you plan to help?'

'Once I get the kids settled and Ben shows up . . . I could drive around, search for him.'

Eve glanced at Ferguson. Normally they'd discourage the offer and tell him to let the police do their job, but this time, she sensed Jake's need to be doing something. No matter how pointless.

'As long as you get some sleep first. If you have any joy, let us know.'

Jake thanked them before walking over to a beaten-up white Fiesta that seemed too small to take his height. Eve couldn't help but watch, fascinated, as he squeezed himself in.

Chapter 76

Saturday, 12 March

EVE YAWNED. SLEEP HADN'T come easily last night. They should've been doing more to find Stephen, to find Brian Logan – but the rest of yesterday had passed with no joy.

She pulled into Queen Street HQ car park, spaces actually available at this early hour, and turned off the engine. Eve pushed back against the headrest, steeling herself for the day ahead.

She yawned again as her phone rang, giving her head a shake as she lifted the mobile from the console. *Jake.* Eve straightened, awake now. 'Hunter.'

'Any luck with Stephen?'

'No. Everything OK last night?'

'Yeah. Kids settled better in the hall than I thought they would. They felt better knowing Ferguson was there so thank you for that. I never got a chance to thank him. He must've left when I went for a nap.'

Eve's blood ran cold. 'What do you mean he left? Are you sure? When I spoke to him last, he said he'd catch some sleep when you were up and about and then he'd stay stationed inside the entrance until he heard from me today. I haven't spoken to him yet.'

There was silence on the other end. 'He's not here.'

Eve's mind raced. 'I'm going to put you on hold. Stay there. I'm going to try his mobile.' Eve didn't wait for Jake to answer before dialling Ferguson. She waited, slouching further in her seat as the phone patched straight through to voicemail. She pressed back to Jake. 'I'm not getting anything. The phone must not have a signal.' Eve stared through the windscreen, trying to figure out why Ferguson would've left, where he might've gone – coming up with nothing. 'I'm going to head over to you, find out what's happening.'

Eve started the engine, her mind whirring. 'I'm on my way.' She hung up and started the car, edging out of the car park as she tried Ferguson one more time, speeding up when it went straight to voicemail again.

Chapter 77

EVE PULLED UP KERBSIDE outside Mannofield Church, abandoning the car and not caring about the hooting horns as cars passed on their work commute. Jake was standing around the corner on Countesswells Road, next to his own car.

'Anything?' She was hoping it had all been a mistake, that Ferguson had gone to the toilet or something.

Jake shook his head and looked at the church entrance. 'I checked again with Beth. She hasn't seen him either. I've left her looking after the kids.'

Eve sighed. 'I tried his home phone on the way here. No one's heard a thing. That worries me. It's not like Ferguson. Unheard of. He would've checked in to say if he was leaving here. Even then, there's no way he would have left you without a replacement.'

Jake shifted from one foot to another, his trainers scuffing against the pavement. 'This sounds crazy, but after us being moved, and you fearing Stephen might pose some kind of danger, you don't think Stephen turned up here, do you? That something might've happened between him and Ferguson?'

Eve agreed it sounded crazy, but she'd couldn't deny having had the same thought in the car – that scenario, or perhaps one involving Brian Logan. She moved towards Jake and leaned her backside against the bonnet of his car, needing the support. 'Let's remove the crazy for a second. We've all been racking our brains since he disappeared, but are we sure we can't think of anywhere else Stephen might've gone?'

Jake was kicking at the pavement now, small loose stones clinking against the underside of his car. 'What about Wellwood?'

Eve scrunched her eyes. 'But there's hardly anything left.'

'It was Stephen's life. Lucas died there. Maybe he needed to see the place again. It's the best I've got.'

Eve wasn't convinced but she had to agree their options were limited. All they knew was that both Stephen and Ferguson were now missing. 'Fine. I can't see why he would be there, but I also don't see the harm in checking. If nothing else, we can tick it off the list.' She moved off the bonnet.

'Can I come?'

Jake was moving from foot to foot, needing to *do* something.

'What about Beth? Does she not need help with the kids? Will she be OK on her own?'

'I told her I'd meet you out here. Ben should be here any minute and I'd be due off shift anyway.'

Eve looked at the double door of the church. 'Fine. Come on then.'

Jake's feet stopped shifting. 'I'll take my car and follow you up there.'

Eve headed back to her car, wanting to flip the bird to those who honked as they drove past. She got in, started the engine and pulled away from the kerb as Jake edged out on to the road.

They had nothing to lose.

At least, Eve hoped they didn't.

Chapter 78

Jake's car came to a stop behind Eve. She'd parked halfway up the concrete driveway to Wellwood, the same driveway where she'd seen Lucas in that body bag. She'd had no idea then that another body lurked beneath the house.

She got out and Jake jogged over to her. The two of them walked fast side by side up the drive; the smell of the blackened ruins of the home still lingered in the early-morning air. The place was eerily quiet. Eve suddenly doubted whether they should be going in alone if something crazy was indeed afoot.

She glanced sideways at Jake, taking in his height and build, figuring the two of them together stood more than a good chance against Stephen if he was there and posing any threat. The idea was hard to believe, but stress, loss and trauma could cause anyone to crack.

Eve walked on, pushing the spooks away. 'Let's check around the back first.'

Chapter 79

COOPER THREW HIS CAR keys on the desk and stretched.

He turned as Mearns appeared in the doorway, seconds behind him. He frowned. 'Did I miss something?' He pointed towards the goldfish-bowl office in the corner. 'Where's the boss?'

'She's not here?' Mearns's gaze followed Cooper's to where Eve normally was. Without fail. Ahead of them all. 'Nope.'

Mearns slung her jacket over the back of her chair. 'It's still early. She's maybe had a rare lie-in, or maybe something's come up with Ferguson at the church. Can I get you a coffee?'

Cooper ignored the offer as he walked over to the corner office, opening the door even though he could see into the space, making doubly sure Eve hadn't been in already. He looked back at Mearns. 'She normally calls if something's on. It's usually me bloody running to keep up with her or heading to meet her somewhere.'

Mearns tutted, trying to make light of it. 'She's a big

girl. She's a little later than usual; let's give her a break before we send out the cavalry.'

Cooper closed Eve's office door and headed over to his own desk. 'Fair enough. I'll take that coffee.' He took out his mobile as Mearns left and started typing. No harm in a quick text.

Chapter 80

THE SCORCHED GRASS STILL lay flattened where the oil drum had been laid down by the firefighters. Eve found it hard to believe that had only been days before, remembering watching it being lifted and carried away, no clue then as to what lay within – the young girl's remains and those of her unborn child on the X-ray now clear in Eve's mind.

'Is it safe to go in?' Jake was staring at what was left of Wellwood.

'I've been in since.' Eve shuddered at the memory, feeling the stickiness of the cobwebs on her face and seeing the stone walls in the thin band of torchlight. The place dark and dank, the circular mark in the rubble indicating where Danny and her child had been. The place where Lucas had been found. It was hard to believe any of the kids had wanted to go down there. Maybe Stephen, like her, had needed to see where Lucas had died. Where Danny and the baby had perished.

She turned to Jake. 'We should check underground.'

Jake hesitated. 'Do you have a torch?'

Eve walked towards the back of the building, to where the ruined doorway led to the hatch, police tape hanging loose and switching in the breeze. She pulled at it, letting it drop to the ground. 'I left the torch hanging on the ladder the last time I was here.'

She stepped over the threshold into darkness, secretly hoping that whatever light they had would uncover nothing but dust.

Chapter 81

'FINALLY.'

'What?' Cooper glanced up as Mearns spoke, expecting to see Eve coming through the door. Gone nine o'clock now and Eve was never this late. She hadn't replied to his earlier text either.

Mearns leaned towards her computer screen. 'CCTV's through. The cameras outside the hostel show Stephen leaving in a white car. You can follow him across Great Western Road before he goes down Duthie Terrace and we lose him. I assume because he's out of the camera angle. From there, there's a few ways he could have gone.'

Cooper raised his head after checking his mobile yet again for an answer from Eve.

'Let me see.'

Mearns shifted sideways as Cooper came up beside her, enabling him to see the screen clearly.

'I know that car.' Cooper had seen it parked at the

hostel but it wasn't Stephen's. He paused the screen, sliding the mouse across the mat, using it to zoom in to the car's windscreen. The resulting image was blurred, but clear enough to tell Cooper that Stephen wasn't alone. 'Oh shit.'

Chapter 82

EVE WENT FIRST, FEELING as though she should, given her position. However, she wasn't sure she'd signed up for being in charge of things underground. She reached the bottom of the steps, torchlight bouncing shakily off the rungs, and stepped back clear of the ladder. Rubble shifted beneath her feet as she looked up at Jake, who was descending the ladder one step at a time. Eve took a deep breath before turning, steeling herself for the black corridor ahead.

The beam of torchlight stretched along the narrow space, exposing wires and pipes above their heads. There was a stone wall at the end of the corridor, mirroring the layout of what remained of the home above. There were other rooms, other spaces, on either side of that corridor.

She was aware of Jake at her back.

He spoke. 'Do you want me to go first?'

The words were whispered, apt for down here, for whatever stupid reason. She did the same in return. 'No.'

She sounded braver than she felt. Eve stepped forward, forcing herself to take another pace, and another. No idea what she was expecting to find.

She froze as she heard something ahead, Jake stopping just short of her heels.

'What was that?' He hissed the words this time.

Eve held up her free hand to silence him.

The noise again. A shuffling sound.

She crept forward. If it was a person, the torchlight had likely already given them away. Her heart thudded as she neared the dark open space on her left. She was conscious of Jake's measured steps behind her. He had her back, but she was dreading what was in front of her.

She stopped at the gap in the wall and turned her head into it, her eyes adjusting to what she could see in the light shining from the torch.

'What the . . .'

Eve felt the blow to the back of her head. Right before everything went black.

Chapter 83

'THAT'S JAKE IN THE car with him.' Cooper's forefinger was pressed hard against the monitor. 'That's Jake in the bloody driver's seat.' His tall frame was clear in the image. 'What the fuck is he doing?' Cooper barked at Mearns. 'Rewind and run it again.'

Mearns clicked on the mouse, her hand trembling, both of them fixed on the screen, watching as Stephen opened the door and got in.

Cooper tore his gaze from the screen and started jabbing at his mobile phone. Mearns turned to him. 'What are you doing?'

'Calling Eve. Something's not right.'

Mearns stood and jogged over to the other desk, grabbing the receiver of the office phone.

'Who're you calling?' Cooper's voice was high-pitched, waiting for Eve to answer and trying to make sense of the last few seconds.

'The church. See if you can follow the car on that

footage from the end of Duthie Terrace whilst you're waiting for Eve to answer.'

Cooper turned back to the monitor, hoping it was possible and that it wouldn't take long.

Chapter 84

EVE WINCED AGAINST THE pain in her head as she tried to sit from where she lay on her back. Her eyes snapped open as she tried and failed to move her hands from where they were tied behind her, her heart thumping when all she could see was darkness.

Confusion blurred the edges of her memory. What had happened? Had Stephen taken Jake out behind her and knocked her out? Where was Jake? She tried to think. To remember.

Eve pulled herself to a seated position, the stony rubble rough beneath her hands and legs. She was still underground. Alone. In the dark.

What had *happened*? She remembered turning towards the space where the drum had been. The torchlight had hit something. No. *Someone*. On the ground.

'Stephen?'

There was a shuffle, the same sound she'd heard from the corridor. 'Stephen?'

She heard muffled cries: two voices. She strained her

eyes as the sound surrounded her, willing herself to see through the darkness, across the space she was in. She tried to stand, stumbling forward and down on to her knees, realizing her feet were also tied together.

She let herself fall back, pulling herself to a seated position again before shuffling forward, digging her feet into the dirt a little at a time, bouncing her bottom to meet them. Again. And again. Moving painstakingly slowly in the direction of the cries. Her head throbbed with the effort.

The muffled sound grew louder as she moved. She was going in the right direction. Eve panted at the effort as she forced herself to keep going. She stopped as her feet hit something hard. She gasped and squeezed her eyes shut as glaring light suddenly flooded the space, ratcheting up the pain in her head.

'All together. Perfect.'

Eve turned towards the light blinding her. It was some kind of floodlight on a stand, in the same place the voice had come from. A voice she recognized.

Jake.

Chapter 85

'COME ON, FOR CHRIST'S sa—Hello?' Mearns's hand gripped the receiver hard as she heard someone answer.

'Hello?'

'Hello, who am I talking to?'

'Beth. Who is this?'

Mearns sighed with relief. 'It's DC Mearns, you haven't met me, I'm a colleague of DC Ferguson.'

'Have you found him?'

Mearns scowled. 'Sorry?'

'The police officer, have you found him?'

Cooper was staring at Mearns as dread crept over her. 'Wait a minute. Before that, have you seen DI Hunter?'

'No. She and Jake left together.'

Mearns closed her eyes. 'Beth, you need to tell me what's been going on.'

Chapter 86

'JAKE?' EVE'S HEAD THUMPED as she squinted, wishing she had a free hand to shield her eyes. Trying, and failing, to make sense of what the hell was going on. If she turned away from the glaring beam, she could see now it was Stephen and Ferguson thrashing beside her, both of them trussed up the same way she was, but gagged, too. 'Jake, what is this?'

Jake stood, his silhouette black in front of the harsh light, so that Eve was unable to see any of his features. She peered over at Ferguson and Stephen. Stephen's eyes were wide above the gag, white lines showing the trail of tears on dirty cheeks. Ferguson was bright red and glowering.

Eve tried again. 'Jake?'

'I'm sorry, DI Hunter . . . Eve, isn't it? It wasn't supposed to be like this. Or at least it was, but Ferguson here was a bonus.'

Eve looked towards Jake, unable to see his face but hoping he was focusing on hers. 'What's going on?'

Jake grunted. 'I wanted Stephen here because that fucker William Alderton's genes run through his veins. Ferguson was a surprise, but I recognized him as soon as you arrived at the church yesterday. Not the skinny runt he was back then but my brother all the same, if you like. Call it a family reunion.'

Chapter 87

FERGUSON FOUGHT AGAINST THE restraints, needing to free his hands, if only to block his ears to the madness Jake was spewing.

All the years he'd spent trying to forget about his past, wanting to block the hurt and pain he'd endured, needing to box away the regrets and fear he felt over Danny's disappearance, and now here he was, facing it all full on. In front of his boss and none other than William Alderton's son. That father of his was as responsible for what had happened to Ferguson as Sally Fields was.

Ferguson glared at Jake. He knew where this was going. What else would be said between these walls, in front of this audience? He wasn't going to let that happen without a fight. No way. It was time for him to put the ghosts to rest.

Chapter 88

MEARNS DROVE DOWN MARKET Street, dodging buses and taxis, blue lights flashing and sirens blaring, Cooper in the passenger seat. The CCTV had come through, making it easy for them to follow the white Fiesta to Wellwood.

Cooper put a hand out, steadying himself against the dashboard as Mearns braked but didn't stop, carrying on through the red light at the junction of Guild Street – Bluebird buses and cars scattering to make way for them.

Cooper had grumbled about her demanding to drive as they'd run into the HQ car park, but he'd shut up since. 'What if they're not there?'

Mearns glanced sideways. 'We've got to hope that they are.'

Cooper held on to the armrest on the car door as Mearns turned on to North Esplanade West, the River Dee on their left, early-morning rowers oblivious to what was happening along the riverbank. They sped towards Duthie Park, en route to Wellwood. 'Why would Jake be with Stephen and Eve?'

Mearns hardly slowed as she went over the round-about at the arches. 'Why anything on this bloody case? The way I see it, getting to Wellwood is our best bet.'

Cooper didn't argue. He could only hope she was right.

Chapter 89

EVE WAS STILL STUNNED by what Jake had said. Stephen's
cries had grown louder beside her.

Think. She had to think, but the beat in her head was
in danger of drowning out everything else. She peered
against the light, trying not to turn her head away when
it was all she wanted to do. 'Is this to do with Lucas?' Eve
was struggling to see what any of this had to do with
Ferguson, but the penny was finally dropping.

Jake's voice was quiet when he spoke. 'He wasn't supposed to die. He was supposed to be in bed. I set that fire
thinking everyone would get out, but he saw me. I
couldn't allow that.'

Eve swallowed the bile in her throat. 'You put him
down here?'

'I had no option.'

Panic was rising in Eve's throat. 'But why did you set
fire to Wellwood?'

'I wouldn't have had to if Stephen hadn't let the kids

down here. If those kids hadn't kept coming here. With them.'

Everything was muddling in Eve's brain – everything except the knowledge that something was very wrong with Jake. She looked down at her feet and saw what they had hit. A rock.

Eve moved her hands, never taking her gaze from the light, from Jake, rubbing her wrists together behind her back in the hope it might loosen whatever was tying them together as she talked. 'I don't understand, Jake.'

Ferguson had stopped kicking, temper fading, eyes darting side to side as Eve waited for Jake to answer.

'You don't need to.' Ice hung from Jake's voice, piercing her skin. She had to keep him talking.

'Who do you mean when you say "with them"?'

Jake moved sideways and Eve was blinded again as she dipped her thumping head to the floor.

Stephen had moved on to his side, away from the light. Eve was conscious of the movement but didn't dare to look away from Jake, her wrists sore from the friction of rubbing harder and faster at the ties. 'Who are "them"?'

The light moved, less bright now as Jake knocked against the pole.

Eve could make out his features now, could see that he was studying her as though she was some unintelligible breed. Her eyes lowered to his hand by his side and saw a knife glinting there in the dark.

Eve could feel the rope loosening a little. 'Tell me, Jake.'

Ferguson was kicking again, trying to talk.

Jake shook his head. 'He's always liked the sound of his voice, that one. Thinks folk want to listen. I guess *she* did.'

Eve was able to loop a thumb between the rope now, pulling at it. If she could get her hands free, she could get to the rock at her feet.

Hoping that help was on its way in case she couldn't.

Chapter 90

Then

SEVEN MONTHS GONE NOW. She's still small which is a god-send as no one has noticed. Yet.

I want to believe we can be a family. That I can have what I've never known. She wants to leave next week. Says she knows a place we can go that'll give us the help we need. I want to believe that too.

I'm scared she's had no checks. No way of being sure the baby is OK. I worry that it won't ever be OK, anyway. Not with a father like me.

But then she takes my hand and places it on her bump as we lie amongst cardboard and blankets and I feel the kick and the wriggle and something that makes my chest burn.

I want it. I do. All of it.

'Scott knows I'm pregnant.'

I snatch my hand away from her, remembering all the times he's looked at her, wanting to know how he knows.

'He noticed, said I should get checked out, but I said we have plans and it'll all work out.'

'Will he be in that bloody diary of yours tonight?' I don't want anyone in there but me and her.

'I wrote about how kind he was. That he cared. And of course, I wrote that I'm with you and I know you'll take care of me and the baby.'

I feel anger. Rage that she shared our secret with someone else. Terror I can't be what she wants. That I'm the same monster my mother was.

And I feel that bubbling in my throat again, sticking there. Thinking of my mother. Is Danny any different after all?

The doubt is in danger of choking me.

And it's making me want to choke her.

Chapter 91

COOPER'S BACKSIDE LIFTED FROM the seat as Mearns took the speed bumps in Abbotswell Crescent too fast. His hand tightened on the door rest. He took a deep breath, remembering the basement, steeling himself as they neared the building. He forced himself to open his door as Mearns stopped the car.

Cooper got out, talking as quietly as he could whilst still being heard. 'Her car's here. So is Jake's.'

Mearns came to a standstill next to Cooper at the bottom of the drive. 'We need to think.'

Cooper didn't say he would rather stand out here all day and think, when the other option was going in there again.

Mearns was staring up at what was left of the building.

Cooper didn't move as she spoke. 'We need to make sure that everyone who is in there, whoever *is* in there, makes it back out. Us included.'

Chapter 92

JAKE MOVED TOWARDS THEM and Eve stilled her hands as he crouched at eye level with Ferguson. 'We're all weak, though. Can't resist what a woman can give us. No matter how hard we try.' He lifted a hand and squeezed Ferguson's cheek.

Ferguson was kicking out, trying to make contact but failing. Jake pushed Ferguson's forehead with his palm, sending him sprawling on to his back.

Jake moved to Stephen, kneeling beside him and stroking his face as he spoke.

'And you, like your father before you, couldn't keep the kids safe. In a different way, I know, but securing debts against Wellwood . . .'

Stephen shook his head from side to side, clouds of dirt lifting from the ground, making him cough and splutter from behind the gag.

Jake stood. 'Not that I give a shit what you were doing, but letting those kids down here . . . I worried about them. Worried about what they were seeing and hearing.'

Eve was pulling at the rope again. 'You worried for the kids?'

'No. Jesus, I was never here for them.'

'What do you mean?' Eve could feel the tension in the rope slackening.

Jake walked towards the circle on the ground.

Eve's head lolled, as if it might topple from her shoulders. She had to stay conscious. 'You put them in there, didn't you?'

Eve was staring at Jake as he sat inside the circle.

He bent forward, deepening the circular indent around him with the blade of his knife. 'I couldn't promise them that I could make things different. I needed to keep them safe. Hidden. Where no one else could harm them. I came back for them when I could. To be with them. To look after them. But he took that from me.' Jake stopped dragging the blade, jabbing the forefinger of his free hand in Stephen's direction.

Eve imagined Jake down here, sitting with that barrel, whilst those above were oblivious to what lay beneath them. The time he'd spent down here with those bodies. The chocolate-bar wrapper making sense now. So the other members of staff and the kids hadn't been lying. They honestly hadn't known anything. And Stephen, as much as he was at fault with his other issues, hadn't had anything to do with the fire or with Lucas's death. It was true that he loved those kids.

Eve was able to work her hands free now, the rope falling to the ground behind her, the rock only inches from her feet.

Jake continued. 'I'll make Stephen pay for that.

Ferguson too for trying to take her away from me all those years ago. And you, DI Eve Hunter, for letting the world know about them. But first, *I* need to know. Where are Danny and my child, Inspector?'

342

Chapter 93

THE PLAN WASN'T EXACTLY dynamic. It couldn't possibly be when they had no idea what they were going into.

They didn't have to search for the hatch; the carpet was already pulled back, the wooden square cut roughly into the floor exposed and open. They peered into the space beneath, the corridor at the bottom of the ladder visible when it should have been in darkness.

Cooper looked up. 'They're down there. There's light coming from further along.'

'We'd better call for back-up.'

Cooper pulled his phone from his pocket and cupped his mouth with his hand, talking in a hushed tone. He hung up and walked a little further into the house, not wanting to wait for others to arrive, motioning to Mearns to do the same. Mearns followed Cooper's lead in looking for anything that would serve as a weapon amid the debris lying damaged or burned after the fire: she grabbed the leg of a broken armchair.

Cooper turned back to the hatch, lowering himself

through the hole, grasping a plank of wood in his own hand.

Mearns watched as he disappeared into the darkness before following him, hoping more than anything that they'd see the light again.

Chapter 94

EVE LUNGED FORWARD, NOT caring what her feet did as long as her hands got to that rock.

Jake was up, jumping out of the circle, coming at Eve with the knife. She grabbed the rock but couldn't get on to her feet, the space around her spinning after her sudden movement. He was almost on her. She willed her arm to lift, needing the rock to make contact with his head as he bore down on her, but her own head was lolling backwards, shifting her balance and taking her arm and body with it.

She was falling, jerking as a sharp pain hit her shoulder, a scream bouncing off the walls around her. She was vaguely aware that the scream had come from her before her head hit the ground and everything went black again.

Chapter 95

MEARNS HEARD THE SCREAM at the same time Cooper started running. Her legs moved instinctively, faster, the copper in her kicking in.

They sprinted towards the end of the corridor where the light was spilling out, Cooper turning left, Mearns right behind him. She crashed into his back when he stopped dead.

Light shone out from the corner, a black electrical lead snaking across the floor, past Eve who lay on her back, eyes closed, blood spreading across her shirt at the shoulder. Stephen and Ferguson lay metres from Eve. Both of them had their feet and hands tied, and both were gagged at the mouth.

Cooper ran to Eve, crashing to his knees and feeling for a pulse. Mearns forced herself to move, heading to Ferguson and Stephen.

She ungagged Ferguson first, then moved to the rope, struggling to untie the knot behind his back. Then the room was plunged into darkness.

'Cooper?' Mearns's voice sounded strong in the black, echoing around them.

'I'm here. She's breathing.'

Mearns knew that Ferguson was OK and, by the movement and muffled groans at her feet, that Stephen was too.

There was silence before Ferguson broke it. 'Jake?'

Mearns's head turned in the direction the voice was coming from. 'Jake, you don't have to do this.'

'Like you'd care.'

Jake's voice was close, moving. Mearns stepped back.

Ferguson's voice again. 'I know you're hurting.'

'Enough of the bullshit. Same shit you tried to serve to her about needing a doctor, like I wasn't caring for her. Wasn't enough for her.'

'It wasn't like that. I meant no harm. I was worried for you both.'

'Right. Anyway, you've done well for yourself. Got away from here at least. Not me though. I never really left. Neither did they.'

Mearns stepped sideways, the hairs rising on the back of her neck. She heard someone moving and realized it was Ferguson as he spoke. 'John? I want to talk.'

Mearns jumped at the sound of a loud click, light flooding the space again.

Jake – or John – was smiling at them, standing inches away from Ferguson, a knife in his raised hand.

Ferguson was staring at him, a sickly shade, rubbing his legs against one another, trying to loosen the rope at his ankles.

'You don't look pleased to see me. This isn't how a family reunion usually goes.'

Ferguson's eyes flickered past John to Cooper, who was creeping forward, a rock grasped in his hand.

Mearns and Stephen remained silent, watching.

'What did you do to Danny?'

Cooper was almost upon him. Ferguson kept his eyes level with John's – the rope at his ankles almost slack enough now to free his feet – as Cooper lifted the rock higher. In the split second that he ran forward, John turned and slashed at Cooper's arm, the rock falling between them. John pulled back the knife and lunged again, striking Cooper in the chest.

'No!' Ferguson jumped on to John's back, knocking him off balance as Cooper slumped to the ground. The two men stumbled towards Eve and Stephen, Eve still unconscious and Stephen shuffling backwards as fast as he could.

John was aimlessly waving the hand holding the knife in the hope of hitting Ferguson and getting him off his back. Ferguson held tight, swinging around as John turned to find Mearns standing in front of him, lifting the heavy wooden chair leg. John let out a cry of surprise before the wood thudded down on his head, knocking him into silence.

Chapter 96

Sunday, 13 March

FERGUSON SAT ON A wooden bench by the dry water fountain in Victoria Park, his breath clouding in the early-morning chill. He pulled his winter coat around him. Spring hadn't given in to warmth just yet, the surrounding trees still bare, their branches swaying in the breeze. Dog walkers passed by briskly as he jittered his leg up and down and waited.

He looked into the distance, across the bustling Westburn Road and into the tranquillity of Westburn Park, comforted by the knowledge that Eve's cottage was minutes away. Knowing that she and the rest of the team would be waiting once he was done, safe, after the events of yesterday.

A movement to his left made him turn, the red coat bright against the green grass. The woman moved slowly, unsure, but she relaxed a little and sped up as he smiled and stood. He embraced her, tightly, not sure if it was the right thing to do but wanting and needing to do it.

They sat close on the bench, puffs of breath joining

together and dancing in the wind. Alive and well. Something that at one stage they'd both thought might never be possible for them.

'Thank you for coming.' He stared ahead, not sure if he was ready to see the pain in her eyes that he knew was mirrored in his own.

'It's so good to see you.' Her voice hadn't changed.

His own cracked against dry lips. 'I've wanted to see you for a long time, but it was enough that I knew you were OK.'

'And you? Are you OK?' She looked sideways at him.

Ferguson sat silent for a moment, turning to meet her gaze. 'I wasn't. But I am now.'

Jane Henderson reached out and placed her hand over Ferguson's, both of them staring up at the branches of the tree above – the smallest of green buds visible, signalling new life.

Pointing towards new beginnings.

Chapter 97

'JESUS, COOPER. STOP MILKING it.'

Eve couldn't help but smile as Mearns stepped aside, making the rare and grand gesture of giving Cooper first dibs on the bacon butties. Amazing what a knife injury could do for you – superficial or not.

A day had passed since the paramedics had brought her and Cooper up from the basement with injuries that, thankfully, hadn't been life-threatening for either of them. A lot had happened since then, and today was the first time they'd all been back together. In her home. As friends, not just colleagues.

Eve leaned towards the kitchen table as the phone rang, grimacing at the movement in her shoulder, her hand shooting up to press against it. 'I should've got first shout on those butties.' She groaned as she lifted the receiver.

'Hunter.' She listened, watching Mearns and Cooper eat breakfast together, glad of the familiar routine, and thankful that they were all still there to do it. 'Yes, we'd

351

be honoured.' She said her goodbyes and hung up, Cooper and Mearns looking her way between bites.

'That was Stephen. They've decided to scatter Lucas's ashes at Wellwood. They want Lucas to be there with them when they return, whenever that may be. They'd like us to be there when they scatter them.'

Their faces said they would be.

But there was one person who wouldn't be there. Jake – or John as she struggled to see him as. He had been charged for his part in what had gone down at Wellwood recently, and what had happened years before. Two terrible crimes that would likely see him imprisoned for the rest of his life.

Stephen had all but crumbled when he'd been told that a full probe would have to be launched into Wellwood's financial position and his debts, but Eve and the team had given their accounts. With professional help and the support of his wife, who had realized how close she'd come to losing him, they were hopeful that he would still have a home to manage.

Danny and her baby were to be laid to rest. Eve and the team would be there for the small service, as they'd been there for Lucas.

So many people harmed, both mentally and physically, by those who should've been protecting them.

Eve looked at Mearns and Cooper before saying what she had to next. 'I hope Ferguson is getting on OK. It'll be a big moment for him. And for Jane. I have something else for him. Another thing that'll lay the past to rest.'

They stared at her. 'Forensics came back with the

findings on that notebook. The one that was in the drum and almost pulp. Turns out they were able to make out some of the pages. A diary.'

She glanced over to the envelope on the dresser, picturing the laminated sheet that lay within, bearing Danny's original handwriting. She hoped it would answer all of the questions Ferguson had been asking himself over the years since leaving Wellwood.

Eve smiled. She still had no idea what he'd gone through. She didn't want to know. But she did know that, in some small way, Ferguson would heal. He'd vowed to support Archie through his recovery, and he would be true to his word. Helping Archie would help him.

She rose from the table and saw Ferguson through the window, walking from the park entrance. His shoulders were pulled back and there was a sense of purpose in his walk. Free. He'd faced the ghosts, dealt with his own monsters above and beneath ground at Wellwood. Today was another step. The start of a new journey.

Acknowledgements

Book three. Who would've believed it?

It's been a tough couple of years and a time that I've been so grateful for the release, and sometimes escape, of this magic of putting words down on paper. You can't beat it, but, as always, even though writing is an insular experience, no book ever makes it out into the world without the help of others.

I'd like to thank Fire and Rescue Service Crew Commander Leon Webster, based at Inverurie fire station, for being so approachable and helpful. I'm sure he rolled his eyes every time his inbox pinged with my emails and daft questions. I also have to thank Ian Donaldson, retired Operational Station Manager – formerly Grampian Fire and Rescue Service – for answering my initial questions so helpfully and thoroughly when I started to play with the idea of a first draft. Their insights into all matters fire-related really helped me set the scene in my head.

Speaking of scenes, the all-important children's home,

Wellwood, came to life thanks to Aberdeen City Council Residential and Youth Services Manager Andrea McGill and her colleague Helen McKenzie, who shared their experiences of working with and within children's residential homes throughout Aberdeen. Their knowledge of the typical set-up, staff provision, day-to-day life for the children, etc., was invaluable. Wellwood has a good pinch of all that input, but I must stress that it is purely fictional and that homes within the city are professionally and expertly run.

Going back to that first draft, I started out writing this book with my fantastic editor Tash Barsby at Transworld Publishers. I was sad when she broke the news that she was moving to pastures new but excited for her next adventure. It was nerve-wracking to think I'd be working with someone else, and therefore I can't thank the lovely Imogen Nelson enough for stepping in to look after and guide me – something she did expertly and with understanding. As always, I'd like to thank all of the fabulous team at Transworld for letting me live the dream.

Special thanks have to go to my wonderful agent, Oli Munson, at A.M. Heath Ltd. Without him, book one would never have been a reality – never mind book three. Thank you for putting up with me.

Then there are those who make Twitter and Facebook a pleasure to be on – fellow authors, bloggers, reviewers, libraries, booksellers and, of course, my all-important readers. Thank you all for your unwavering support. You are the best.

I'm also fortunate to have friends and family who

make my life brighter and better – thank you for being there always and for all you do for me.

And finally, to my two mini monsters, Holly and Ellis. I'm so proud of you both. Thank you for letting Mummy write when those deadlines were looming. I love you.

**Don't miss the first book in the gripping
DI Eve Hunter series**

A brutal murder.
A young woman's body is discovered with
horrifying injuries, a recent newspaper cutting
pinned to her clothing.

A detective with everything to prove.
This is her only chance to redeem herself.

A serial killer with nothing to lose.
He's waited years, and his reign of terror has only just
begun ...

AVAILABLE TO BUY IN PAPERBACK AND EBOOK

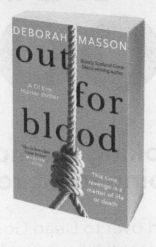

dead good

Looking for more gripping must-reads?

Head over to Dead Good –
the home of killer crime books,
TV and film.

Whether you're on the hunt for an intriguing
mystery, an action-packed thriller
or a creepy psychological drama,
we're here to keep you in the loop.

Get recommendations and reviews from
crime fans, grab discounted books at bargain
prices and enter exclusive giveaways
for the chance to read brand-new releases
before they hit the shelves.

Sign up for the free newsletter:
www.deadgoodbooks.co.uk/newsletter